the Tuscan Sister's Secret

BOOKS BY DANIELA SACERDOTI

THE TUSCAN SISTERS SERIES
The Tuscan Sister

STANDALONE NOVELS
The Italian Villa
The Lost Village
The Italian Island
The Bookseller's Daughter

GLEN AVICH QUARTET
Watch Over Me
Take Me Home
Set Me Free
Don't Be Afraid

SEAL ISLAND SERIES
Keep Me Safe
I Will Find You
Come Back to Me

DANIELA SACERDOTI

the Tuscan Sister's Secret

bookouture

Published by Bookouture in 2025

An imprint of Storyfire Ltd.
Carmelite House
50 Victoria Embankment
London EC4Y 0DZ

www.bookouture.com

The authorised representative in the EEA is Hachette Ireland
8 Castlecourt Centre
Dublin 15 D15 XTP3
Ireland
(email: info@hbgi.ie)

Copyright © Daniela Sacerdoti, 2025

Daniela Sacerdoti has asserted her right to be identified
as the author of this work.

All rights reserved. No part of this publication may be reproduced, stored in any retrieval system, or transmitted, in any form or by any means, electronic, mechanical, photocopying, recording or otherwise, without the prior written permission of the publishers.

ISBN: 978-1-83525-773-9
eBook ISBN: 978-1-83525-772-2

This is a work of fiction. Names, characters, businesses, organisations and events other than those clearly in the public domain, are either the product of the author's imagination or are used fictitiously. Any resemblance to actual persons, living or dead, events or locales is entirely coincidental.

For Auryn

PROLOGUE

CASALTA, 1944

It was like being in a dream, Viola thought, kneeling among the paintings. Her arms were clasped over her head against the deafening thunder. But it wasn't a dream, and the noise wasn't thunder.

The paintings were covered with white sheets, now dusty with the debris that fell off the roof every time a detonation shook the ground. One of the sheets had come loose: the perfect face of a Renaissance girl, bronze hair and dark eyes, a pearl hanging from a gold circlet on her high forehead, was staring at Viola. Bianca de' Medici, a little dame immortalised in paint and gold.

Viola was shaking more and more at every roar that threatened to shatter her body and everything around her, and a prayer learned in childhood came to her lips. Thunder crashed around her, trees on fire glimmered beyond the broken windows – any moment now the wooden ceiling above her would go up in flames and the paintings with it, and she, too, would be obliterated. She prayed and prayed and said goodbye to her family, to her life, to her love, who was lost somewhere, maybe wounded, maybe dead.

A moment of silence. The world seemed to hold its breath and hush, unmoving: the hills, the trees, the flames, the paintings scattered on the attic floor.

The serene eyes of the young Renaissance dame peeping through the sheet met Viola's once more – she saw Bianca's eyes blink slowly, her dark irises disappearing beneath her lids with the long, long eyelashes, and then reappearing. In her terror, Viola didn't question that a girl in a painting had blinked – and she didn't question hearing the little dame's voice in her head.

Viola. All will be well. I promise.

The thunder began again, and Viola curled up into herself.

So this is how dying feels, she thought, waiting for the final blow to end it all.

CHAPTER 1

CASALTA, 1985

BIANCA

I leaned my shoulder against the stony wall, warm after a day of autumn sunshine. Perched on the stairs that climbed the side of my Tuscan home, I took in the lilac sky, the rolling hills crested with cypresses and, beneath me, the gardens of Casalta.

How come there are always roses blooming here in Casalta?

From April to November, crimson, white, pink and yellow, in all their shades and gradations of colour, roses dotted the bushes, and in the winter the rosehip bushes exploded with bright red berries. Now, October regaled me with my favourite, a delicate pink rose with yellow-orange hearts; each one was unique.

To think we almost lost all this; to think we almost lost our beloved Casalta.

So much had changed for me. It seemed impossible that only six months had passed since our lives had been turned upside down. I was still reeling from it all.

The four Falconeri sisters – me and my twin, Lucrezia, our middle sister, Eleonora, and the youngest of the four of us, Mia, were together again, at last. And I had no words to describe the joy and relief this gave me, having been my sisters' keeper for so long, forced to keep my twin away so that our father wouldn't hurt her, to watch over my younger sisters so that what remained of our family would be free from harm...

Now, finally, I could breathe.

The marriage of our parents – a young whimsical artist from Scotland, and an older, traditional Italian man from a powerful family – had been as unhappy as it was unlikely.

Our father, Fosco Falconeri, not-so-beloved patriarch and tyrant, had died, leaving the family business of wine and oil in tatters.

While our mother, Emmeline McCrimmon, had only just returned after years of absence. We were convinced she'd passed away years earlier – we'd been to her funeral, visited her grave, grieved until our hearts were in pieces, believing she was gone forever... but we'd been deceived.

Our mother wasn't dead.

She'd been forced to stay away from us, her daughters, to leave us behind. My father had separated her from us, and then ripped my twin Lulu away too, destroying our family.

But in the end, our father's cruelty couldn't keep the women of Casalta apart. His death freed us. Mum came back, now a successful painter, prosperous enough to save our home, our Casalta, and the business from bankruptcy; and my beautiful, wilful, courageous twin sister, Lucrezia, the other half of my heart, returned to me, to us, to her home, from the exile imposed on her by our father.

A flicker of movement from below made me look down – a dark little head moved in the grounds beneath. My youngest sister, Mia, was off for an evening walk. Recently, she'd taken to walking by herself every night – I followed her with my eyes, as the dusk turned her figure into a fairy vision, a blurred black silhouette almost gliding over the hill. I knew that she was mulling over Mum's invitation to go and visit her at her home in London, so they could paint together.

All of a sudden, this sweet, warm evening seemed a little melancholy, a little wistful. I wrapped my shawl tighter around myself and shivered – the impulse to call Mia back before she disappeared came over me all at once.

Where did this restlessness come from? It was an uneasy feeling. Life had cut all our knots; what more did I want?

I reached into my dress pocket and took out a brochure, folded in two. I followed with my fingers the words printed on it: *Scuola di Restauro*. Three years to learn restoration of paintings and sculptures. A dream condensed into twelve small pages of glossy pictures.

But would this ever be within my reach?

'*You're such a practical little person, Bianca. Practical, but not clever,*' is what Father used to say to me – when he noticed my existence, that was. '*In the womb, Lucrezia took all the brains.*'

'Bianca?' a voice that still retained a hint of a French accent from its owner's years of living in Paris called from behind me. I turned around to see Lulu climbing out of my bedroom window.

Seeing her was like looking in the mirror. Lucrezia and I were identical twins, but there were subtle differences in us: we both had red hair, blue eyes and fair skin, inherited from our Scottish mum, but Lulu's hair was a mahogany shade, and I was closer to a strawberry blonde.

My younger sister, Mia, instead, had the darker skin and hair from the Falconeri side of the family, while genetics had played a game with her eyes: one was hazel-brown, and one was blue with brown speckles. The difference was only startling in bright light, but even when it wasn't that visible, it did give her a magical, slightly eerie look.

It was an unspoken truth, though, that Nora, the middle

sister, was the beauty of the family: slanted green eyes and golden skin, a mop of black hair she kept short to highlight her long, graceful neck, and a way of simply *being* that fascinated the people who met her. The clothes she usually wore, outdoorsy and casual, enhanced her beauty instead of hiding it – though I was probably biased, as I found all three of my sisters the prettiest creatures on earth.

Lucrezia came to sit beside me, and I slipped the brochure back into my pocket. She clasped her hands around her long, doe-like legs – she and I and Nora were taller than average, especially Nora, while Mia was petite, like a little fairy.

I composed my expression quickly, to hide any hints of melancholy – but concealing my mood from her wasn't easy at all. Not only was she my twin, but she also had the ability to see people's auras, a halo of colour around their bodies, giving away their thoughts and state of mind. This happened only when someone's emotions were strong enough to be manifested, or when Lulu had a connection with the person in question. I wondered which colour mine was, now.

All of us Falconeri sisters had inherited gifts from our mother. And the gifts that our mother's heritage had bestowed on us hadn't made our family life easier: Father had been repulsed and terrified by them.

Lulu could see auras; Nora, in her vain attempt to win our father's affection, had denied her gift to such an extent that we didn't even know what it was; Mia was the most magical of the four of us, with her uncanny way to *know things I'm not supposed to know*, as she put it. As for me...

I could see scenes and people from long ago, flowing parallel to the current day, so that my life had always been suspended between the present and the past. For some mysterious reason, this only happened to me in Casalta: to my eyes, my home and gardens were the background to eras gone.

But my abilities had disappeared when Lucrezia was exiled,

and never returned. It was as if when my twin had gone, she'd taken my deepest soul with her. Now that she had come back to me, I kept hoping to find my own gift again – but so far, it hadn't happened: I was blind of my sixth sense, unable to see Casalta's history come to life as it was happening there and then, in front of my eyes. I preferred not to think about what I'd lost, but at times I couldn't help it.

'Finished for the night?' I asked.

'The work here is *never* finished! But well, it's what I do.' Lucrezia shrugged. Even after a long day's work, she looked radiant – what a difference from when she first returned, diffident and bitter, so much so that I was afraid I'd lost her forever!

I mirrored her smile – seeing her so contented in work and love, after all she'd been through, filled my heart. My eyes traced her features that were also my own, took in the unique shade of red of her hair, a hue I'd only ever seen in my twin, and in paintings. She'd been back for six months now, but there were still moments when I was disbelieving that she was here, and I contemplated her just like that, like a painting in a museum, trying to convince myself that yes, my sister really was with me, now.

'What's on your mind, Bianca?'

'I'm good,' was my knee-jerk response. I wasn't used to being asked how I was; I wasn't used to being the person people worried about. *I* was the one who worried for others.

Lulu raised her eyebrows; as expected, she wouldn't be deflected.

'Your aura is wan tonight. Not that I need to see it to know how you're feeling.'

I tried to translate my vague feelings into words. 'Everything is sorted, now, isn't it? You're home with us, Mum is back in our lives… We're a family again.'

'But?' Lucrezia encouraged me.

I took a breath. 'But… nobody *needs* me as much as before.'

Oh. Those words had come out of me unplanned, unexpected. It was as if they had a will of their own, overcoming mine.

'That's not true! Everyone needs you. Especially me, after all the years we spent apart! I need you more than ever, Bianca. And so do Mia and Nora, though Nora will deny needing anyone. However...'

I waited.

'Everyone is finding their way, now,' Lucrezia continued. 'You took care of this family; you kept everyone safe. You can let go a little. It's your time to take care of yourself.'

There. She'd read me like an open book.

I took the brochure out of my pocket again and handed it to Lulu without a word. She opened it, and a smile spread on her face.

'This looks amazing. Are you thinking of applying?'

'Well, I don't know...'

'But you *have to*! You have all my support! And our sisters' too, I'm sure!'

'There's a list of problems to be sorted before I can do this...'

'There are *always* problems. Nothing comes without problems. They just need to be faced and sorted. You're not alone, remember? Tell me, what stands between you and this?' She waved the brochure like a fan.

'Well, just for a start, I need a job that pays. *Actually* pays. So I can save enough to apply in the new term.'

In my current job, I ran a charity called Legami, with my friend Camilla. We helped vulnerable people with everyday life: collecting prescriptions for them, doing groceries, paying bills and generally taking care of those little things that can become huge, when age or illness get in the way. I supposed looking after people was a bit of a theme, in my life.

The wages Camilla and I paid ourselves were meagre and I didn't want to rely on my sisters. Our father had left us bankrupt – yes, our mother had bought Casalta back for us, but the Falconeri business was still recovering, thanks to Lucrezia's canny administration. Nora had a riding school; Mia sold her paintings: now I needed to contribute, too.

Lulu shook her head. 'That's not an issue; our business is doing better now...'

'No. I want to support myself. Non-negotiable. And also...'

'What, Bianca?' she coaxed gently.

'I'd be leaving Camilla, I'd be leaving the people we look after. They *need* me.'

'Camilla is very capable, so you tell me. She can find someone else; you both can look for the perfect person to fill your shoes. I know Legami is your baby,' Lucrezia added when I opened my mouth to protest. 'But I'm sure there's someone out there who can take your place with just as much commitment. And heart.'

'That's the word, *commitment*.' I sighed. 'I *committed* to them. I owe it to them to be around.' I was thinking of the elderly at Villa Lieta, the local retirement home, of the families I followed, of all the people who relied on me.

'You owe it to yourself to chase your dreams, Bianca. What you want and need and desire is in the equation too. Not just us sisters, the family, Legami, Camilla... where is Bianca in all this?'

'I used to love what I do. I still love what I do. But...'

'...but you've outgrown it. It happens. Like I'd outgrown my life in Paris, and I'm here now,' Lucrezia said with a smile.

'They'll miss me, and I'll miss them,' I insisted.

'Of course *you* will, of course *they* will, but that's what change is all about. You bid goodbye to things and people, leave them behind, welcome the new into your life. And one day, you'll say goodbye to that too, and something new will come.'

'Yes, of course.' My stomach clenched. My twin might be

easy with change, but I wasn't. In my book, change equalled anxiety.

'You won't be disappearing off the face of the earth! You can still see them, make sure they're all right, make sure Camilla is good...'

Finally, my deepest, most secret fear came out all at once.

'I don't know if I can do it, Lucrezia. I'm not *clever*! You're the one with the brains, remember?'

The hills of home were now black outlines against the lilac sky, white puffs of mist gathering at their feet. Stars appeared in the sky, glowing like pearls in velvet.

My harsh words hung between us for a moment.

'*What?*'

I looked at my twin; her eyes had grown dark.

'I might simply be incapable...' I began.

'Where has this come from? This idea that you're not clever and I *got the brains?*'

'I don't know, that's the way it always was...'

'No, it *isn't*. It's not like there was one dollop of intelligence in our mother's womb, and somehow I got it and you didn't. *Father* said that to you, didn't he? And like pretty much everything he said, it's not true. It's rubbish! He said it to keep you down! To hurt you. He'd have told us anything to stop us from challenging him. He used to call me mean, remember? I was mean, you were stupid, Mia was weird and Nora didn't even *exist*. Is this all true, Bianca? Because if you're not that clever, then I'm mean and nasty.'

Even in the dusky light, I could see that Lulu's cheeks were flushed pink.

'You were never mean or nasty.'

'You were never stupid.'

Sudden tears filled my eyes.

Maybe what Father told me, told us, *was* rubbish.

Maybe it'd been a lie all along. And I always believed it,

somewhere deep in my soul, I always thought the world was too complicated a place for me.

Lucrezia took my hand. 'Go for it, Bianca. Grab your life. Promise me.'

'Yes. I will,' I said, and in the twilight gloom I kissed her smooth, cool cheek.

Later that night, our conversation kept coming back to me. I tossed and turned, unable to sleep. Lulu was right: *alarm* had been my middle name all these years. And when it first overcame me, my gift, the deepest and most precious part of me, disappeared – as if there wasn't room for both in my heart and soul.

There wasn't a single memory from my childhood that didn't have my gift as part of it. I cast my mind back to that time of innocence, before my world fell apart around me, when I was still whole – to when a strange woman appeared in my room, sitting on my windowsill and singing a song from long ago...

CHAPTER 2

CASALTA, EIGHTEEN YEARS EARLIER

BIANCA

I can't remember the first time my gift manifested itself – I was too little, a baby in her mother's arms. But Mum told me that I used to point to empty corners, clap my hands and laugh, or wince as if I'd heard a sudden noise, and even cry out in fear. Even as a baby, I was seeing people and scenes from the past of Casalta come alive in front of my eyes.

I do remember, though, the first time I was made aware that Lulu couldn't see what I saw, and neither could my other sisters, nor the rest of the world. I must have been five or six, and still convinced that the world began and ended between the walls of Casalta, with my family, and that my gift was simply a sixth sense that everyone had.

I was sitting on my bed, in the room Mum had decorated with white roses and meadow flowers, facing the window, and Lulu was waving a hand in front of my enraptured face.

'Bianca?'

'*Shhhh!* The lady is singing!'

There was a woman in a long blue dress sitting at my

window, holding what looked to my child's eyes like a stick, with some kind of thread all around it – only later I learned that it was a spindle – and she was spinning wool and singing in a language I didn't understand.

Lulu looked towards the window, which opened out onto the stone stairs where I'd sat just that morning. She touched the windowsill and looked out, before turning to me. 'There's nobody here.'

I was sure she was joking, making fun of me – because the lady in blue was sitting just there, and her singing filled the room. It was in my eyes, in my ears, impossible to miss. A white bonnet covered her head, and her hands were dark and slender…

'She's right *there*!'

'I can't see anyone! And if there's someone here, how come I can touch the stone?' My twin slapped the windowsill several times.

How could she do that? How could Lulu's hand touch the stone, and the woman be sitting there with her spindle, at the same time?

'She's there, she's *there*!' I cried in frustration – the horrible feeling of not being able to trust my eyes filled me.

The incident ended in tears from both of us. Lulu was upset for having upset *me*, and I was shaken and confused – all of a sudden I wasn't sure of my own eyes, of my own ears. Mum gathered us in her arms, and between sobs and tears, we told her what had happened.

'She says the lady isn't there, but she *is*! I can show you, Mum!' I took her by the hand and began pulling her towards my room. When we crossed the threshold, the white roses painted on the ceiling and walls seemed to quiver and rearrange themselves as if to point towards the lady, who was still humming a tune.

'Look! She's *there*!'

Mum turned towards me and smiled. Her serene expression told me that there was nothing to worry about, that what was happening to me was right and good.

'Come out, girls.'

When there was something to discuss away from prying ears, we always took refuge on the stone stairs that ran outside the length of our house. Even back then, when we were so small, there was a sense of two worlds inhabiting our home – one belonging to Father and his men, and one belonging to the women, Mum and her daughters, and our housekeeper, Matilde. In those private, almost clandestine times when us sisters were alone with our mother, she spoke to us in English. Father had forbidden it, believing that we'd grow confused between the two languages – and so, it'd become the secret idiom we used with Mum only.

I was still in tears and hot and upset; Mum wrapped an arm around my shoulders and met my eyes – holding her gaze calmed me a little.

'I believe you, of course,' she said softly. 'But neither Lucrezia nor I can see her. Nobody else can. I think this is your gift, Bianca. You have the Sight.'

I didn't fully understand, back then. How could I?

'Don't be afraid of anything you see; they can't hurt you, I promise. And remember, never speak of this to anyone but me and Lulu, and your little sisters. Never, *never*, let your father know of it, or even suspect. It's our secret, yes?'

'It's our secret,' I repeated.

In the years to come I'd say this to myself over and over again: *It's our secret*, every time Mum reminded me not to talk about it. She wanted to instil this into me, so that there wouldn't be even the smallest chance of a mistake.

It was only years later, after what happened to Mum and Lulu, that I fully grasped the depth of my father's fear and repulsion when it came to our gifts, and the consequences of him finding out about them.

It took me a while to understand the Sight. For me, the past and present were mixed together, and time worked in layers – I could unpeel them and fall into eras long lost. My little world was populated not only by my family, by Matilde, by the people in flesh and blood who came and went around Casalta; but also by bygone folk who became familiar to me, interwoven with my life.

I saw soldiers in armour marching along the profile of the hill, and lighting a campfire in our garden; girls in wide dresses and hats promenading among our roses; children playing hopscotch in the courtyard while their mother did laundry, bent in two over a wide wooden tub.

Rock walls appeared beyond our plastered and painted ones, and instead of stepping over terracotta tiles, I walked over perfumed grass scattered on stone floors; I saw tapestries over our windows, an open fire instead of our fireplace. I heard the howls of wolves hunted to extinction hundreds of years ago, the sound of ancient drums and flutes, soft voices chattering in corners.

Sometimes I was delighted and lost in wonder; sometimes I was scared and ran to my mother, who helped me navigate it all: but it was always normal to me, mundane, a sixth sense that was as much mine as the other five.

Soon I came to understand that this only happened to me in Casalta and nowhere else – to this day, I still don't know why. But the rest of the world seemed rather uninteresting to me, when I compared it to the rich, strange sights of my home. Sometimes I asked myself how much this was *my* gift, and how much belonged to Casalta, with me being a conduit. As if I was a human metal detector, but instead of metals, I detected memories. Because I came to understand that the people I saw weren't ghosts, souls trapped between worlds: they were the imprints of the past.

And always, always, Mum reminded us to keep our gifts to ourselves. Only Matilde, our housekeeper since we were babies, knew, or had a vague idea of it – though I suspected she didn't quite believe we really had those talents; we were simply too imaginative for our own good. Matilde was a practical, solid woman who had ironclad loyalty to Mum and to us.

But it wasn't my imagination. The past materialised in front of me in ways so intense, so immersive, that I either felt I was there, or that the people I saw were *here*, alive, with us. Sometimes I couldn't even tell the difference. It was disconcerting for the people around me, but my sisters and I were used to our lives feeling that way.

Viola came to me for the first time when we were toddlers. She was playing on the living room floor with a little wooden house, and wooden dolls shaped a bit like skittles, her head with its wavy black hair bent over the toys and white Mary Janes on her feet. A woman dressed in lilac – her mother, I knew instinctively – sat with her. I remember the pearls around the woman's neck dangling in front of Viola's eyes, and how her small hand was trying to grab them. I seldom saw her father, and this was comforting: my own father's presence was heavy and troubling enough.

While other apparitions stayed the same, Viola changed and grew alongside me, from toddlerhood to the age of twelve, the point at which my Sight disappeared when Lucrezia was sent away, and I lost her.

Up until then, Viola had been my constant companion, an imaginary friend who wasn't imaginary at all, but simply long gone. And yet, I was as fond of her as if she'd been living there with us – and her timeline, somehow, seemed to flow alongside mine.

And with her, I could see her family – her father with the

dark moustache and her graceful mother with silk and chiffon dresses, a little out of place in her rural surroundings. I saw Viola at the kitchen table on rainy days, doing homework, writing in thin black books; I saw her celebrating birthdays and Christmases, twirling in front of the mirror with a new dress, coming home from school with her leather pouch across her chest, sneaking into her mother's room with a friend, and both of them painting patchy make-up on their faces.

There were many times when we sat in silence, me reading a book and Viola embroidering or sewing like her mother had taught her to – her silent presence in Casalta was as habitual to me as that of my sisters. As strange as it may sound, she was my best friend – we were separated only by rivers of time.

Lulu was even jealous of Viola, and we sparred over her.

'I wish I could see her. You love her more than *me*!'

'I don't! You're my sister. She's my friend.'

'She can't even *speak* to you.'

But privately, I wasn't sure about that.

One day I spoke to her, whispering so that nobody else could hear – and Viola looked around, as if searching for the source of the sound.

I didn't try to explain it. The logical complications of any communications between Viola and me were too much to tackle for my child's mind, and anyway, my instinct told me that I'd find no answer. I just took it all at face value and let it happen. She was part of my life.

And then, when I was twelve, my family fell apart. Mum disappeared, and we believed she was dead. Father sent Lulu away, because she insisted she'd seen our mother in the rose garden, and wouldn't back down. We all believed, at the time, that it'd been wishful thinking, or yet another manifestation of her gift: it was only years later that we discovered Lulu *really* had seen our mum, alive, that night.

For the first couple of days after we were told that my twin would never again come home, I was too distraught to notice that my gift had gone. And then I began to feel that the house was even emptier than it should have been without Lucrezia...

For a time, I was in denial. My world had changed too fast for me to keep pace. It simply couldn't be: my gift *couldn't* have disappeared. It simply wasn't possible that I'd fallen asleep one night with my Sight intact, and woke up blind the next day.

Of course, I told myself, the woman spinning wool would be at the window.

Of course the soldiers would sit around the fire in our garden.

Of course Viola would go to school every morning in her gingham dress, her hair in plaits with a hairclip by the side of her face, and disappear beyond the gate; she'd eat supper with her family alongside us; she'd run out to climb into her father's car, where he waited for her wearing driving gloves and glasses; she'd lie prone on her belly, reading a book, her legs scissoring the air.

Then came the wait.

Maybe I wouldn't see Viola today, but tomorrow, for sure. Or the day after, or the one after. But it never happened, and my loss and despair deepened day by day. My world had been cut in half – I didn't have my mother and my twin any more, nor the sights and sounds that had been all around me for as long as I could remember.

I walked on blind, disconcerted, unsure in an incomplete world. I didn't know how to move in it – I almost had to put my hands in front of me to sense what was around me, take uncertain steps through a reality alien and empty. It seemed to me that *all* my senses had been turned off, that my eyes and ears perceived muffled sights and sounds, that food had no flavour and that whatever touched my skin didn't leave an impression. I wasn't really there.

I'd dissolved into thin air, like Viola. I didn't know who I was any more.

Now, years later, a thin, almost inaudible voice awoke me in the night.

Bianca.

I opened my eyes in the gloom. There was no lull between wakefulness and sleep: the calling awoke me in an instant. I knew that voice; I'd waited to hear it for years!

Bianca.

Viola was calling me; her voice was like the wind in the trees and in the rustling grass, and yet clear to my ears.

Is my gift back? I sat up in the darkness. *After years of wishing, wishing with all my heart...*

I switched the light on – but I was alone. Maybe it'd been a dream? Disappointment filled me like cold mist, until—

Bianca.

Again, I heard my name being called – *Bianca, Bianca* – they were like sighs, like the words you might believe you're hearing in the creaking of footsteps on wood, in the breeze blowing around the windows.

There was nothing but darkness around me – but this was the first appearance of my gift after so many years!

I waited until the small hours, not daring to move and almost not daring to breathe, in case I missed Viola's call – but the silence of the night was broken only by night birds and the rustling of tall grass in the distance.

Finally I fell into a restless sleep, full of hope and expectation.

CHAPTER 3

CASALTA, 1985

BIANCA

The next morning, despite my sleepless night, there was a spring in my step when I made my way to the empty kitchen.

Soon Matilde, Lulu and Mia joined me – Nora was still away on a riding competition – and we began setting up the breakfast table outside. The autumn morning air was crisp, but not too cold – a fresh wind swept the hills, and the chill made my skin pucker and tingle.

'You look different,' Mia said with her usual forthrightness.

Mia had no filter, and in social situations the uncanny way she had of reading people coupled with her sincerity made for a dangerous combination. Thankfully she preferred our company to that of anyone else, and Casalta to any other place in the world, so I seldom had to soothe wounded egos or repair cracked bonds.

'No, I don't. Same as yesterday, sister of mine,' was my cheery answer. I laid a basket of croissants on the table, courtesy of Matilde, who always stopped at the bakery before starting work at Casalta. She was just behind me with another tray, laden with coffee cups, a jug of milk and the sugar bowl, while Lulu followed with a teapot.

'No sleep?' Lulu asked after studying my face. The pros and cons of having a nest of sisters: constant support, but also living under watchful eyes. We'd been a house of secrets for so long: it seemed that keeping one now was much harder.

'Not much, but I'm good,' I said.

I didn't quite feel ready to share Viola's call and the hope it had instilled in me. I was afraid that if I put it in words, this renewed spark I felt inside me would dampen and die. It was too early. Like a newly started fire, I wanted to cup it with my hands to protect it, blow a nourishing breath on it so it could grow – and not to expose it to the winds of comments and opinions.

'You need to eat, rest and sleep, *figlia mia*,' Matilde admonished me. 'Especially with the work you do, so demanding for you.' I resisted a smile: Matilde always saw us four sisters as something fragile, to be protected. When really, the only one of us who was fragile was Mia.

'I promise you I'm looking after myself,' I said, laying a hand on Matilde's arm.

'*Brava, bambina mia*,' Matilde said.

I was twenty-five, not exactly a *bambina* – but for her, me and my sisters would never grow up.

We finally settled around the table, and I poured myself a cup of tea, while Lulu sipped her espresso and Mia cradled a cup of hot chocolate in her hands.

My sisters' styles couldn't have been more different from one another. Lulu was dressed in the height of fashion as usual, in her favourite blue dress with padded shoulders, round gold earrings and black high-heeled pumps – she looked the portrait of a businesswoman, the perfect image for the Falconeri company. Mia wore something black and flowy that looked billowy on her slender frame, and a stained painting apron that had belonged to Mum and began as white a long time ago. This was pretty much her uniform.

As for me, I always wore dresses, mainly flowery, and my hair half up, half down, held with a clip. More 1885 than 1985, I supposed. It was my style – old fashioned, but *me*. I hadn't changed it since I was fourteen, and I wouldn't have known how.

In middle school I'd tried to dress more like my classmates, but I didn't feel right in jeans or miniskirts. When it became clear that Mia needed to be homeschooled, and I chose to stay home with her so she wouldn't be alone, we were both free to wear whatever we wanted, without any peer pressure.

'Did you hear from Mum?' Lulu asked Mia, interrupting my musings about clothes.

Mia was suddenly absorbed by a speck of fluff on her skirt.

'Yes, just yesterday. She'll come any day now.'

'She didn't say when, did she? Just so we can prepare.' Lulu's efficiency and Mum's unpredictability were colliding again. No surprise there.

'What about you going to see her in London? Any progress there?' Lulu enquired. I bristled a little. For Mia, going to visit Mum in London would be no mean feat, and she was trying her best to summon the courage to do so. Mia didn't even like going down to the village, let alone taking a plane to another country.

'I'm thinking about it,' Mia said in a small voice.

This was the reason for her evening walks, she'd told me – to consider the journey, to gather the courage.

'Well, I'm off,' I said, rising. I wanted to end the conversation: I knew that Lulu just wanted to encourage our little sister to spread her wings, but Lulu didn't know Mia the way I did, and she didn't know how anxious Mia could become.

'I'll walk you to the car. I have a work meeting in Florence,' Lulu said.

'For that export deal?' I asked my twin as we circumnavigated the house to get to the gate, where we kept our cars.

'Yes, with Britain. It'd be a lifeline for us,' she said. Even if our mother had bought Casalta for us and saved it from the banks, it was still an uphill struggle to get the business, which had been ruined by our father, profitable again.

'Listen, about Mia,' I said gently. 'Don't put pressure on her. You know that...' I said, as Lulu bent towards the car mirror to apply lipstick.

'...she's special. I *know* she is. But she's twenty, and she behaves like a little girl. She needs to grow up a little. Gently, don't worry.' Lulu put her hands up. 'I know you want her here...'

'I don't! I mean, I do. But I want her to be where *she* wants to be!'

Lulu gave me a meaningful look.

'Yes, well, maybe where I can keep an eye on her.'

'We're trying to convince her to see Mum. Not to go on an expedition to Patagonia.'

I had to laugh. 'You're right. Bear with us, Lulu. We hunkered down for many years. It's not easy for any of us to open up to the world again.'

'Baby steps,' Lucrezia said, and gave me a peck on the cheek. While I rubbed my skin to get rid of the inevitable lipstick stain, she got into her car.

Her return and that of our mother had restored what had been broken by our father a long time ago, but also changed the balance we'd established while they were away. Everything was changing again, I considered as I climbed into my small blue Fiat 500. Life doesn't care how much we cling to the status quo; it charges on no matter what. Just like Lulu had said, we have to know how to let go, love what comes to us, then let go of that too, for yet something else to arrive...

The road between Casalta and Biancamura was a little gem,

perfect and beautiful, offering me mini surprises – a goshawk or a buzzard perched on a branch, a fox crossing the road, a grey heron watching over one of the small ponds.

The light of morning kissed the fields with a warmth that seeped into my skin, filling me with a quiet joy that felt as natural as the air I breathed. The sweet Tuscan countryside, which at the beginning of October was only just leaving the heat of summer behind and entering autumn, rolled alongside; smooth, rounded hills covered in grass and pine trees followed one another like notes of a symphony, farmhouses, hamlets and churches dotted here and there. Cypress trees lined the road like sentinels, their dark silhouettes standing against the sky like ink strokes on a watercolour painting, whispering secrets. In each season, this enchanted road looked subtly different: now, a golden, sideways light had replaced the blinding white-yellow of summer, and it made everything gleam equally golden.

This was more than a place to me – it was a part of me, my own heartbeat. I loved this land with devotion, as though it were an extension of my own body: every hill, every olive grove, every line of cypress trees was woven into the very fabric of who I was. The rhythms of the land, its shifting colours and quiet whispers, mirrored something deep within me, a connection so profound that it defied words. The hills rose and fell like the soft contours of a resting body, their curves familiar, comforting. In the early morning, as the mist clung to the slopes, I could feel the stillness settling into my chest, as if the land and I were breathing together.

The precise rows of grapevines were a testament to the land's patience and generosity, a reminder of the abundance this land offered to those who tended it with care. Now that the *vendemmia*, the grape harvest, was done, they seemed to rest after having given their all.

Even the imperfections of the land – the rough patches of brambles, the stubborn weeds that grew in forgotten corners –

were beautiful to me. They were part of its story, part of life. Its imperfections mirrored my own. Everything was a reminder of resilience, of the land's ability to create something extraordinary from the simplest, hardest of beginnings.

I didn't just see fields and villages and groves. I saw a part of myself reflected back, a love that was as vast and unending as the hills themselves. I couldn't imagine being anywhere else, because this land wasn't just my home – it was my body, my soul, my heart. And I loved it with everything I had.

Half an hour later I was in Biancamura, a village with a few shops and facilities that, compared to Casalta, made it look like a small town. I parked at the retirement home, Villa Lieta, a small red-roofed building that housed both elderly and disabled people who couldn't live independently. Every Wednesday I went to visit the guests, put out little fires for them and keep them company, and I enjoyed this part of my work. But today, something was different, something I couldn't define.

As soon as I opened the car door and put my feet on the ground, I felt uneasy, somehow. It was as if a tiny electric charge had run over my skin. Hearing Viola's call and praying my gift was back, the conversations with my sisters about Mia leaving: these events seemed to me like the little tremors that precede an earthquake.

My world was shifting.

'*Ciao*, Ortensia!' I called to a woman clutching a doll to her chest. She was dressed in bright colours, her hair cut short and held with a pink hairclip to keep her fringe away from her face. Ortensia always waited by the door for me to arrive. She would eternally be ten years old, and needed so much looking after that her elderly parents had entrusted her to the home, coming to see her every weekend.

She threw herself in my arms and squeezed me tight. 'I missed you!' she said, like she did every time she saw me.

'Me too! How are you, *cara?*'

'I'm good. Can we do a jigsaw?'

Her favourite pastime. 'Of course. Go wait for me in the common room, get everything ready, and I'll come in a minute,' I said.

Ortensia obediently skipped away into the common room: here guests gathered in the morning and late afternoon, to chat and dedicate themselves to their hobbies. Some read, some did their crosswords, some just sat and soaked in the light coming from the wide windows. This was where family and friends of the guests could spend time with their loved ones, during visiting hours.

Ortensia had just disappeared into the common room, when a short man with a pair of glasses on his nose and another on his head stepped out of a side door, in front of me. It was Dottor Artibani, the resident doctor and director of the home.

'Bianca, *buongiorno*! It's great you're here today of all days!'

Was it? I frowned slightly. I came every Wednesday, after all.

'Thank you,' I replied.

Dottor Artibani was always welcoming towards me and Camilla – he perpetually stood on the precipice of not having enough personnel, time and funding to provide for the guests, so he cherished any help he could get. But today he seemed positively enthusiastic about seeing me.

He turned towards his office. 'Signor Orafi, have you met Signorina Bianca Falconeri before?'

My heart stopped.

Signor Orafi?

And then Lorenzo Orafi appeared from behind Artibani, dressed in an immaculate suit as always, his black hair now tamed and slicked back – but I remembered it wavy and thick, silky between my fingers. The scent of him, a fragrance I knew so well but couldn't have named, hit me and filled me with memories – his body close to mine, all my senses full of him.

The deep-set, diffident, guilty-until-proven-innocent eyes, the features of a Roman statue, his stalwart body, stalwart heart... a heart that I used to be sure only I knew.

Yes, we had met before.

Lorenzo's face looked at me from the corkboard over my desk every day, where his picture had been pinned for years.

I did my best to keep my composure.

'Bianca. Hello,' he greeted me calmly. His expression didn't change. The contrast between my memories and his present indifference gave me whiplash.

When my family had fallen apart, and I'd felt broken, when I'd descended into darkness, secretly and silently – because on the surface, I had to keep smiling and be strong for my little sisters – his hand had appeared out of the dark to hold mine, saving me like I was saving him. I found love where I had least expected to find it. He became the seventh person to know about our gifts – us four sisters, our mother and, by force of circumstances, Matilde.

And I entrusted my lost gift to him to keep safe...

Probably seeing me wasn't a big deal to him any more – even when Father died and he'd attempted to buy Casalta from us, he'd kept his distance from me.

My family, the Falconeri, had a complicated history with the Orafi clan, and only with my mother's return had we sisters grasped the full extent of those complications. Our grandparents had been allies, even friends; but something had happened between our fathers – since then, we'd been forbidden to even talk to anyone belonging to the Orafi clan.

But Vanni, the younger brother, and Lulu had a bond that proved to be unbreakable, a friendship stronger than our families' rivalries. As children, they met in secret at a little treehouse Vanni built in the hills, between Casalta and the Orafi's estate in Biancamura.

When Lulu was sent away there was a long period of

silence between them; after her return, they picked up where they'd left off – on the verge of adolescence, when their friendship was about to turn into something more. Now they were together, and more in love than ever.

But when Lulu had been away, something had happened to me too, at the same treehouse she and Vanni had left behind. I was supposed to meet Vanni in secret, to explain to him the reasons behind my twin's imposed exile, and I did – a glimmer of friendship and goodwill sparked between us and we resolved to meet again. But one day, instead of Vanni, it was Lorenzo who came to the treehouse...

Stop.

Better not remembering all that now, or I'd get flustered, and that was the exact opposite of what I was aiming for.

Cool and collected, Bianca, I reminded myself.

After all, it wasn't the first time I'd seen Lorenzo in all those years – and every time I'd been successful in hiding my emotions. Or at least I hoped.

'...Bianca and Camilla, we couldn't do without them,' I heard Artibani saying when I came back to myself. Between Artibani's comment on our indispensability just at the moment when I was planning to look for another job, and Lorenzo's presence, I went into short circuit. Everyone turned towards me, but any words got stuck in my throat.

'Lorenzo,' I managed to articulate finally, sounding more aloof than I wanted to. When I looked down, I thought I would see icicles growing from my fingertips.

'Bianca. Can I introduce you to...' But Lorenzo didn't get to finish his sentence.

'Bianca! Lucrezia's *twin!*' A petite, blonde woman appeared from behind him. She wore a silk scarf around her neck, a short linen dress in spite of the chill in the air, and strappy sandals. She was perfectly groomed, from her lipstick to her highlighted waves to her manicured hands. Her smile was bright and wide. Like a crocodile...

Bianca, stop it.

But I really disliked her at once. I couldn't help it.

'I'm Tamara, Lorenzo's *girlfriend*! I believe you met my mum!' She was a walking, talking exclamation mark.

She was Lorenzo's girlfriend.

Oh.

That wasn't supposed to happen. Lorenzo never saw anyone else in all these years, I was sure. Not since...

Oh, this was just stupid. Why had I assumed he'd never meet anyone? Yes, he'd been devoted to looking after his brother and his father ever since the accident, much as I'd been looking after my sisters – but surely that wouldn't last forever?

There was no reason to be so stunned.

'Bianca?' Tamara squealed. I shook myself out of my reverie.

'Nice to meet you,' I managed. *Oh, a real joy.* 'I know your mum?'

'Annasara! She did the interior design for the Orafi house. That's how Lorenzo and I met. It was meant to be,' she added with an adoring gaze towards Lorenzo.

Oh, yes. I remembered now. Annasara, the woman with the red talons and the enormous perm.

Dottor Artibani intervened. 'Bianca, Signor Orafi is here because he's generously funding the refurbishment of the upper floor. And you know how much we need it!'

'That *is* very generous,' I said sincerely. 'Thank you, Lorenzo.'

'My pleasure,' he answered coolly.

'Let me show you the rooms.' Dottor Artibani extended a hand towards Lorenzo, to lead him towards the stairs. That was my cue to go.

'Well, I'll get to my work,' I said. My hands felt icy – all of a sudden I realised I was cold, freezing. My heart had been galloping a few minutes before, but now it seemed to me that it was beating slow, slow. Cold and inert and apathetic.

Now I knew why I'd had that strange feeling when I first arrived, like something was about to happen.

'Nice meeting you, Tamara.'

As nice as being stung by a wasp.

Lorenzo and the doctor moved on and I was about to step into the common room, when Tamara's small fingers closed around my wrist and made me turn around. What did she want from me?

'With you two being childhood friends you'd think he'd talk about you at some point, but he never did,' she said, eyes wide.

Oh. Snake in the grass. Still, maybe I was reading into it. Maybe it was a perfectly innocent statement.

Then how did she know Lorenzo and I were childhood friends?

He must have told someone. He must have told *her*. Which contradicted her statement.

Anyway. I had nothing to comment on what she said, true or not.

'I really must go...'

'So, is this your job?' She did a thing with her hand, a little wrist twist landing with her palm upwards.

'Part of it, yes. Did Lorenzo tell you?'

'He said something, yes.'

'I thought he never mentioned me?' I said, and regretted it immediately. That was a cheap shot. I wished I could scrap the whole conversation and start again. 'And what do you do?' I asked with a smile, as sincere as I could.

'You don't know me? I work on Toscana TV.'

Oh, yes! That was why I thought I'd seen her somewhere. She was the perky, high-pitched girl on the local evening news.

'Of course! We watch it sometimes. I didn't recognise you.'

Tamara tilted her head. 'It's funny, you know?'

'What's funny?'

'You look *just* like your sister. Lucrezia, I mean.'

'Well, we're identical twins.'

'I know, but she's always *so* put together.'

And I'm not. I knew what she was implying.

'Don't get me wrong, your dress is so pretty. My *nonna* had one just the same.'

She *really* was a snake in the grass.

'Wait, what does your look remind me of... Oh, I know! *Little House on the Prairie*? *Anne of Green Gables*?'

I couldn't find anything to say. I knew that later I'd think of a thousand dignified, yet biting replies. But for now, I had nothing.

'Well, I'd better go,' she concluded. 'Oh, wait. I was wondering if you wanted my hairdresser's number?'

My hand went to my hair. 'No, thanks?'

She put her hands up. 'Just wondering.'

She followed Lorenzo, tottering on her high heels, and I was left a little dazed. Poison served in honey has a confusing effect – because of the sweetness of the honey, it takes a little while to feel the poison. I ran my hands over my hair again, and down my dress.

So, I looked like Anne of Green Gables. And like Tamara's *nonna*.

The thoughts that burst into my mind were *way* beneath me.

CHAPTER 4

CASALTA, 1985

BIANCA

I was trying to take a deep, calming breath, when a tiny woman with a grey bob and thick glasses came into the hallway, walking with little steps.

It was Amarilli, my friend, surrogate granny for me and my favourite among all the people we assisted – though I probably shouldn't have had favourites.

Amarilli had been small in her youth and was even smaller in her old age – like a grey-haired fairy. Her eyesight was bad to the point that she struggled to read, but books and magazines were her passion – so, every Wednesday when I visited Villa Lieta, I read aloud to her. I often took her out at the weekend too, because her eyes made going out by herself unsafe.

'Morning, my dear,' she greeted me and threw a glance at Tamara, who was about to pivot and tackle the second set of stairs. 'How does she walk in *those*?' Amarilli said loud enough for Tamara to hear and stop for a moment, before reprising her climb like Amarilli wasn't even worth a reply.

'*Shhh!*' I whispered, taking Amarilli by the arm and leading her gently towards the common room. 'Honestly, you have no filter! You remind me of my little sister!'

'Well, Mia is an outstanding little person. And, at my age, I've earned the right to say what I think.'

'Aloud?' I said and she giggled, a mischievous look in her eyes, like a little girl caught being naughty.

But I also noticed that she looked a little pale. And she'd been late in coming downstairs this morning.

'I have a couple of things to do, then I'll come and read you a magazine?' I always tried to leave her last, so I could give her as much time as possible. Amarilli didn't receive many visitors: friends and distant relatives came, but her beloved daughter and grandchildren lived in Rome and were about to move to the United States.

'I'd love that, dear. I'll go sit in my sunny corner over there and wait for you.'

I busied myself, which wasn't difficult – everyone needed something, and I enjoyed fixing little problems, giving encouragement, holding wrinkled, fragile hands. Thankfully, doing the rounds of my duties didn't leave much room for me to brood about the unwelcome morning encounter. Not *much* room, but a little room, sadly yes, and thoughts of Lorenzo whirled in my mind, like sand rising up in a pond that had been disturbed.

The walls of Villa Lieta seemed to be closing on me, and I was suffocating. I recalled the strange, tingling feeling that had overcome me when I arrived there – like my own skin had become too tight on me – as if something long pushed down yearned to be released.

I was sitting with Ortensia, helping her with her jigsaw, when one of the nurses passed by our table.

'Paola?' I called. 'Amarilli looks a little under the weather,' I said in a low voice, careful that nobody else would hear me. 'Is she well?'

'So-so,' Paola answered, throwing a glance at the elderly

woman, who was soaking up the autumnal sun in her window seat. 'A little tired. Nothing major, but we're keeping an eye on her.'

'I will too.'

Finally, Amarilli and I sat and read *La Signora*, a magazine packed with sweet, tame, real-life stories she loved – and I did too, though I was about thirty years younger than their average reader.

'So... where were we?' I said, opening the magazine. Amarilli laid a hand on my arm.

'*E' un bel ragazzo,*' she murmured. *He's a handsome man.*

'Sorry?'

'The Orafi boy. Lorenzo.'

I'd been so good at hiding everything that had happened between Lorenzo and me – even the simple fact that we knew each other, which in small villages like Casalta and Biancamura wasn't easy at all. I couldn't give myself away now.

Why, *why* did he have the bright idea to come into my sphere of existence? The retirement home was *my* territory. And now, I had to deal with it.

'I suppose.' I resumed my reading, but barely a sentence in, Amarilli spoke again.

'He turned around.'

I took a deep breath. I really didn't want to continue this conversation, so I said nothing. Amarilli patted my knee. Her eyes were like two raisins beyond the thick glasses.

'When you said goodbye he went but then he turned around when you weren't looking,' she breathed out, making the sentence sound like an extra-long word.

'I have no idea what you're talking about!' But she smiled a knowing smile, and I felt compelled to protest some more. 'Did you not see his *girlfriend* was with him?'

'Oh, I did.'

'Well, then.'

'Well, then.'

I once again resumed my reading, and tried to ignore what Amarilli stubbornly whispered under her breath once again.

'*He turned around.*'

CHAPTER 5

❦

CASALTA, 1985

BIANCA

When I finally returned home, I was exhausted. For the rest of the day, I just couldn't concentrate on anything.

I sat on the windowsill in my room, just where the lady in blue used to spin her wool. Unwelcome thoughts kept coming at me, dark and so tangled up that I could hardly tell them apart.

Tamara.

Amarilli looking so frail, just when I was considering moving on from Legami.

The fear that Mia would crumble under the pressure of going to London.

The joy I'd felt when I heard Viola's voice for the first time in years melted into this jumble and turned into longing and disquiet. It wasn't enough, to hear Viola call my name! I desperately wanted – I *needed* – my gift back...

And Lorenzo.

Lorenzo.

The tremors in my life had indeed grown into an earthquake, like I knew they would. Solid ground had turned liquid and I swam in novel emotions.

Lorenzo's cold, inexpressive face when he'd seen me kept coming back to me, and Tamara's cruel words too, which she'd had no reason to utter: there was nothing between me and Lorenzo, and it had been that way for years. I was no threat to her now, surely?

And yet, Lorenzo's picture had been pinned in my room, on my heart, for years.

I rested my chin on my hand and threw my gaze across my room. Hanging over my desk, among postcards and cinema tickets and to-do lists, was a newspaper cutting. It'd been there forever, and the paper was a little curled at the edges.

Lorenzo's smiling face stared back at me, forever fixed in a joyful moment that happened years before. He was dressed in running gear and holding a medal wrapped around his neck. He'd come third place in a fundraising race for the physiotherapy centre Vanni attended after the accident that left him in a wheelchair. A local paper had written an article about the event, and I'd carefully cut it out and kept it.

Lorenzo's picture was pinned on my heart.

A shameful thought bubbled up to the surface of my mind, a realisation that shattered me: I'd been *waiting* for him. I'd been waiting for something to happen between us, and somewhere in my heart I was sure it would.

I should have known better, considering what I'd done to him...

I walked to my desk and touched the paper lightly, following its contours with my fingers.

Who was I fooling? Tamara had plenty of reason to be wary of me, and what I hid inside, so deep not even I could find it.

The impulse to rip the picture into pieces filled me – but I couldn't. Instead, I removed it gently and placed it in the desk drawer.

The empty space was as sad as I thought it'd be, a Lorenzo-shaped hole in my life, in my memories, in my history... but maybe I could fill it with something else. New dreams, new stories, new ambitions. A new Bianca, free from the chains of the past, free from vain hopes and delusions.

I stood in front of the mirror that hung beside my wardrobe, and studied my reflection. I hated how Tamara's words had taken residence in my mind, but maybe it was time to reconsider.

The light green dress, with the colour-on-colour embroidery around the neckline and hem, and my hairstyle *were* a bit grandmothery. It *was* an old-fashioned look, after all, and as much as Tamara was venomous towards me, there was some truth in what she'd said.

The *witch*.

I supposed my clothes suited my job, working with elderly people, frozen out of time, dealing with medicines and bills and complaints of arthritis, reading aloud stories from *La Signora* and *The People's Companion*.

I thought of Tamara on her TV set, glamorous, fashionable, perfect like I could never be. Was I stuck in time? Was I stuck pretending to be someone I no longer was?

Lulu's admonishment – *don't let your life pass you by* – and Tamara's comments on my clothes and my work echoed in my ears. Lulu loved me and wanted the best for me – Tamara was nothing to me, but she seemed to be the collective voice of the outside world, the world beyond Casalta.

I opened my wardrobe – dresses and more dresses – and closed it at once.

I needed expert help. I made my way to Lucrezia's study, where she was still working, and knocked at my sister's door.

'Perfect!' Lulu beamed at me, an hour later.

My heart gave a little jump when I didn't recognise myself in the mirror, but it was a happy kind of jump. Happy, and a little apprehensive.

Courtesy of Lucrezia, the new Bianca wore a pair of jeans and a light peach-coloured T-shirt that left one shoulder bare. I let my hair down, and it fell in waves over my shoulders. As the last touch, Lulu secured a pair of green earrings in my ears, a triangular shape that I would have never picked for myself.

No more *nonna* style for me.

I did like the girl I saw in the mirror... It was just that this girl didn't really look like me. I chased my doubts away. Of course I didn't look like the old Bianca any more! This was the *new* me.

'Are you sure you don't mind lending me your clothes?' I asked Lulu.

'Not at all. That's what sisters do; that's what we'd have done had we not been separated! Now you have a whole new look for whole new projects. A new job, higher education...' She began picking items from the pile of clothes on my bed and hanging them up in my wardrobe. I looked at my discarded dresses, destined to be put away, with some nostalgia.

'Actually, that's not the only reason why I wanted a change. Someone today told me her *nonna* has clothes like mine. That I look like Anne of Green Gables – remember, the book we had when we were little?' I sighed. 'She offered me the number of her *hairdresser*. And asked me why you always look so put together, and I don't.'

'What?' Lulu's eyes were murderous. 'Who told you this?'

'Tamara. Lorenzo Orafi's new girlfriend.' I tried to keep my tone casual.

'She didn't... I could *strangle* her!'

I had to laugh. 'Please don't.'

'Did you see her at Villa Lieta? Vanni said they're financing work there.'

'Yes.'

Lulu studied my face – she could see through me and I knew she would be watching my aura. I'd kept the secret about Lorenzo and me for so long, afraid that it would complicate our lives further – to the point that when she first returned, Lulu had mistakenly believed there was something between me and Vanni. I knew she suspected something had happened between me and the other Orafi brother, and I longed to open up to her.

A hairline crack opened in my reserve...

But instead of saying any more I shrugged again, to drive home the point that it wasn't that important. I'd become used to keeping everything inside. Every fibre of my being yearned to be secret, to hide my feelings as much as I could.

'Look, I *know* there's history between you and Lorenzo. Something you never spoke about.' Lucrezia pointed at the empty space above my desk where Lorenzo's face used to be. 'Also, remember I saw you together? It's clear to me that there's history between you.'

You could say that, yes.

The hairline crack opened a little wider. I looked down. Regret and shame always took a hold of me, every time I thought of *us*, Lorenzo and Bianca... the *us* that never was. 'Lulu, did you meet Tamara?'

'Oh, yes. Up at their house. It was a surprise for everyone, including Vanni and their dad,' Lulu continued. 'They thought Lorenzo would be a bachelor forever. I know exactly where you're coming from. She's *horrible*.'

Lucrezia was always direct. Also, she had little consideration for shades of grey – everything was always black and white, with her. Out of fairness, I would have liked to say, *Maybe you should give her a chance*. But I didn't.

'She reads the news on Toscana TV,' I said, trying, and probably failing, to sound nonchalant.

'Oh, I know.' Lucrezia began imitating her, making up a piece of local news and stressing every word, all the while fanning her hair about and making intense expressions. 'The village of Biancamura has a new *fountain*,' Lulu made up as she went along, 'full of the tears of all who *crossed me*. Have a good night everyone, bye from *me!*' She tilted her head in a way that made me bend in two with laughter. Sometimes, when my twin and I were together, we reverted to children.

'Anyway. Tamara's comments didn't affect me,' I made sure to say. 'I didn't care.'

'You cared enough to change your look,' Lulu said truthfully. 'And...' She threw a glance towards my desk. 'The photo is down.'

'It's time to move on,' I said, though my heart struggled to keep up with my brain. 'It was nothing more than a childish crush, you know that.'

'No, I don't, Bianca. I can't say what it was or what it wasn't. It belongs to the time of secrets, remember? The time when we had to guess and fill in the gaps and got it wrong so many times...'

It was those words that finally broke my reserve, and a stream of confidences began to pour out of me. But I couldn't tell her *everything*. I never could. There was something I'd always keep for myself.

'When you were sent away, I saw Vanni at the treehouse, to tell him what happened to you,' I said. Lulu frowned a little, remembering those grim times – and probably remembering how she misunderstood the relationship between Vanni and me. 'Both of us missed you so much. We arranged to meet again, so I could give him any news I had of you. But Lorenzo turned up instead, to order me to stay away from their family. Not just because of the rivalry between our fathers – only later we all found out that something had happened between Mum and Gherardo Orafi...'

Lulu nodded. She'd found out about Mum and Gherardo Orafi when I did – when our mother told us, not much longer than six months before. Gherardo had been in love with our mother for years – nothing had happened between them, nothing more than a deep friendship, and Gherardo had tried to help her, to help us, when Father threw her out of Casalta and forced her to leave us behind.

There'd been nothing Gherardo could do. My father's wrath fell on him: his men tampered with the Orafi car and caused the accident that left Vanni in a wheelchair, Gherardo chronically ill, and Lorenzo traumatised. At the time I couldn't believe that Father was responsible for the accident, but Lorenzo was always convinced of it.

'Lorenzo told me to stay away, but I went back to the treehouse; I don't know why. And I don't know why he returned too. But we both did. I can't quite explain... nobody can understand unless they've felt it, and I think you did, with Vanni.'

'Yes.'

'Every time we could, we escaped there. It wasn't often, because we were both so involved with our families... but when we did... it was perfect. And our friendship became... more than a friendship.'

'Oh, Bianca,' my twin whispered. The feeling of being known, of being understood, was heady, almost painful – like the pain in muscles contracted for so long that they screamed when they were let go. I wasn't used to it any more – I didn't know the sweetness of confidences, of leaning on someone.

'The accident brought us even closer. There was so much on Lorenzo's shoulders... We leaned on each other. And then...'

Matilde's voice called us from downstairs. 'Girls! Dinner's on the table!' The call broke the spell, and for a moment I almost regretted confiding in Lulu. My story wasn't finished. I'd have to tell her what happened next – the hardest, worst decision of my life, one that I'd regretted ever since.

'Anyway. Everyone has moved on with their lives,' I said, standing up. 'He's moved on too. And so will I.'

'I'm sorry that with Vanni and me being together you might have to see him... well, the family... from time to time...'

'I'm fine with it. Seriously, I am.'

'You know Gherardo's sixtieth birthday is coming up. There'll be a party, and I'm sure he'll want us all there.'

'And I'll be there.'

'If Tamara *dares* to open her mouth...' Lucrezia said with a dark look in her eyes.

'Sometimes you scare me, Lulu.'

'Well, good. Every woman should know how to be scary sometimes,' she said and left the room, with me behind her.

After today, I had to agree.

CHAPTER 6

CASALTA, FOURTEEN YEARS EARLIER

BIANCA

I don't know why I went back to the treehouse.

I was thirteen years old, and I lived among the ruins of my world. The first time I was there, it was to tell Vanni about Lucrezia's exile.

The second time I was there, it was to spend time with Vanni, so that we both could feel closer to our lost Lulu.

The third time, I found Lorenzo there.

The brothers were very alike, so for a moment I didn't recognise him – I thought it *was* Vanni, and I was preparing myself to tell him that there was no news, that none of us knew where Lulu had been sent, that Father was behaving like everything was normal and Matilde's eyes were perpetually shiny...

But something wasn't right. Vanni wasn't that tall, that big – he was slight, and his hair not that dark, and he never stood so straight and still. And then I realised it wasn't Vanni: it was his elder brother, Lorenzo. His face was hard in a way that didn't suit his features – as if he was wearing a mask. He was fifteen, a teenager; but just like me, he'd had to grow up fast.

A small part of me considered turning around and running away – but pride stopped me. I wouldn't run away in front of an Orafi. Or anyone else, for that matter.

'Falconeri,' he said. He knew my first name, of course, but he decided to greet me by my family name. Just to make things clear from the beginning.

I crossed my arms. Things were bad enough for me at home without having the Orafi boy treat me like this.

'I have a name,' I said coldly.

He seemed taken aback. Maybe he expected me to cower?

'Bianca.'

'Lorenzo.'

'Stay away from my brother. You, your twin, all of you Falconeri, stay away from my brother and from all my family.'

'Why can't he tell me that?'

'He won't be coming back here. Your twin is gone, anyway. And you have your father to thank for that.'

And with that, my defiance went. I burst into tears.

The shame, the shame! I covered my face with my hands but it was no use, of course – my tears were a child's tears, unstoppable, my shoulders trembling, sobs and all. Like a dam had broken.

'I'm sorry,' I heard Lorenzo say quietly.

'Lulu is not gone! She's just away for a little while! Everything will go back to normal!' I cried out and stared at him, as if challenging him would change things.

Lorenzo gave me a long, long look. Back then, I had no idea of what was going through his mind – I had no idea of what had happened in his family, of the secret bond between his father and my mother at the time of Mum's disappearance.

After a minute of unbearable embarrassment, I dried my tears and took a long breath. Neither of us moved.

Tentatively, awkwardly, Lorenzo came close to me and

wrapped his arms around me. We held onto each other, two teenagers who'd seen their families fall apart.

I had a few moments in his arms, and then I turned around and ran, ran all the way home.

CHAPTER 7

CASALTA, 1985

BIANCA

A few days passed quietly, along the blueprint of the usual routine. But what nobody knew was that I'd kept the promise made to Lulu, to grab my life with both hands. I'd planted a seed in the form of a phone call, and I was hoping it'd take.

We were gathered on the patio for breakfast, as usual. My sisters were chatting, but I was quiet – I was waiting for news about something that mattered a lot to me, and I hoped with all my heart that the phone would ring any moment now.

All of a sudden, Nora's familiar alto voice resounded from the inside of the house. 'I'm back, everyone! Anybody home?'

'In the garden!' Mia shouted, jumping up to welcome her.

Nora appeared through the French doors: she was dressed in her riding gear, her worse-for-wear brown backpack on her shoulders. She was glowing: the summer always turned her skin golden, and when Lulu and I were beside her, with our milky complexions, we didn't look like sisters. There was something about her that reminded me of an ancient Roman goddess: a hunting goddess, a woodland one, running with hounds and deer.

'Welcome back, *cara*,' I said and gave Nora a hug, as soon as I could disentangle Mia from her. Nora smelled of cut grass, and of horse – an earthy, warm scent that was her signature.

'Was it good?' Lulu asked. She hugged Nora too, and then proceeded to sweep her dress with her hands. 'Horse hair,' she muttered.

'It was brilliant. Just *brilliant*. I need a shower. And food!' She grabbed one of Matilde's croissants and took a hearty bite. Then she looked at me. 'Oh.'

'Oh?' I asked, heat rising to my face.

'You look different.'

'Different, how?' I teased her. She sensed the smallest changes in the weather, the scents in the air, the hues of plants and trees and the faintest animal noises, but she was usually oblivious of almost anything regarding humans.

'I don't know...' She tilted her head in that graceful way of hers – the line of her long neck, exposed by the pixie haircut, exquisite as ever. Nora turned heads wherever she went – not that she noticed it, and when she did, she balked just like a wild horse.

'Bianca is wearing jeans,' Mia said seriously.

'Oh. Yes, that's it! I haven't seen you in jeans since we were... *twelve*? You look lovely, Bianca. Anyway, keep me some food, please. Oh, hi, Matilde,' Nora said as our housekeeper appeared behind her, and kissed her on the cheek, bending down a good deal.

'*Ciao, bambina mia*. Welcome back,' Matilde said. 'Well, it's good to have everyone under the same roof. And the signora is coming soon, isn't she?'

'Yes! Mum will be here any day now,' Mia said, beaming.

'She'll probably just turn up at the door,' Lulu said with a resigned sigh. She liked to plan everything well in advance and in great detail, but with a family like ours, it wasn't easy.

The shrill sound of the phone reached us, and I jumped out of my skin.

'Bianca! For you!' Nora shouted my name; blood rushed to my head and my heart started pounding against my ribs. I ran inside as quickly as I could and took the handset from my sister – a blade of grass was stuck on it from her hand, and I would have smiled, had I not been so nervous. I knew it was the news I'd been waiting for.

'Hello, this is Bianca speaking.'

'Bianca, it's Hilda Matteusz from the Uffizi Museum,' said a German-accented voice.

'Yes. Yes, hello.' *Sound nonchalant. Confident. Sound like someone employable.* 'Thank you for getting back to me.'

'No problem at all, Bianca. Luigi is an old friend of mine and I'll be more than happy to see you, if you're still keen?'

Luigi was known by us sisters as Signor Pero, my father's old friend and one of the few who'd had kind words when we discovered he was bankrupt. He knew pretty much everyone in Florence, so I'd hoped he could put me in touch with someone at the Uffizi – and he did. I made a mental note of visiting him, armed with a case of the best Falconeri wine.

'I am! I'm very keen.' Deep breath. 'Thank you.'

'I have half an hour tomorrow at ten? Or is that too soon?'

'Perfect. I'll be there,' I said, my mind immediately rushing to rearrange my duties with Legami.

'Well, bring your CV. It'll be lovely to meet you,' Hilda answered.

'Good news?' Nora called from halfway up the stairs.

'I have an interview!'

'You're changing jobs?' she asked.

'I'm changing *everything*,' I said happily, while my sisters reached me in a flutter of congratulations and questions.

'And now, the hard part!' I said.

'Finding the perfect outfit for the interview.' Lulu was as pragmatic as ever.

'Well, no. Telling Camilla that I might be leaving soon. I didn't think it'd be so quick. I hate to leave her in a tough spot.'

'She'll be fine. They'll all be fine. And you,' Lulu said triumphantly. 'You'll make all your dreams come true.'

~

I made my way down the hill to the village of Casalta, where Camilla and I had our informal headquarters. The road to the village was narrow and winding, and not asphalted – our father had insisted on that, and for once we all thought he'd been inspired. It added a touch of isolation and aloofness to our beloved home.

It was a clear morning, warm still – here, winter came sudden and cold, but late summers always lingered before falling into autumn, and we always had a few weeks of deep blue skies and tepid air, only lightly touched by the first chilly winds.

As I walked down, bend after bend, my thoughts were whirling – what would Hilda offer me? Would I be good enough, capable enough to do whatever was asked of me? I'd never had a job outside of Legami – all I knew was looking after people...

But there was too much beauty around me, and I was too happy and expectant to leave much room for frightened thoughts. I was almost skipping along the wild fennel, laurel and myrtle, the fig trees, the grass browned with the summer sun; and beyond the road, the woods of chestnuts and holly oaks. Our hill was as wild as we could keep it – it was only beyond Casalta that the fields and hills were domesticated, covered in tidy vineyards and olive groves: the heart of the Falconeri estate, together with Nora's stables.

At the foot of the hill the hamlet of Casalta announced itself with the first vegetable patches, neatly divided by hedges and short fences, dotted here and there with apple and cherry trees. I walked down a tiny alley between two houses, paved with the brown-rose-golden stone of our villages.

Everything about Casalta whispered of history: the weathered stones of the homes, the uneven cobbles underfoot, the carved lintels above the doors. The houses stood huddled together and their walls, shaped by years of sun, wind, and rain, bore patches of moss and ivy that climbed and curled as if they were part of the architecture itself. Small windows peeked out from these walls, framed by wooden shutters painted in shades of green and blue. The paint was chipped and faded in places, but it only added to the charm, as did the flower boxes beneath the windows, overflowing with flowers. The roads that wove through Casalta were narrow and winding, paved with cobblestones polished smooth by the tread of countless feet. These roads were too small for cars, and even the occasional bicycle seemed to move through them with caution. It was a place made for walking, for wandering at an unhurried pace.

Elderly residents sat outside their homes, their wooden chairs pulled into the shade of doorways. They watched the children playing, their weathered faces and hands betraying a lifetime of hard work. Their conversations rose and fell in a symphony of voices, discussing the day's events or reminiscing about the past. Some worked with their hands as they chatted – knitting, shelling beans. Others simply rested, soaking in the peace of the afternoon.

Washing lines were tied onto balconies, displaying all manners of clothing except the women's underclothes and newborns' clothes, which were traditionally hung inside – the first because of modesty, the second because of superstition. It was believed that babies' clothes could be cursed by witches, especially after dark, and had to be protected.

Traversing the village would have taken fifteen minutes at the most, but there was always someone to greet, chat and exchange news with. My sisters and I had grown up almost isolated from the people of Casalta, except for church on Sundays and errands in the small shops; also, we were homeschooled from our early teens. For years, the link between us and the community had been Matilde. But now my work had created strong ties with the people in the area, Nora's riding school meant that she knew many of the local schoolchildren, and Lulu employed some of their parents and grandparents.

Now the Falconeri sisters were not as isolated and unapproachable as we used to be, except for Mia, who preferred remaining so – not because of snobbery, as it was often misinterpreted as, but of shyness.

The heart of Casalta was its central square, small but full of life, bordered by the hamlet's most important landmarks. At one end stood the *panetteria*, a small bread shop, and the scent of freshly baked bread, warm and inviting, wafted out into the square, mingling with the sweet aroma of pastries and cakes. Matilde's house, a paragon of neatness with its doorstep swept and the windows polished, stood only two doors down from the shop. Matilde stopped every morning to buy croissants for our breakfast, a tradition she'd started when we were little and never stopped. Beside the *panetteria* was a coffee shop where us children bought ice cream from, local mums got their coffees and cappuccinos, and men drank red wine and discussed football after work. In the summer, tables and chairs spilled out onto the square, covered by striped awning.

In the centre of the square, overlooking everything, stood the main church, grand and beautifully decorated even in such a small village, its steps carved in stone and its heavy, wooden door made smooth by countless hands opening it.

More chapels were dotted here and there at the edges of Casalta, built in the Middle Ages to mark its borders and protect the place from war and disease.

Just beside the church were some rooms for community use, and one of them had been kindly given to us. It was small, with a tiny table and four foldable chairs besieged by boxes of donations, but it was perfect for Legami.

Camilla's Fiat Panda was parked in front – she was there already. I stopped at the coffee shop across the street and bought a cappuccino and pastries, a minuscule and futile attempt to soften the blow.

'*Buongiorno*,' I said and laid the round metal tray on the table.

'Oh hello, my dear. Why, thank you for breakfast! I didn't have a moment to eat this morning. My daughter threw a strop because she doesn't like her new haircut and refused to go to school, and my son lost his football kit. You are the best,' she added, lifting her cup.

I wonder if she'll still think that after I give her my news, I thought anxiously.

Camilla was only a little older than me, but already she had two children and had been married for a few years. Her demeanour was always calm and seraphic, which was perfect for our line of work. I'd met her at Villa Lieta when I first set up the co-op. At the time I had so little funds, the co-op was really just me running around from case to case doing my best. Camilla was there visiting her grandmother, and we clicked at once. We became Legami, and the rest was history.

And now I was about to leave.

'I have something to tell you that you might not like. Well, that you *won't* like.' I breathed deeply. Better tell her all at once, like ripping a plaster off. 'I'm going to apply to the Scuola di Restauro in Florence. And look for a job in the meanwhile. There, I said it.'

Camilla's mouth was like a little *o*.

'I won't leave until we find someone else, of course! I'll go part time. And I'll always be here if you need anything. Please, say something...'

'I'm so happy for you,' she said with a smile that really, really tried.

'Please, Camilla. *Be* happy for me.'

'I *just* said that I am!'

'I mean, for real.'

'I promise you, I am. But... I miss you already! And so will our people. Oh, listen to me, guilt tripping you! It's not fair of me.' She laid her hand on mine. Her fingers were chubby and short and full of rings, and her hand felt warm – Camilla was always warm: being beside her was enough to feel toasty. 'I'm just a little surprised. Don't let me rain on your parade! This is wonderful news.'

'I'll be working part-time hours,' I repeated. 'You won't be rid of me yet, I promise. Until we find someone suitable.'

'I'd better start spreading the word, then. Don't worry, we'll find someone soon.'

Someone. Someone to take over my baby.

I won't feel guilty, I won't feel guilty, I won't feel guilty.
Or at least, I'll try.

∼

That night, in my bed, I felt something brushing my cheek. I was in a sleep too deep to awake from, but I felt the touch, and I knew it wasn't a dream. And then, the long-awaited call came again.

Bianca, Viola whispered in my ear. *Find me.*

I woke up at once and switched the light on. *Find me?* What did that mean? Find her where? In Casalta? Was she there somewhere, and finally I'd see her again?

I got up, fully awake, and grabbed the torch I kept in my desk drawer. When I stepped outside my room, fear gathered in the pit of my stomach. I couldn't help remembering the times that my gift had frightened me, when I was little – when sudden, unexpected apparitions opened the door between my time and theirs. Sometimes I'd even cried out in fear. And tonight, Casalta looked huge and dark and full of whispers.

I made my way down the corridor lined with our rooms. and stepped inside the turret that hosted Mia's studio, the stone floor cold under my feet. Her frescoes covered the walls, and silent faces painted on canvas watched me from all around. The studio was so wide that my light couldn't reach its corners.

'Viola?' I whispered. Fear was beginning to seep into the excitement. I was desperate to get my gift back, but couldn't help shivering and trembling a little among the canvases.

'Viola?' I repeated – but only silence answered me.

At that moment, out of the corner of my eye, I caught a flicker of movement – a girl in a long white nightdress and with long hair was looking at me from across the room. I let out a gasp – but a moment later I recognised myself, reflected in the dark window.

A sigh escaped my lips, and I kneeled on the floor.

Maybe I'd imagined it all? Maybe I'd been dreaming?

The desire to be whole again, with all my six senses, gripped my heart, my soul, my gut. With elation fading, I felt colder and colder. I got back on my feet.

'Viola?' I whispered.

The white rays of the moon pooled beneath the windows. Something brushed against me, and I turned around quickly – there was nobody there, but a force pulled me towards the frescoed walls, where the moon made a tiny white pond. My reflection seemed to walk towards me as I advanced towards the window.

I saw the depiction of Judith and Holofernes, with Judith

beheading the evil chief – Mia had painted this just before our father's death. Bit by bit, she was filling the whole wall with little scenes; since the last time I'd looked at that corner, she'd painted more, adding another small scene.

It was a tableau of us sisters, with our mum. Lulu and I were painted close, so that our hair mixed with each other's – then there was Nora, slanted eyes like a cat's. Mia had painted herself slightly below us, so that the three of us surrounded and protected her. She was the baby of the family, after all. Our effigies were encompassed with a garland of roses, white, red, yellow and pink, with thorns among their petals. I looked closer – there was another face, a little removed from ours – dark as Nora and Mia, with long black hair – it was Mia as a young girl. Maybe now that she was about to jump into the unknown, she was reflecting on her childhood.

The sweetness of that painting comforted me, and eased the frustration of my fruitless search for Viola. But something nudged at me; something wasn't right, in the painting.

I lifted the torch to the wall once more – and I noticed that Mia had made a mistake in her self-portrait as a girl. She'd painted both her eyes brown, and not one blue and one brown...

But all of a sudden I felt the pull of sleep trying to drag me down there and then – all energy left me.

I lay down on the hard floor, and darkness closed around me.

CHAPTER 8

CASALTA, 1985

BIANCA

The next morning, my feet pounded the asphalt as I ran from the car to the platform. I could see the train to Florence sitting there already – it'd leave any moment now... Why, oh why had I decided to stop at the office on the morning of my interview? Why had I chosen to take the train instead of driving? Yes, I hated driving in the city, and I wanted to go over what I'd planned to tell Hilda – but now I was going to be late! Stupid heels – stupid tight skirt! I was wearing a navy dress Lulu had loaned me, with a fitted blazer of the same colour, blue tights and navy and white high-heeled pumps – perfect for an interview but extremely, extremely uncomfortable if you had to run.

I was almost there...

'Bianca!'

I froze. That voice...

'Bianca!'

I turned around, and just as I saw Lorenzo standing in front of his car, I heard the train preparing to leave, making those mechanical noises that sound a little like the train is breathing. I was unprepared. Unprepared for how much I loved his face, his familiar features: the man he'd become, superimposed on the boy I remembered, how handsome he was in his own unique way. Only Lorenzo could ignite such a reaction from me. And I resented him for it; I resented myself.

A part of me wanted to run away; a part of me wanted to run to him.

No panic. No panic.

No, actually, *panic*.

I tried to race for the train, I really did. But my feet refused to obey. I jerked my neck towards the tracks – I could still make it – but I didn't.

I stayed put, and let the train leave.

Oh, sometimes I hated myself.

Lorenzo walked towards me, slowly and coolly as he always did, looking at his feet. But when he lifted his eyes to me, I sensed his apprehension. He was never fully relaxed when he was around me, and neither was I when I was around him.

'Was that your train?' he asked, unnecessarily. There was only one service, to and from Casalta: the Florence line.

'It was. Had you not called me, I would have made it.' Not true. But I was still touchy after the Tamara encounter. At least now he was alone, I didn't have to see him with her, and be subjected to more of her comments about my looks.

'Sorry. Lift?' he asked in his usual laconic manner.

'I'll take my car. Thank you, though.'

'But you hate driving in the city.'

'How do you know?'

'Lucrezia mentioned it to me, at some point.'

Didn't his girlfriend say he never spoke about me?

Bianca. Stop. You moved on. You have other plans, remember? All that was finished. And I'd prove it to myself by not avoiding him. After all, Gherardo Orafi's birthday party was looming, and I couldn't avoid Lorenzo then. I might as well bite the bullet.

'Are you going to Florence?' I asked.

'Not far from it. Get in,' he said in that slightly commanding way he had, and opened the car door.

I did.

We didn't speak, as we left Casalta and drove through the Tuscan countryside, under a deep blue sky – but I was acutely aware of his presence. This was the first time we'd been properly alone since we'd broken up. We'd had a little time together the day he came to pay his respects after my father's death, but Vanni and Lulu were there. I remember every second of that day – the guilt for having let him down, the distance between us. And his coldness, even if covered by flawless manners. I also remembered the longing to hold him, to ask for forgiveness...

'You look smart,' he said after a while, and I almost jumped. The car was gliding along silently – it looked more like a starship, compared to my little 500.

'Thank you.' I refrained from reporting his girlfriend's venomous words about my usual dresses. 'I have an interview at the Uffizi Museum today.'

'I know. It's great news. I'm rooting for you.'

'How did you—?'

He raised his eyebrows.

'Vanni?' I said.

'I might have asked him how you're doing.'

'The plan is to go back to school next year. I applied to do a course in art restoration.'

'Bianca, that's brilliant!' His usual composure was broken by enthusiasm. 'You always wanted to study art. I remember it well.'

'Thank you. Yes, I've wanted it for a long time. But you know... it wasn't possible.' No need to explain why – he knew it all too well. 'But now, I'm taking the leap!'

'Bianca. I'm so proud of you.'

Oh.

I don't know why, but those words took my breath away.

He's proud of me.

Maybe, just maybe, he has forgiven me?

I turned my face away, towards the hills, so he wouldn't see how much his words had affected me.

'Bianca. I've been wanting to speak to you for a long time. After your father died...'

No. I couldn't have that. We couldn't have that. 'So, how's Tamara?' I said instead.

I was looking out of the window, but I still felt him freezing, stung. There was a shift in the air between us, and the sensation of him clamming up was almost physical.

'She's good. Thank you for asking,' he said formally. I could almost *see* ice crystals forming all over his skin, and mine.

There was silence until we reached the station of Santa Maria Novella, where he stopped the car. My heart sank. In spite of all my resolutions and good intentions, saying goodbye to him, ending our ever-so-short time together, broke me a little.

Contradictory? Oh, yes. For sure.

'I'm sorry I can't park any closer to the museum,' Lorenzo said.

'No, you saved me a lot of time. Thank you. I hope I didn't take you too out of your way.'

'Nah. I'm off to Siena.'

'*Siena?* But that's in the opposite direction!'

He shrugged. 'I enjoyed our chat. Good luck for your interview.'

I couldn't help it – I took a few steps away from the car, but I had to turn around.

Lorenzo sat there, his hands on the steering wheel and his dark, deep-set eyes following me. A moment to see his profile, the raven hair tamed back with rebel waves on the top, those full, full lips I used to drown on – and he started the car just as I turned away.

Memories can be comforting.

Memories can be thoroughly, thoroughly wicked.

Remembering how I lost Lorenzo was definitely in the second category. I tried to never think about it, because it still hurt – but now, with Lorenzo's scent still in my nostrils, with his voice still in my ears, with his presence lingering in all my senses…

I remembered the day I lost him.

CHAPTER 9

CASALTA, SIX YEARS BEFORE

BIANCA

Lorenzo and I were side by side in the treehouse, our fingers woven together and my head on his shoulder.

It was our secret haven, high in the hazelnut tree, hidden where no one would think to look. The branches held it steady, as though the tree had woven its limbs together just for this. No stairs led here, no sign marking the way – we had to climb, rough bark under our hands, until we were wrapped in the treehouse's quiet. Inside, the floor was layered with old rugs, threadbare and soft, their edges curling up like the pages of a book. Cushions were scattered everywhere and books piled in a corner, their familiar weight ready to pull me away when I needed it most.

Above, the branches twisted into a roof that wasn't really a roof, just a net of leaves and light that shifted with the wind, and a few planks to protect from the rain. When it rained, we huddled under a blanket and watched the drops slip through, glittering as they caught on the edges of the tree.

The air inside smelled like earth and bark, grounding me

when everything else felt too much. It was ours, mine and Lorenzo's, but I could still hear Lulu's voice there. Her presence lingered, one of her scarves forgotten, her doodles tucked into the pages of a book. In the treehouse, I felt close to my lost sister as well.

But now, our haven was full of Lorenzo's frustration. I could feel it on my skin, like static.

'Do you trust me, Bianca?' he said suddenly.

I'd sensed his agitation, his impatience for weeks now, and I knew the reason for it. I knew it was coming; I knew that this precarious situation, our secret relationship, our frustrated desire to have more of each other, to be together fully, properly, was going to come to a head. I knew things couldn't continue the way they were now.

'Of course, *of course* I do, Lorenzo…'

'Bianca…' he began, and I held my breath. I buried my face in his shoulder. I didn't want to hear it.

'You know what I'm going to say, don't you?'

I nodded. He took my chin in his hand, gently, and made me turn my face so I'd look at him. When our eyes met, I wanted to lose myself in them and stay there, in peace, basking in his love like a sunflower in the sun. But I didn't know how to deal with what he was about to ask of me.

'I want us to stop hiding…'

'Lorenzo…'

'No, let me finish! I want us to be *normal*. A normal couple. We're not doing anything wrong; why should we hide?'

'Is this not enough for you…' I started, but I knew I sounded uncertain, unconvinced of my own words.

'Of course it's not! Is it enough for *you*? Meeting here in secret? I know it isn't. I want you to come to my house, to spend time with my family! I want to go speak with *your* father and tell him that nothing can keep us apart. Please, Bianca, let me!'

'I can't let you! You don't understand. You don't really know what he can do...'

'You mean, worse than destroying your family and trying to kill mine? What else can he do to us?'

I squeezed my eyes shut.

There was something else he could do to me, and he would – but at that time, I didn't know yet.

I hadn't accepted my father's responsibility for the accident, yet; I hadn't accepted his involvement in the car wreck that left Vanni paralysed and Gherardo, Lorenzo's and Vanni's father, an invalid.

'Then why do you want to put yourself in the line of fire again?'

'Because I love you!'

His words were beautiful and painful, and I didn't know how to deal with them. Thoughts of my mother, whom I believed dead, of Lucrezia, exiled and alone, of Nora and Mia young and vulnerable and in my care, whirled in my mind.

But Lorenzo was there, in front of me, his scent and the feeling of his skin against mine so familiar, so right – the pull towards him overwhelmed me, confused me. I was desperate to do what he asked; I was desperate for us to come into the light: to be normal, like Lorenzo said. The two of us walking down the street arm in arm, not counting the minutes and hours we could spend together before we inevitably separated, going back to our homes in secret, like criminals. Looking forward to a future together, instead of tumbling on in the dark, not knowing what was ahead of us.

How I wanted to say yes. To let go of fear and truly trust my Lorenzo. To believe that maybe my father wasn't almighty, all-reaching. Maybe he could be stopped.

'I'll protect you and your sisters. Do you not believe me, *amore mio*?'

'I do. I believe you, and I believe *in* you.'

'Let me speak to your father, then. We'll be together properly.' He held me and he kissed me, and in that moment I was so happy and so afraid. It was like coming too close to a flame, warm and luminous, knowing that you might get burned but being unable to look away, or step away.

I was on the verge of taking flight, to free myself and be with my love.

That night, at home, I was beside myself with anxiety. I paced up and down in my room; I stared out of the window to see if a car was approaching. I tried to do chores, to pick up a book, to tidy my little sisters' toys.

Every night, aside from when he was away for business, Father wanted us to have dinner in the dining room, formally, with all the best crockery. Me and my sisters all hated that. We preferred eating in the kitchen, just the three of us and Matilde, in peace. Eating with Father was an exercise in fear and restraint; if we didn't exhibit perfect manners we'd be reproached, but sometimes not even that was enough to save us from poisonous words.

And that night was no different; but there was an edge to his mood that terrified me. It couldn't be a coincidence. There was something in his eyes, something in the way he looked at me, looked at us.

Oh my God, I realised. He knew.

He *knew*.

'You're flustered, Bianca,' he said. 'What's wrong?'

Had he been a normal parent, you might have thought he was worried about me. But being Fosco Falconeri, what I saw was a snake circling a mouse before gobbling it.

'I'm fine.'

Then came words that left me with no doubt, no doubt at all, that somehow he had found out. 'Are you *waiting for someone?*'

I froze, and my sisters too. They weren't aware of what

Lorenzo and I had planned, but they recognised the threat in Father's voice.

'No, of course not.'

'You know, something I appreciate in you, Bianca,' he began, as sweat beaded my forehead and my hands tingled with panic, 'is that you're wise in choosing your friends.'

My sisters had put their cutlery down and were both staring at our father, their faces white with fear.

'You know that certain friendships and acquaintances carry consequences,' he said slowly, deliberately. 'And these consequences travel all the way back to your sisters,' he continued in a pleasant tone. 'Should you be here or far away.'

He knows he knows he knows...

'You're a wise girl, Bianca. Aren't you?'

'Yes,' I said in a whisper.

Consequences that travel all the way back to my sisters.

He didn't need to say anything more.

As soon as I could, I ran upstairs and wrote a hurried note to Lorenzo. Bitter tears smudged the ink as I told him to not come to my house, that we couldn't be together, to stay away from me, from my sisters.

I told him something unforgivable: that if something happened to my sisters here, or to Lulu in her exile, I'd blame him. It was a cruel and horrible thing to say – and I wrote it because I wanted him to be hurt enough to stay away forever.

I felt like I was writing with my blood, my own life blood leaking out of me and leaving me empty.

I sneaked downstairs, grabbed a torch from the kitchen and ran all the way to Biancamura – my lungs hurt, but I couldn't stop. At the time the property was walled and had an iron gate – it looked like a small fortress, like the family who lived there was besieged.

This was what the war between the Falconeri and the Orafi had done.

I stood at the gate searching for a suitable place to leave my letter, all the while praying that nobody back home noticed I was gone. The barking of their guard dogs started somewhere and got closer and closer – I was terrified – I left the letter between the bars of the gate, and prayed Lorenzo would find it.

My heart broke then, an almost physical sensation that took my breath away and made me bring a hand to my chest. I sobbed all the way back to Casalta, running in the dark, grass rustling under my feet. The second I crossed through the Casalta gate, I swallowed the tears, swallowed the pain – nobody was to see the storm inside me. I have no memories of that night, spent curled up in a bubble of loss and pain.

Lorenzo did find the letter: because the day after, he wasn't at the treehouse. Why did I go there, anyway? Because I hoped against all hope that we could keep meeting in secret, coward that I was. I kept going for a long time, and I hated myself for what I'd done.

But there was no going back. And I didn't see Lorenzo again until my father died.

CHAPTER 10

CASALTA, 1985

BIANCA

Enough!

I was about to have the first job interview of my life, and I had to collect myself. I had to be in the here and now, not wallowing in the past.

I looked around me and took in the solid, exquisite harmony of the city of Florence – with its statues and churches and palazzos, century upon century of wealth and power translated into pure beauty. When we were very little, Mum had often taken us sisters to the Uffizi, to contemplate the paintings – it was her love of art that'd led her from Scotland to Florence in the first place. At the Uffizi, Mum had seen the four portraits by the painter Bronzino that inspired our names: Lucrezia Panciatichi, Bianca de' Medici, Eleonora di Toledo and Maria de' Medici.

I passed the Basilica of Santa Maria Novella, with its square and round lines that formed a perfect symmetry, and the Duomo appeared in its harmonious beauty: even after having seen it a hundred times it still took my breath away, with its tower falling upwards into the sky, reaching for the divine, and its dome that seemed to defy gravity. The skill that must have been required to manoeuvre such materials without modern machinery was incredible: no wonder it had taken two hundred years to finish.

I walked down Via dei Calzaiuoli until the heavy, solid Palazzo Vecchio appeared, with its colourful strip of coat of arms. It always gave me a sense of stability and immortality: powerful families and governments would come and go, but Florence stood unmoved and unchanged in its loveliness and grace. I waved hello to *David* – this particular *David* was not the original statue by Michelangelo, but a copy set there at the turn of the century – maybe that was why it seemed a little sulky and frowning, because it was the lesser twin.

Bit of a Freudian thought there, Bianca.

And there I was, at the Uffizi, in between the two colonnades with the statues of famous Tuscans cooped up in the alcoves: Dante, and Giotto, Machiavelli, Galileo Galilei... I couldn't remember them all... looking down at me from the recesses of history.

There were a few tourists in line to enter the museum, and locals going about their business: this was hallowed ground for history and art, but if you lived here and saw it every day, it became simply the background to your life.

Thanks to Lorenzo's lift I had almost half an hour spare before the interview, so I walked the few steps that separated the Uffizi from the riverbank. I leaned on the worn stone wall, looking out to the Arno's placid waters. Placid, yes, but mighty in their quiet strength: the liquid heart of Florence. This river had been the key to the city's survival and wealth, the root of all the beauty I saw around me now.

My gaze moved to the Ponte Vecchio, the old bridge, where my parents had met for the first time when Mum was working in a jewellery shop. She'd been so brave, to come over here all alone! I couldn't help comparing her youth, so adventurous, to mine – not sheltered by any means, but still spent in one place, where I was born and bred.

A thought hit me: all these years, I'd had good reasons not to step out into the world, to be there as my sisters' protector. But as hard and painful as these reasons might be, they did suit my shy nature, my desire to always remain as private and hidden as I could. The *reasons* were now *excuses*. Because the threat was gone; because my sisters didn't need me as much.

And now it was time to overcome my fears, set my shyness aside, and start living.

~

Hilda was the epitome of a chic woman working in the arts, and I was a little intimidated as soon as I saw her.

She wore a colourful pashmina around her shoulders, held in place by a silver brooch, and her ash-blonde hair was cut in a sharp bob. After some small talk, though, I relaxed a bit – though I was still rigid on the chair across from her desk, and my smile was a little fixed.

'Let me see your CV,' she asked, and I handed her my one-page resumé. Homeschool. Charity co-op. No other jobs. Shame I couldn't include my lived experience on it, because I had quite a lot of that.

'I can see you're full of enthusiasm, and clearly art is a family passion. But you have no experience,' she said in her Italian tinged with a German accent.

'Yes, however I built a social enterprise by myself, before my partner joined,' I said, more boldly than I felt.

'Working part time can be a little restrictive for us.'

'You see, I need to phase out from the co-op. We haven't found the right person to take my place, yet. As for qualifications, I'm planning to apply for higher education when the new term starts. I'd like to apply to the Scuola di Restauro, here in Florence.'

She smiled. 'I see... It's hard to get into that course; I wish you the best of luck. You're in our files now; I'll keep you in mind for any cover, or if a position becomes available. It may be some time, though.'

I was deflated. And, although I really, really hated to admit it, I felt a little pathetic. What did I think was going to happen? That she'd offer me a job on a silver platter?

'Thank you.'

She stood, and I imitated her – it was over. 'I hope I'll see you again soon.'

'I hope so too. *Arrivederci.*' I turned around and heard the door of Hilda's office closing behind me – a metaphorical shove in between my shoulder blades, to push me out and away. I knew I was being overdramatic, but I couldn't help it.

I'd never been to an interview before, never applied for a job before: the one I had, I'd built it myself. In my fairy-tale mind, I had already seen myself working here...

Even with my family history, even if my work at Legami had further exposed me to the difficulties of life, I was naïve about the world in many ways. I had no street smarts and no knowledge of how to negotiate the world of employment. There was so much to learn... and learn I would, through trial and error.

Well. It was time for a pep talk to myself! *There are other museums, heaps of them. Art galleries as well – maybe I can speak to the gallery that buys Mia's paintings? I set my heart on working at the Uffizi, but beggars can't be choosers, like Amarilli says. It's just the first try, after all...*

I was still busy telling myself why I shouldn't be discouraged *at all* while I walked down the first flight of stairs to a small hall with a window – the glare of the autumn sun blinded me for a moment, and I miscalculated the next step down the second flight. I was about to roll down onto hard stone and possibly break a bone or two, when someone held me and stopped me from falling.

A deep scent of sandalwood and old books filled my nostrils as I opened my eyes against a forest-green jumper, and slowly looked up to meet two wide brown eyes topped by dark blond eyebrows.

'Are you all right?' the man asked me.

'All right enough,' I said, when my shoes touched the floor. I straightened the dress with my free hand, while the other held my handbag.

To my relief, the man – too close for comfort – set me free, and when we'd pulled apart enough to see each other's faces, I saw recognition in his eyes.

'Bianca?'

He knows me? I had no memory of this man. But wait – if I took the glasses away... Of course! Brando Pacini. We'd gone to middle school together before I left to be homeschooled.

I remembered a boy who couldn't sit still, with a mop of curly dark blond hair and who was always doodling. Except the lanky boy was now a man... a man whose looks made me do a double-take. Very much so. Something told me he was used to such a reaction, because he blushed and looked away with a humbleness that contrasted with his appearance.

'Brando?'

'Yes. I know I've changed, but you're unmistakable, Bianca. It's been years!'

'A long time, yes,' I said with a smile.

'Feel like a coffee? To catch up? It's fine if you don't...'

I thought of the million things that needed to be done at home, how I could possibly squeeze in a bit of paperwork for Legami...

But no. I was out in the world; I'd stay out a little longer.

'Sure, why not?'

The coffee shops and restaurants still had tables set up outside, in the warm air – the *ottobrata* had started, that period of unseasonal warmth in the middle of October.

Brando and I sat outside at the Caffè Medaglia, across from the Basilica di Santa Croce, from which the square took its name. I contemplated the Gothic naves rising to the sky, and the blue star in the middle... here rested Michelangelo, and with him many other Florentine geniuses.

However, embarrassingly, my eyes kept returning to Brando's face and his fair, northern looks, as if an ancient Celt had sprinkled some of his DNA in this corner of Italy. The dark blond shade of his hair invoked a vague sense of familiarity in me, shared as it was by my twin, my mother and me.

He was gorgeous.

'So, what have you been up to?' Brando asked amiably. 'You didn't finish school with us...' His words tapered away, and he looked a little flustered.

'I didn't, no. I was taken out of school and homeschooled with my sisters until the diploma.'

'Really? The Falconeri sisters are a bit of a legend around Casalta, shrouded in mystery,' he ventured.

I clammed up every time an outsider elaborated about my family. People seemed to enjoy all the drama that surrounded us, and tongues ran. I looked away, my gaze moving to the church and the square and a pigeon tottering around the table. There was a pause, and I knew Brando was looking for something to say that wouldn't make me close up and stop talking entirely.

I felt a little embarrassed at my reaction. Outside of my family and the people we assisted at Legami, I must have become a little thorny. I supposed that was what endless vigilance did to you.

'I'm sorry. Bianca, I didn't mean to pry. Oh, I feel like a bull in a china shop, now. Please, let's start over.' He put his hands up. At that moment a server came to take our orders and gave us a moment to clear the air. 'Espresso? Cappuccino?' Brando asked.

'Tea, please.'

'An espresso for me. Thank you,' he said to the waiter, before turning back to me. 'So. I'm Brando, remember me? We went to middle school together.' He gave me an apologetic smile.

'And I'm Bianca, the local legend.'

'Ah, no! I said I was sorry,' he laughed.

'I'm just not used to talking about my family.'

'No problem. Let's talk about *me*. Artsy types have big egos, so I enjoy that,' he joked. I thought of Mum and Mia – not so much big egos, but big personalities for sure. 'Since you last saw me, my family moved to Florence. I went to high school here, graduated in Art History, and here I am.'

'You work at the Uffizi? I just applied for a job there,' I said.

'Not exactly the museum. I work at the Sovrintendenza alle Belle Arti. *We* supervise all the art heritage in Tuscany, from museums to archaeological sites, churches, castles, you name it. We're in the same building as the Uffizi administration.'

'So when you say *a day at the office*, you mean this,' I remarked, making a gesture to encompass the square and its basilica, like the backdrop of a theatre. A steaming cup of tea and Brando's espresso were laid before us.

'Yes, it's a stunning place to work. Sometimes I can't quite believe it myself... Although I never fainted, overwhelmed by beauty,' he said dramatically. 'You know, like Stendhal. Apparently, the whole thing happened here, in the Cappella Niccolina, inside the church. He was so affected by the perfect beauty of the place that he took ill.'

'Oh, yes, Stendhal syndrome. Just as well you don't suffer from it; it'd be quite inconvenient to faint at the workplace every morning.'

'It would be, yes,' he laughed. 'So, did you have a meeting with Hilda? What did she say?'

'That she'll keep me in mind, but there are no openings at the moment. And that the chances are very slim.' I couldn't hide my disappointment. 'But it was the first place I applied to, I'm sure there's something for me, somewhere. I just have to keep trying.'

'Absolutely. I'll keep an eye out for you, of course. What exactly are you looking for?'

'Anything, really. Part time, for now... I have to find a replacement for my current job. I don't have any official qualifications, yet. I'm going to apply for the Scuola di Restauro in the new term.'

'It's not easy to get a place there. A lot of people have to apply multiple times. Sure, I'll keep an eye out for you,' Brando said and looked at his wristwatch. 'I must go back; they'll think I ran away. Well, this was my treat, of course. Just give me a moment.'

He stood and went inside to pay. I was left alone in the square, while the autumn sun disappeared behind a cloud and cast the place in gloom. A gust of wind played with my hair, lifted dead leaves and sent birds in flight, black against the white clouds. When Brando came out, I expected a wave and a hurried goodbye, but he offered me his hand to get up in an old-fashioned way.

'It was nice seeing you again, and thank you for the tea,' I said as formally as I could.

'It was nice seeing you too, Bianca Falconeri. Local legend,' he added mischievously with a smile. 'I hope it won't be another ten years before I see you again.'

'Yes. Me too.'

He lifted his hand as a farewell gesture – and yet, our eyes lingered on each other for a handful of seconds after we'd exchanged our goodbye.

Now, that *was* unexpected.

∼

On the way back, my mind was full of sights and thoughts and hopes, new things appearing and old things returning.

Lorenzo and I, alone in his car, unspoken words between us, memories rising from the scent of him, the sound of his voice, the profile I knew so well.

The disappointing interview.

And then meeting Brando Pacini after all those years, but really, meeting him for the first time: *I hope it won't be another ten years before I see you again.* The first time I'd even *seen* a man who wasn't Lorenzo. That in itself was momentous.

I was charged and excited and yet exhausted, and my mind whirled for a while until the landscape outside the window – the gentle hills dotted with villages and farms, the deep blue sky of the Tuscan autumn, the cypresses and pines lining country roads – soothed my thoughts and lulled me into almost-sleep. Oh, going home to the countryside was good, even after a city as gentle and beautiful as Florence…

'How did it go, how did it go, how did it go?' A bouncing Mia came to welcome me, her black hair held up in a loose bun with a paintbrush slipped in.

'Well, nothing for now, but I took the first step,' I said, hanging up my bag and blazer and taking off those pesky high heels.

'You did! And something tells me you'll have good news soon.'

When Mia said *something tells me*, or *I have a feeling*, we all took her seriously. It was part of her gift, after all.

I ran upstairs to change, and slipped into the jeans and T-shirt that constituted my new informal look. It seemed to me that the forsaken dresses folded in the rattan bag at the back of the wardrobe were forlornly calling to me.

I was studying the new me in the mirror, still not quite convinced, when the phone rang from its cradle on my bedside table.

'*Pronto?*'

A German-accented voice answered – I recognised it – my pulse quickened. 'Hello, this is Hilda, from the Uffizi office. Can I speak to Bianca Falconeri, please?'

'Speaking, hello!' I took a breath. *Cool, calm and collected, Bianca, remember?*

'Bianca, I have good news for you. It's not exactly a post at the Uffizi, but they need a temporary assistant at the Sovrintendenza. What do you think?'

I think that Mia was right once again!

'It sounds wonderful!' I had no idea what a job as an assistant at the Sovrintendenza would entail, but any job in the field was an answer to my prayers. 'Could you tell me more?'

'All I know is that an awful lot of boxes arrived at the archive last week,' Hilda laughed. 'I think it has something to do with that, but it's not my domain, really. They'll explain better... if you want to pursue this, of course.'

'I do! Of course I do. *It sounds wonderful!*' I repeated – I knew I was a broken record, but I was too excited to articulate. Where was a thesaurus when you needed one?

'Wait until you're buried in papers from the archive before you thank me,' she said, her voice deadpan. 'But you'll want to discuss things further. Let me give you the number of the co-ordinator here. Brando Pacini. Do you have a pen handy?'

Brando Pacini?

'Bianca?'

'Yes, sorry. I have a pen.'

I wrote the number down in my little address book, thanked Hilda again and sat there for a moment.

Brando did say he was going to keep an eye out for me, but I didn't think he'd find me a position in the space of a few hours. I was grateful, and yet I didn't want to feel indebted to him.

I needed details so I typed in the number.

'Brando? It's Bianca.'

'Did Hilda give you the good news?' There was a smile in his voice.

'She did. I'm delighted, but... you shouldn't have.'

'It's a temporary position, and not the most riveting of projects...'

'Oh, no, it's a great chance for me. But... I feel a little embarrassed. A little... well, *indebted.*'

'I know what you mean, but in all honesty, we were looking for someone. I wanted to tell you earlier, at the coffee shop, but I had to check with my boss. You appeared in the right place at the right time... The staff is being computer trained...'

'For our sins!' called a voice in the background, and Brando laughed.

'But we've also been sent some new documents from all over Tuscany. They need to be registered and set in order. You might not thank me when you see the boxes and boxes and boxes we must work on.'

'I don't know anything about archives, Brando. I was really aiming to be a tour guide or something along those lines, something I could learn quickly. I...'

'Don't worry about that, it's really just practical work.'

'You'd be doing us all a favour!' I heard the same woman's voice in the background.

'That was Adriana, the boss in question,' Brando said. 'Really, like she said, you'd be doing all of us a favour. So, will you join the team?'

I still had a moment of hesitation – self-doubt raised its ugly head again. Could I do this? Or would everyone soon realise what an impostor I was...

No, I'd not entertain these thoughts. I fought my desire to hide away, to stay where I was and never challenge myself. I'd gone too far to step back now.

'I will. Of course I will!'

'Brill—'

'Part time, though, remember?' I added hastily. I needed to make that point clear – I couldn't leave Legami completely yet, and I'd said that to Hilda too. 'Just until I find a suitable replacement for me at my current job.'

'Yes, part time suits us. Tomorrow at nine?'

'I'll be there!'

Once the phone was back in its cradle, I did a little dance around the room – and the girl who looked back at me from the mirror seemed years younger than I'd felt only last week, and full of promise. I was off to new shores, and nothing could hold me back – nothing that belonged to the past.

Not even the words I'd heard this morning: *I'm so proud of you.* Or the man who had uttered them.

Also, if I really had to admit it... knowing that I'd see Brando again, and so soon, didn't feel bad at all.

Not in the slightest.

∼

I woke up in the middle of night and opened my eyes in the dark. There had been no calling of my name, but I felt her presence – Viola. I didn't need to go searching for her, because she was already there...

A faint scent of violets filled the air, and the curtains at my window danced, just a little.

I took it as a message from my old friend. I was on the right track.

CHAPTER 11

CASALTA, 1985

BIANCA

'*Buongiorno!*' Brando said warmly the next morning as he opened the door. 'Welcome to our office.' He really was as cheerful as I remembered him. Was that smooth brow even capable of furrowing? It didn't seem so.

'*Buongiorno,*' I replied and stepped in.

I couldn't believe this would be my workplace. Beamed ceilings, stone frames around the windows, stone floors polished by centuries of being stepped upon. This place had been built hundreds of years ago, and hundreds of people must have come and gone between these walls – and now, here I was.

'So, these are the unfortunate souls stuck here with us. Paolo...' An older man came to shake my hand – he wore sleeve protectors, like a clerk in a Dickens novel.

'...and this is the boss of us all, Adriana,' Brando said, gesturing towards a small mountain of boxes. A mop of dark-purplish hair surfaced from behind the boxes, followed by a small, pinched face.

'*Benvenuta*, Bianca,' Adriana said. Her fingers were stained with nicotine and thick glasses rested on the bridge of her nose. When she got up, I saw that she barely came to my shoulder – she looked like a little mole, surfacing from the ground to smell the air.

'*Grazie*, Adriana.' I looked around. Modern office furniture, three desks and chairs, table lights clamped to the desks, calendars and whiteboards contrasted with the historical setting.

'Come, Bianca. I'll show you your bit. The computer guy should be here any moment,' Adriana offered.

Paolo rolled his eyes. 'I'm too old to learn all this new stuff.'

'No, you aren't! Computers are the way of the future. You'll see,' Brando said encouragingly. Paolo didn't seem convinced.

I followed Adriana and Brando across the room. Beyond the mountain of boxes she had emerged from was a short wooden door ensconced in a stone frame – when she opened it, the scent of old paper and mould and dust hit me.

The high-ceilinged room was full to the brim with documents, some on shelves, protected by glass, some in filing cabinets and some in boxes. There were modern-looking folders full of papers, and parcels of documents held together by string.

'That's a lot of documents,' I whispered, overwhelmed, staring at the layers upon layers of history stacked together.

'We just gathered a lot of material from all over the region,' Brando explained. Oh, yes: I remembered Hilda mentioning it.

Boxes and boxes sealed with tape sat among the shelves. 'These,' Adriana said with a certain glee, 'are your load. All you have to do for now is open them and sort the folders inside, possibly by date. We'll do the rest. Your back won't thank you, but you're young.'

'And hopefully soon we'll have more funding to hire a few more hands...' Brando interjected.

Adriana scoffed. '*As if!* We're lucky to have Bianca here. I told you you'd be doing us a favour, *cara*.'

'You see, we're among the first digitalising documents,'

Brando explained. 'Hopefully it will count for something... for funding, I mean. But as you know, in Italy we have more history and art than money to maintain it all.'

'*Digitalising?*' Should I know that word? My old friend self-doubt reappeared all of a sudden. There was so much I needed to learn.

'Transcribing them on computers,' Adriana explained. 'They're making so much progress every day, I'm sure the time will come when everything will be digitalised. There'll be a way to photograph images straight on computers, like we do with microfilm.'

'Hopefully I'll be retired by then!' Paolo said grimly.

A shrill noise interrupted us – the doorbell. Brando went to open the door, and returned with a young man who beamed at us.

'Everyone, this is Giacomo, the computer technician. He'll teach you all you need to know.'

'Welcome to the future,' the young man said, quite theatrically.

'You can certainly make an entrance,' Paolo answered, his voice chilly. He tapped one of the grey cubes. 'Now, how do you switch this thing on?'

∽

I shouldn't have worn Lulu's suit.

I was kneeling on the floor surrounded by boxes and dust, my nose running and my hands sweating in latex gloves, as I took out parcels of documents and piled them neatly. I hoped I wasn't going to run out of space. At the other end of the room sat Brando, Adriana and Paolo, their backs to me, laboriously following Giacomo's instructions.

Time flew, and before I knew it my colleagues were heading out for lunch.

'You coming?' Brando asked and offered me his hand to get up. I was about to take it, when something stopped me.

Bianca.

'Bianca?'

I blinked over and over – Viola's call and Brando's voice had overlapped, and I was still on the floor, my hand extended to take Brando's but not quite reaching it.

'Not today. I'll finish unpacking everything...' I said, and it was like hearing someone else talking: all my being was focused on listening out for Viola. Like the tips of our fingers were close, but hadn't quite met...

'Sure. I'll bring you something up. Thank you,' Adriana said from behind Brando.

The call came again.

Bianca.

Before I could control myself, I turned my head towards the labyrinth of floor-to-ceiling shelves and, beyond it, room after room of memories transformed into paper and parchment. Brando looked at me curiously. I met his eyes and smiled – but I knew I must have looked a little strange, a little distant.

As soon as I heard the door closing, I stepped into the maze of shelves packed with folders and boxes – the call might stop at any moment, and I'd lose her...

'Viola...' I whispered. *'Viola?'* Fear was beginning to seep into the excitement. I was desperate to see if my gift was back, but couldn't help shivering and trembling a little.

Maybe I'd imagined it all. Maybe I'd been daydreaming?

Bianca.

The call resounded so clearly this time. I was sure I wasn't dreaming it. I lifted the dusty box at my eye level and placed it on the floor. I began emptying it carefully, delicately, until a little book came into my hand, bound with the Florentine traditional motif, the lilies, blue on a black background.

The moment I touched it, Viola's call resounded again, and

this time it was followed by a sigh, a sigh of relief – I'd done what she wanted; I'd let her guide me. Whatever she wanted me to have was now safe in my hands.

Tears of joy filled my eyes – she'd communicated with me through time, somehow.

With shaking hands, I opened the small book. The pages were yellowed and soft, as if the dampness of many years had seeped into the paper.

Casalta, 1944

Everything is changing in my life and in the world, and I want to remember these days, so I'll record my life here. Little diary, may you be the witness to the events to follow, big and small, joyful or sad. Hopefully all joyful!

Yours,

Viola

I clasped my hand to my mouth. What I had in my hands was Viola's *diary*!

At that moment I knew, I knew with all my heart and soul, that fate had taken me here, to this job. This was the closest I'd got to my gift in years.

Viola had called me here.

What to do now? I held the diary to my chest – I couldn't possibly relinquish it. A few moments later I was standing above my open bag.

Wait. I was stealing a document from the Uffizi archive. This was theft. *Theft*, no other way to define it.

Not the best way to start my new job.

I had to put it back, now. But I found I couldn't. I was sure Viola had led me here; I was sure I was meant to have it!

Suddenly Paolo's booming voice filled the room.

'I can't believe I'll be staring at that black and green horror for another few hours...'

They'd returned from lunch – why, why had they been so quick?

I froze for a second; I couldn't have put the diary back in time, or that was my excuse anyway. I watched it disappear into the black mouth of my bag. It was done. I ran back to my workstation – the floor, at the opposite end of the room – and almost landed face first among the boxes.

'We cut lunch short to pack in an extra hour of training. Are you sure you don't want anything?' Brando asked. I felt like the diary in my bag was all lit up, with red arrows materialising in the air and hovering over me. I probably had the word THIEF written on my forehead in capital letters.

'I'm sure,' I said in a tiny voice, trying to look innocent. How do you look innocent when you've just stolen something? I had no idea. It was my first time as a criminal.

Brando leaned over me and picked something out of my hair, ever so gently. 'Cobweb.' He shook the gossamer from his fingers, and then offered me his hand to get up.

Bliss at having found the diary, dread at having stolen it, and the unfamiliar emotion of having my hand in Brando's were mixed together, stirring me in heart, soul and body.

It seemed to me that one step had been followed by another, and another, and another, until before I knew it, I'd found myself in uncharted territory.

'Brando, we're starting back!' Adriana's voice broke the moment, and I pulled back my captured hand, moving my gaze away too. But Brando was still looking at me with his kind, intuitive eyes.

Hopefully not too *intuitive*, I thought as the hidden loot tugged at my conscience. I remembered reading a story, somewhere, about a hidden beating heart that wouldn't quiet, and each thump reminded the protagonist of his guilt.

Viola's little book, concealed among my things, was beating like a heart, and I was sure Brando could hear it...

'Everything good?' he asked me, and I jumped out of my skin.

'Everything great, thank you,' I said quickly.

But I could almost feel the word *THIEF* pulsating on my forehead.

CHAPTER 12

CASALTA, 1985

BIANCA

I couldn't get to the station fast enough.

I prayed I didn't meet anyone I knew and was forced by my good manners to chat, instead of reading Viola's diary. My back was in bits after being on the floor for so long, my plait had come undone, I had a ladder in my tights and my clothes were dusty, but none of this mattered. Anticipation filled me whole.

The second I sat down, I opened my bag and looked left and right. Like a thief.

And you are a thief; you stole something from the archives, a little, impudent voice inside me said, and I tried to ignore it.

The inscription on the first page was like the first sip of a sweet drink: the anticipation made me want to gulp it down, but I made myself savour it. I began to read.

Casalta, 1944

Dear diary,

> *It's the middle of the night and I'm listening to the sound of the cicadas coming through the open window. It's the song of summer. The scent of roses is filling the air – there are always roses blooming here in Casalta, at any time of year.*

I smiled to myself. Viola's thoughts mirrored mine... two girls living in the same place, many years apart.

> *Today was the happiest and the saddest of days. Both! It was my birthday, and we had a party, and all of my friends and family came, and we danced and ate and laughed until late! I'm twenty years old, can you believe it? When I'm with my friends I feel fifteen; when Papà is around I feel eighty and tired with the weight of the world on my shoulders.*
>
> *But Papà was away today and life seemed perfect, in our little bubble here at Casalta...*

'Oh, Viola! You, too?' I whispered under my breath. *You too lived under your father's shadow; you too carried the weight of the world on your shoulders when he was around?*

To think you were there, in my home. And not so long ago. If only I could reach out and touch you through the rivers of time. If only I could see you again!

Reading those words was like reuniting with a long-lost friend. It filled me with sweetness and sadness and regret for the years spent apart, and the joy of having found each other again.

I brought the diary to my face, closed my eyes and inhaled – a faint scent of violets filled me, the same I'd smelled in my room when she first called me, a few days before.

> *I received so many gifts, and now they're all lined up on my desk. Caterina gave me a musical box, Anna gave me Acqua di Parma, and I adore the scent of violets! Marita gave me you, my*

dear diary, this little book, with Florentine lilies all over the cover. I love this gift so much that I began writing as soon as the guests were gone! Zia Agnese gave me Signorsì, *a novel by Liala. Liala is one of my idols. She writes books and also articles in magazines, she's an aristocrat and lives a glamorous, adventurous life. You were my favourite present, I promise. But* Signorsì, *oh, it's perfect: so romantic!*

I've decided: I'm going to write my diary like I'd write a novel. Or at least I'll try. And address it to her.

So: Dear Liala,

This is what I want for myself... to fall in love, real, proper love, the kind that sets your heart on fire! I want to learn to drive, cut my hair like the blonde woman on the cover of your book, do something meaningful, build something that is all mine! But none of this might happen...

And now to tell you the hard part of today, the part I wish hadn't happened.

After the party I was giddy and happy and a little tired, and after all the dancing I did my hair was all over the place. The tune of 'Un Bacio a Mezzanotte' was stuck in my mind and I was even humming a little...

I smiled to myself. This was the Viola I remembered! Exuberant, full of life, happy.

...until I saw Papà coming through the door. He and Mamma exchanged a quick word, and then I was summoned to the living room.

'Well, happy birthday,' Papà said.

'Thank you.' I'm always brief with him, wary. I try to speak as little as possible, just in case.

'I received a proposal today. Well, it's been on the cards for

a while, and it came to fruition. Count *Federico Valsecchi asked for your hand,'* he said, and he looked triumphant. *'You met him a couple of times, remember?'*

The room swam around me. It couldn't be him; I was thinking of someone else, the wrong man. The Federico Valsecchi I was thinking of was old enough to be my father...

My head spun. The dizziness was such that I had to lean my head back on the seat. An avalanche of memories engulfed me and took my breath away.

I hadn't told anyone, not Lulu, not Mum, not Lorenzo, nobody: but not long after I'd written that letter to Lorenzo, my father had decided that his wayward daughter, who'd betrayed his trust to the point of having a relationship with an Orafi, needed a tighter leash. Why not catch two birds with one stone, and make an alliance as well, while taming a daughter?

I was nineteen when Father invited Enrico Rinaldi to our home. He was the mayor of a nearby town, a powerful man with many connections, and Father wanted him on his side. Obviously, I didn't know that at the time: his affairs, business and otherwise were a mystery to us.

But I'd soon find out.

That evening, Mia was skittish and agitated like a cat during a storm, but I didn't realise what was happening, even though it was in front of my eyes. The idea of Father having some twisted, wicked design that involved me and a man as old as him was too outrageous to even form in my mind.

But he did, indeed, have a plan for me and Enrico.

I still remember Enrico's hand on my knee, his arm around my shoulders, the smell of cigarettes on his breath...

Those memories still made me feel nauseous.

Before reading some more, I had to open the train window a little and breathe in the wind. I couldn't believe how much

Viola's life and mine had overlapped. I wished it hadn't been because of this.

> 'Valsecchi is close to our Duce himself. He's a man of substance. We're very fortunate.'
>
> We?
>
> 'He's old,' I said helplessly. 'I don't even know him.' I looked to Mamma, but I realised at once that as always, she'd agree with whatever Papà wanted. She laid her hand on mine in a way that wanted to be soothing, but made me even more anxious.
>
> 'Viola...' Mamma began.
>
> 'She's fine. Aren't you, Viola?' Papà's look was searing, and my eyes filled with tears.
>
> Nobody could help me; nobody would.
>
> 'Yes. Of course.' How could I say no? If I did, he'd make our lives impossible. He'd make Mamma's life impossible. I couldn't do this to her. And still, tears overflowed and fell on my cheeks, and there was no stopping them.
>
> 'This is ridiculous, Viola! A gentleman asked for your hand, and you're sitting there crying? He's coming for dinner tomorrow night, and you'll be in a good mood.'
>
> 'I don't know him,' I repeated, weakly. I whispered, but I wanted to shout. I'd never, never contradicted or disobeyed my father. I couldn't have Mamma pay the price for my rebellion.
>
> 'You'll get to know him,' Mamma said and opened her hands as if to beg me – please, don't make your father angry, please do what he says.
>
> A sense of inevitability came over me, but I fought. 'He's too old for me. He must be your age, Papà!'
>
> 'Well, would you rather marry a boy with nothing? A boy who can't take care of you?' he shouted, and Mamma wrung her hands in fear. 'You're being so very ungrateful. Well, if you

behave like a child, you'll be treated like a child. Upstairs, now.'

I shivered. Ungrateful? For being given the privilege to marry an old man? The image I had of Viola's mum, the sweet woman I'd never seen dressed in anything other than silk, with pearls around her neck, sweet and almost fairy-like, changed in an instant. From someone living a charmed life, to a prisoner in her home.

Like my mother had been. Like we'd been.

Dear Liala,

I ran away from Mamma. She keeps tormenting me about what I should wear tonight and what I should say and how I should do my hair. I ran down the hill and took refuge at Zia Agnese's house.

Agnese never married, and she lives alone. Mamma feels sorry for her, but Zia Agnese doesn't seem sad to me at all, just the opposite. She loves her work as a seamstress, even if Mamma tears her hair out at the idea of her sister working for a living. Zia Agnese has often said to me that she'd rather jump in the Arno river than live like my mother does, and I agree.

When I finished telling her what had happened, she was furious.

'That bastard father of yours.'

'Zia Agnese, please, don't...'

'That's what he is, Viola! He ate my sister alive; she doesn't even know who she is any more! She doesn't know what she wants, what she likes; she's a puppet in his hands. You're going the same way!'

'He's coming for dinner tonight. I don't even remember what he looks like. Just that he has a moustache and a beard

and he speaks in a loud voice, like he wants the whole room to hear him. I don't understand; it was so sudden...'

'Your father's business is not doing well. Your mother didn't go into details, she's proud, as you know, but I filled in the gaps. I think that's why your father is so keen for you to get married. I assume this man is wealthy?'

I knew there was something more, something else, to this sudden decision! It took me a minute to wrap my head around it. And even after that minute, it still didn't sink in.

'Yes, he's wealthy. He's a count; he owns a palazzo in Florence... Oh, they should have told me... I had no idea. Yes, Papà has been angry all the time recently, but you know him. They should have told me! I could have helped... I can help!'

Zia Agnese rose and lit herself a cigarette. 'That's how your father wants you to help. Marry a rich man. You must tell him no. No, no, no. A million times no!'

'I can't. You know Papà...'

'Oh, I do. I know your father,' *she said. She despises him for how he treats Mamma, but also despises Mamma because she lets him.*

I don't think Agnese realises how much Papà has chipped away at Mamma's heart and soul through the years. It seems to me that she's been hollowed out, and now all that's left is a husk dressed in fancy clothes and wearing fancy jewellery. She's not the woman I remember from my childhood, when her eyes were still sparkling, her soul was still intact.

'He's selling you.' *Agnese's voice was hard.*

'He's not selling me.' *Is he?*

'What else would you call it? You can come and stay with me. You have a choice...'

I shook my head. 'I'm not doing this to Mamma. If I refuse, Papà is going to take it out on her.'

'She doesn't have any fight in her!'

'You don't understand...'

'Your mother is not standing up for herself; she's not standing up for you.' Her words hit even harder, because they were true. But Agnese will never understand what happened to Mamma in the years she spent with Papà. Never. *'It's not fair. They can't do this to you. They can't.'*

'They're not doing this to me. I'm choosing to go along with it.'

She gave me a long, hard look. *'It's not up to you to save your parents. You can find a job like you always wanted, and Giusy could come here too...'*

'He wouldn't let her go,' I said and shivered, a thin shiver of fear. *'Maybe I'll like him,'* I repeated, and Zia Agnese let herself fall backwards on her chair, defeated.

CHAPTER 13

CASALTA, 1985

BIANCA

The doleful hope Viola had expressed knotted my chest.

But I had to stop reading: the train was coming into the station. I slipped the diary back into my bag and began my short journey home. Now that the sun had set I was cold, and looking forward to ending this long, eventful day.

Poor Viola, I thought as I walked under the darkening sky. She tried so hard to protect her mother, but more and more was being asked of her. I knew what that was like, and I knew what she meant when she said that her *zia* Agnese didn't understand what it was like, to be hollowed out – like Viola had called it – by years of forced submission and fear.

Would she be able to set herself free?

The hint of pink in the west would soon disappear, swallowed by the night. Dusk had turned into evening, and I hurried towards the lights of Casalta. The evening star shone just above it – I hurried on, hugging myself to keep warm. I couldn't wait to tell my sisters all about my first day at work. Nora greeted me first – she was the most introverted of us four, and the most reticent to express affection, but behind her dour exterior was a soft heart, and she was always there for us at key times of our lives.

'How did it go? I've been thinking about you all day,' she said as I came in. I noticed happily that the fire had been lit against the chilly night.

'It was *great*. I spent hours on the floor and I'm sore everywhere, but I loved every minute! I'll tell you everything. Let's gather the troops and see what Matilde left us for dinner.'

'Tonight it's *fettuccine ai funghi*,' Lulu said, emerging from the study, her glasses pushed over her forehead.

'Thankfully nobody is ever on a diet, in this family!' I said, taking my shoes off and walking on stockinged feet. Matilde's dinners were always substantial and abundant. 'I'll go call Mia.'

'I'll go. Camilla phoned; she says it's urgent,' Lulu said.

There had to be a problem. She hadn't been exactly ecstatic when I'd told her I found a job so soon, and I didn't blame her. I sat on one of the leather sofas, watching the flames, and dialled her number.

'Oh, Bianca! Thank goodness. Want the good news or the bad news first?'

'Bad news first, I suppose.'

'Amarilli has taken unwell. She was in the hospital all day and they decided to keep her overnight.'

My stomach churned. I knew she wasn't looking good when I saw her last. And I'd chosen just this time to leave... 'What happened? How is she now?'

'They suspect a heart attack, but they aren't sure yet. If everything goes well she'll be out tomorrow, otherwise they're talking about a few days of observation.'

Guilt clasped my heart in a vice. Moving on from Legami just as Amarilli's health took a blow... my timing was lousy. 'Can she have visitors?'

'Not today, I was told most likely tomorrow. The visiting hours don't leave much wiggle room, though.'

'I'm working tomorrow and the day after... I can try and call in, see if maybe I can swap days...'

'See what you can do.'

'I wonder if Anita will plan a trip over.' I was sure that Dottor Artibani would have let Amarilli's daughter know that her mother was in hospital, and I made a mental note to ask if she planned to come and see her as soon as she could.

'She's very busy with the move,' Camilla said in her kind, thoughtful way. We both knew that Amarilli's daughter simply didn't have much time for her mother, but I never heard Camilla speaking ill of anyone. It simply wasn't like her.

'Yes. She is.'

'The good news, now. I might have found your replacement. I met her today and she's lovely. Her name is Teresa. If you like her too...'

It felt like the boulder I was carrying on my shoulders fell to the ground and rolled away. *What a relief!* 'That's great news. I hope I can meet her this week. Thank you for letting me know. And...' I paused. Camilla waited patiently on the other end of the line. 'I'm sorry I wasn't there today...'

'Don't say sorry. You made a decision; now you must embrace it. Everyone will be fine, all round. Including Amarilli. How was your first day?'

'Brilliant, actually. Eventful.' To say the least! My thoughts kept returning to Viola's diary, and I couldn't quite believe I'd found it.

'Well, enjoy it then,' Camilla said warmly.

'I will.' But the thought of Amarilli in the hospital cast a shadow over me, one that I couldn't shake.

When I reached my sisters in the kitchen and sat in front of my *fettuccine*, a sigh escaped my lips.

'What's wrong?' Mia asked. She was a living palette, paint on her hands and a lick of blue on her left ear.

'Amarilli's sick. She's in hospital.'

The news was met with a chorus of commiserations -my sisters had met Amarilli many times and they knew how close we were.

'Can you go see her?' Lulu asked.

'In the evening, yes. Unless I ask for a day off. On my second day of work,' I said desolately.

Nora shrugged. 'It's a family emergency, after all. Amarilli is like family to you.'

'Ask. You don't have much time,' Mia said.

'True, Camilla said they'll probably send her home tomorrow.'

I met Mia's eyes – she didn't say anything more, and it hit me. The words *You don't have much time*, pronounced by Mia, suddenly took on another meaning, and cold fingers travelled down my spine.

∾

I called Adriana that same evening – thankfully she'd given me her home number in case of emergency – and she agreed I could go see Amarilli in the morning and go to work in the afternoon.

I'd barely started my new job, and already I felt torn.

I grabbed a blanket, my booklight and Viola's diary, and climbed out onto the stone stairs. Night had fallen, and again I found Venus shining over the black outline of the hills. The familiar Tuscan scent of pine and juniper filled the air, and I breathed in peace and breathed out anxiety.

The evening was too lovely, Casalta too beautiful: cares and worries, or even pain, didn't come between me and the joy my home brought: no, they heightened it. The sky and the hills and the solid stone against my cheek, the sound of the autumnal breeze in the distance and the wild roses at the edge of the garden, all this was a balm to my troubled soul.

I wrapped the blanket around my shoulders and opened the diary. The tiny booklight illuminated the pages. I couldn't wait to know more about Viola's life.

Dear Liala,

Federico Valsecchi came for dinner, as promised.

I was upstairs reading Signorsì, *sitting upright at my desk so I wouldn't wrinkle my dress, the lilac one with the matching shoes. My long hair was tied in a knot at the nape of my neck, grandmother-style, which added to my misery.*

'I hear you, Viola,' I said with a little smile. From one 'grandmothery' girl to another...

I heard the noise of a car and ran to the window. I'd have preferred having a chance to look at Federico for the first time by myself – yes, I'd seen him before, but I hadn't really looked at him, if you know what I mean.

But I only had a moment, as he stepped out of his car in full gear, gloves, goggles and all, as if he'd been piloting a plane – I barely caught a glimpse of him before Mamma burst into the room and, without ceremony, grabbed my hand to lead me downstairs, through the living room – and out the front door.

He was small, not much taller than me, and thin; his hair was thinning on top and greying on the sides. When he saw me, he straightened, and I thought he'd click his heels together.

'Well, well, well, if this isn't a beautiful horse!' Papà said genially, holding out his hand for Federico to shake.

For a second, I thought he was talking about me.

'Lancia Ardea,' Federico answered, turning towards his car. 'I'm the third person in the country to own one, the first two being our Duce and his son-in-law,' he boasted. Federico is devoted to Mussolini. He even imitates his trademark stance,

with legs apart and the chest puffed out, and his way of speaking. Both of which look ridiculous enough on the Duce, but even more so on puny, thin Federico.

'Oh!' Mamma breathed and turned her head towards me, in a silent invitation to join in the awe. I endeavoured to smile, but I really did not care that he was one of three people in Italy to own that car.

I remembered myself, nodded and smiled – I had to work hard to make my lips stretch.

After we'd finished admiring the new and thoroughly manly car, Federico took off his driving paraphernalia. Now I could see his face. He has a pinched face and a goatee and a little moustache, and he looks so old. So old!

I wanted to cry.

He took Mamma's hand and kissed it, and she giggled and pretended to wave him away. Then he turned towards me.

'It's a privilege meeting you, Viola,' he said. He took my hand but thankfully he didn't kiss it.

The evening was like a dream, and not in a good way. It seemed to me that I was watching myself from somewhere far away. There were two Federicos sitting at our table, that night: one, when he spoke to my parents, was loud and boastful and full of stories about his piloting past. The other one, when he spoke to me, was gentle, extremely gentle, like he was talking to a child.

Understandable, considering I'm half his age.

Unwelcome memories stirred me. Enrico Rinaldi didn't speak to me like he'd speak to a child, but to someone not very bright. He almost shouted at me like I spoke a foreign language. But that first night I thought nothing of it, because I had no idea of having been earmarked for him, like a prized cow sold at the market.

When we moved to the living room, he'd just finished telling my parents some story about his plane falling in the Black Sea and him having to swim to safety – it'd have been quite riveting, had I not felt sick about the whole situation. Mamma had poured rosolio for all of us, pink, sweet liquid in tiny crystal glasses. Words unspoken hung between the four of us, until finally Mamma took the lead.

'Well, your stories are heart-stopping, Count. I don't want to think what would happen to us women if we didn't have men like you to fight for us... in war or daily life. Us mothers have no other hope for our daughters than that they find a protector! You see, my sister never married. Your aunt Agnese, dear,' she said to me, as though I might have forgotten my aunt's name. 'Our parents tried and tried to make her see sense, but she refused to marry! She said she wanted to keep her independence. Her life is hard, without a husband to care for her. She regrets her choices,' Mamma ended in a whisper, as if revealing a shameful secret.

Federico shook his head at such a foolish choice.

'Nobody understands more than me, signora! My hope for a family was dashed years ago by someone who doesn't know what loyalty is. I don't want to speak ill of her, but I know for sure she reaped what she sowed! I spent many years in solitude, but solitude weighs heavy on a man's heart.'

I had to give it to him, he had the gift of eloquence. Magniloquence, really. Your characters, Liala, have nothing on him.

'I'm sure it does,' Mamma said gravely.

'I am now ready to embrace life again,' Federico said, and looked to Papà, and then my mother again, solemnly. *My heart sped up and I hoped that the way my chest was rising and falling would go unnoticed.*

'...and I hope to do so with your lovely daughter, Viola.'

Finally he moved his gaze to me, and acknowledged me. At

last. Previously you'd have thought he wanted to marry my parents.

'Signorina Innocenti, I assume your father spoke to you about my proposal.'

'Viola,' Papà murmured. There was no need for him to raise his voice. I knew what I must say. I knew what I must do.

'I'm honoured.'

My parents almost crumbled with relief. I think my fate is sealed.

I took refuge in my room, and glanced at the rag doll on my bedside table, my favourite, my little Bianca...

I leaned the diary against me for a moment – I had to digest that bit of information.

Viola had given my name to a doll, her favourite doll?

Was it a coincidence?

Or had my existence had been known to her, like hers was to me?

I couldn't believe that Viola, too, had had to go through what I went through, and my mother and my sisters. That history had repeated itself in Casalta. How disappointing to find out what her parents were really like, how little they valued her happiness.

I had to stop reading and say goodbye to Viola, for now. I couldn't wait to know more, but my eyes were closing.

It'd been the longest day, and yet, when I climbed back into my room and into my bed, I couldn't help remembering, even if I didn't want to.

After that first dinner at our house, Enrico Rinaldi kissed all of us, sloppy kisses that left us girls revolted. Mia wiped her cheek on her sleeve and Father frowned, but Enrico laughed, a belly laugh. Only then did I realise that something was up: Father was jealous of us and careful of our reputation, and it certainly wasn't customary for any associate of his to slobber all over his daughters. But Enrico was allowed. Why?

When the door closed, Father called me into his study. That room held more bad memories than I cared to remember. I still didn't like to go in there, even if we'd cleared away all his things after he died; Lulu had imbued the room with her essence.

Father wasn't one for speeches or lengthy explanations.

'Enrico will be taking you out sometime next week,' he announced.

It had taken me a moment to get his meaning. I remembered my heart sinking lower than ever before.

I didn't recall what I said, but I remembered what my father told me: 'You'll go, and I'll be content and satisfied and proud of you, my dear. You know that if I'm content, and satisfied, and proud of you, your sisters will be happy too.'

His veiled threats were now familiar to me. What could I do? If one hasn't been in the situation, it's impossible to explain powerlessness. It's impossible to explain that no, you can't just leave, you can't just say no. Just like Agnese, Viola's aunt didn't understand why Viola's mother *stayed*.

If Father was kept happy, my sisters would be safe.

I realised now I was shaking. How could I have thought that I'd left all that behind? It was all still in me, still in my memory, in my mind, in my body. And Viola's diary was bringing it all back, like a wound that still needed cauterising.

It took a long time to fall asleep, but when I finally did, troubling images came to darken my dreams and I woke up covered in sweat.

I know what that feels like, Viola. I know what you went through.

CHAPTER 14

CASALTA, 1985

BIANCA

Amarilli was pale, but two pink blotches on her cheeks bloomed like sick flowers. Seeing her in her hospital bed, helpless and weak when she was always so feisty and energetic, broke my heart.

'Take that sad look off your face, my dear. I didn't die. And I'm fine, just a little tired.'

'You gave us a fright, Amarilli,' I said, and leaned over to kiss her forehead.

'No need to be frightened, dear. What are you doing here, anyway? You should be at work! Are you pulling a sickie already?' She smiled a weak smile.

'I swapped my hours so I could come see you. And I brought the *La Signora Omnibus*. Lots of stories. We can go through them while you recover.'

'That'd be good. Thank you, *cara*.'

'You're very welcome,' I said, and I squeezed her hand. I was dismayed to feel it was cold and clammy to the touch.

I walked out of the hospital with a heavy heart.

Amarilli needed me now. I had the horrible feeling that walking on to my future meant leaving loose threads behind, and each of those threads was a person...

But Teresa would be there. I was sure I was going to like her, if Camilla did... I looked at my watch – I was a little late, so I hurried to the Legami headquarters. When I stepped inside, a white-haired lady in a long beige cardigan and jeans sitting at the small Formica table turned to me and smiled. She looked vaguely familiar, but I couldn't quite pinpoint when and where I'd seen her before.

'Hello, Bianca! You probably don't remember me, but I taught you and your sisters in primary school.'

Now I recognised her. 'Oh! Of course! Maestra Teresa!'

'That's me.'

My whole self gave a sigh of relief. Teresa had taught generations of children in Casalta and Biancamura, she had a spotless reputation and nobody could say a bad word about her. I truly felt we were home and dry.

'Oh, thank you for being here! We couldn't have found a better person!' I said, truthfully.

'Thank you for this opportunity! I'm so glad I can help you. And it'll be good for me too. I'm used to being busy, and the days are so long when you don't have enough to do! Retirement is a double-edged sword.'

'Well, you won't be short of things to do from now on, I can assure you,' I said. 'I must run; I'll be late for the train!'

Now I could move towards my future with no guilt. Well, less guilt. A *little* bit less.

∽

Twenty minutes later I was at the station, breathless but excited to be going to Florence. I'd barely stepped past the tiny ticket booth when I spotted the van, with its blue inscription on the side: *Toscana TV*.

Oh, no. Hopefully it was another reporter and not...

No such luck. It was indeed Tamara, and she was in front of a cameraman, clutching a microphone with both hands like her life depended on it. I made out some of her words here and there, something about a line to Siena being added to the schedule.

How come I'd never seen her around before, and now she was everywhere I went?

I hoped she wouldn't spot me as I walked with my head down low – maybe Lucrezia's black suit would make me anonymous. Sadly, red hair never quite makes you anonymous *enough*. And it's hard to avoid people in a one-platform station. She gestured to the cameraman that the shoot was over, and jumped on me. Not literally, though it felt like it, because her presence was as heavy as an incubus on my back.

'Bianca!' she called. She was trying to sound cheerful, but her tone had a shrill edge. Somewhere between calling an unruly puppy and screaming at a scurrying rat.

'Hello,' I said without enthusiasm. Tamara made me feel like I wanted to crawl out of my skin. Because I didn't like her, not because she was Lorenzo's girlfriend, of course. I didn't care about that, I told myself; I had moved on.

'Look at you, wearing Lucrezia's clothes!' I noticed that the cameraman turned away diplomatically – had I just imagined him rolling his eyes?

For a moment I wondered how she knew it was my sister's suit: maybe she'd seen it on Lulu – my twin was often at the Orafi house, of course, to see Vanni. Tamara seemed obsessed with what I wore, for some reason. I was about to say just that, but the noise of a train coming stopped me. That was my cue to disappear and end this pathetic excuse for a conversation.

Never had anyone been so thankful to see a train rolling into a station.

'Well, sorry, I must catch that. Bye,' I said, trying to infuse my voice with a semblance of regret, and failing.

Her grip on my wrist was unexpected.

'What happened between you two?' she hissed, low enough that the cameraman wouldn't hear her, but I would.

'It was a long time ago,' I said curtly and shook my arm free.

'Oh, really? Why did you get into his car the other day?'

Of course. The small village grapevine never failed. 'I missed my train. He gave me a lift.'

'Right.'

'Yes. I have to—'

'I know the likes of you! Look at yourself. All these ridiculous airs and graces! You Falconeri sisters think you're special, don't you? You have no idea what the real world is, the modern world. Did you let Lorenzo hold your hand? Or even kiss you on the cheek? Now that would be a huge step for you!'

It was like being punched in the gut. What was wrong with this woman? Why did she hate me so much?

'You don't know me. You have no idea who I am.'

'My dear Bianca, *there's nothing to know*.'

I almost took a step back, hit by her words, but I stopped myself. I had to stand my ground. 'Does Lorenzo know *you*?'

'He likes what he sees, that's for sure.'

The effort to keep my face composed took everything I had.

'I wonder if he'd like what he *doesn't* see,' I said, and walked away. I was desperate to hide my emotions – I couldn't let Tamara see that her words had upset me.

I was still shaking when I let myself fall into a seat by the window.

That witch. I indulged in the fantasy of slapping her – but a voice in my mind came to poke and prod me.

Can you truly, honestly say that Tamara has no reason to be so hostile to you, when being with Lorenzo turned you inside out?

'Oh, shut up, conscience,' I whispered.

I had to put a stop to all this. I had to stay away from Lorenzo no matter what. For him, for me. And for Tamara, even if she truly was a witch.

I almost grabbed Viola's diary out of my bag, to lose myself in her life and, just for a little while, forget about mine.

CHAPTER 15

∝∞∝

CASALTA, 194-

VIOLA

Dear Liala,

My story seems to be turning out like one of your novels. Yes, there's a count and former pilot, and a young girl who (I hope) knows her own mind. Except there's no love nor passion. Not on my part anyway.

Federico took me out for the day. Forte dei Marmi, the renowned sea resort, baked under the sun, and the beach was full of people sunbathing and swimming. Seagulls cawed at one another in the sky. We walked along the promenade and stopped for ice cream from a little cart painted blue and cream. Marita says I could chat with a stone, but apparently I've lost the gift of the gab, because I couldn't find anything to talk about. I just interspersed Federico's monologue with an occasional 'Yes,' 'Oh,' and 'I didn't know that.' The long and detailed descriptions of his undertakings during the war completely lost me; my attention re-emerged a little when he talked about his travels, because I'd like to see the world; and then he started listing his possessions.

We sat on the low stone wall that separated the promenade from the beach – the salt wind played in my hair and the light of the sun was that yummy golden-orange hue, you almost want to drink it in.

I shaded my eyes with my hand and as Federico gazed out to sea, I had a moment to look at him properly. He wore a cream linen suit and the tufts of grey hair at the sides of his head were pomaded back. His beard was slick with pomade too, and his moustache had been coaxed upwards. He was so thin, I thought he might be blown away by the sea breeze.

'I know I'm as old as your father,' he said suddenly.

'Federico—'

'No, no, let me finish. I know I'm as old as your father, and I know why you're here with me. I promise you I'll restore your father's business. I'll take care of you and your signora madre, and make sure that your signor padre will not be shamed.'

I was speechless. He'd stripped away all hypocrisy and told it like it was.

'Thank you,' I said.

'I know you'll love me, in time.'

A thought came to my mind. Was he going to call my parents Mamma and Papà, like affectionate sons-in-law do? Because he's my father's age and older than my mother. I laughed to myself a little – but immediately turned melancholic.

Maybe he won't like me. Maybe he'll call this whole thing off, because I'm not the girl he thought I was?

Maybe there's hope...

I silently rooted for Viola – for her to find a way out of that terrible predicament. I shuddered. But what she'd written next dashed my hopes for her.

'I suspect you know why I asked to venture out with you...'

I nodded. 'You want to propose to me.'

He opened his mouth in surprise, then he smiled. 'True. I thought I'd be the one to introduce the subject, that you wouldn't be so forward, but yes.'

All of a sudden I was overwhelmed. The impulse to run and the obligation to stay fought in my mind, and I was trembling all over.

'Oh, cara, I know you're frightened! But I promise I'll always be kind to you. You have nothing to fear from me.'

I'm not afraid. I'm unhappy. You're old. I had hopes; there were things I wanted to do before getting married, I wanted to say. Only then I noticed that there was a little black box in his hand. He opened it – inside was a ring, a ruby mounted in gold.

'So, will you marry me?'

The little scenario of running away and letting my parents deal with it all themselves made an arc through my mind like a comet.

'Yes,' I said instead. I felt like I was signing my death sentence. No: a life sentence. A life in prison.

Federico slipped the ring onto my finger – it was a little big, but it stayed put. He laid one hand on my waist, the other on the back of my neck, and kissed me. From now on I'm not going to talk about his kisses, or anything of the sort. I can't.

Oh, God. I remembered that feeling well.

We were walking back to Casalta arm in arm, to give my parents the good news, when I stopped and let go of his arm.

'Federico, I have a request.'

'Of course, cara. Anything. If it's appropriate, of course.'

'It is appropriate. It's extremely appropriate. I'd like to work for a little while, until we marry.'

'But... why? Why would you want to work if you don't need

to? Our Duce says women should be wives and most of all mothers. Is that not enough for you?'

No.

'It will be enough once we marry.'

'We'll marry soon; I don't see why we would wait.'

'Oh, but I want my wedding to be in the spring! I've always dreamed of a lace dress! Autumn and winter are dark and cold... Also, Mamma and I have a lot to do, a lot to organise!' I scrambled.

'Well, I didn't really want to wait that long, but if it makes you happy...'

'So I can work?'

'In some noisy, stinking factory? You're so pure, Viola... you should stay home with your family and then come to me. Unsullied. You don't seem to grasp what it means to become Countess Valsecchi!'

'I do! And I know there must be something for me to do that's appropriate for your future wife...'

He took my arm and we resumed walking. I was looking down at my feet, trying to hold back tears of frustration.

'Wait. I thought of something,' he said and stopped again.

I held my breath.

'My family has always been a patron of the arts; Giovanni Poggi is a friend of mine. He's the Sovrintendente alle Arti... in layman's words, he oversees Florence's museums and galleries. He's a nice fellow, though sometimes I doubt his political inclinations...'

And? And? I was hanging from his every word – maybe, maybe...

'...and they have a little team at the Uffizi. Factotums really, they give guided tours and make sure visitors behave, general duties...'

The Uffizi! Maybe Viola would work there; maybe that was

why her diary ended up in that box! And that was how our lives entwined again. It was fate, I was sure.

'Yes! Absolutely yes!'

Federico laughed again. 'It's an appropriate position I suppose, a little pastime until the wedding.'

'Thank you, thank you, thank you. Thank you,' I said, and in this moment of enthusiasm, I threw my arms around his neck. I was grateful: but oh for a world where I don't have to depend on a man's kindness and whims... to be able to decide for myself! Like every woman should.

Was this really a thing of the past, for us girls and women? To have to depend on a man's whims. To have our lives decided by fathers and husbands. There are many ways to control a woman's life, not all as overt as the ones Viola's parents had used. Some are covert, subtle, based on emotional blackmail.

Not a thing of the past at all...

My parents were waiting, Papà sitting on the sofa smoking and Mamma standing at the window. I could see her as we came in, arms crossed with one hand on her lips. When she saw our smiling faces – though the reasons for our happiness were different – she ran to open the door.

'Well, I am exceedingly grateful and honoured to announce that your daughter has agreed to marry me,' Federico proclaimed, as Papà rose to shake his hand and Mamma embraced me, tears in her eyes.

'I'm going to work at the Uffizi,' I said when they finished congratulating us.

And silence fell.

I had to laugh. How I loved Viola and her way of distilling her dream out of the situation! But before I knew it, tears gathered in my eyes. Maybe if she'd been less generous, if she'd let her parents deal with their financial situation without being forced to help, she could have freed herself. But she was too selfless. My sisters had been children, little girls, when I shouldered the family situation and accepted to go out with Rinaldi; but Viola's mother was an adult!

And yet, Viola said, her mother had been 'hollowed out'.

With sheer willpower, I didn't let my tears fall. The train would enter the station of Santa Maria Novella in a few minutes: I couldn't turn up at work with a puffy face. *Hold on, Viola... hold on for a better future,* I said in my mind.

Dear Liala,

Zia Agnese and I went to Lina, the village hairdresser, together. I didn't tell Mamma, of course. But at this point, her reproach means nothing.

'Oh, your hair is beautiful, such a nice chestnut colour! And down to your waist!' Lina said.

'Chop it all off.'

I swallowed when I saw my dark locks all over the floor. But only little girls and old ladies have hair that long, and I'm not a child any more and not an old lady yet, though I'll be married to an old man soon.

Lina curled my hair – I can't deny I was a little horrified when I smelled burning, but apparently it's normal when your hair is heated – and then styled it with two waves rolled back at the sides of my face.

'You look lovely,' Zia Agnese said. But I could see the wistfulness in her eyes. I know she'll try until the very last minute to convince me to refuse the marriage.

'Well, if I can't choose my husband, at least I want to choose my hairstyle.'

I laughed again, dried the rogue tear that had escaped from under my lashes, and walked out of the station towards the Uffizi. I understood Viola; I knew what she was going through. I knew what it was like to live in fear, to walk on eggshells in case you said or did something wrong, and then paid the consequences. I knew what it was like to see your mother suffering, shaking every time he came into the room. I knew what it was like to feel the touch of a man as old as my father. To pretend it was Lorenzo, to dream I hadn't bent to my father's will, to cry in my bed, late at night, and have Mia slip in the bed with me and hold me, trying to comfort me.

It still hurt. The memories made me shake, as if I still was a dam that stood between my father and my sisters and held back an ocean of rage, just like Viola was between her father and her mother. The years spent in terror had shaped who I was; they were laced in my identity, in my story. I'd never be free of them.

I never stood up to Fosco Falconeri, not me: our mother tried, and she had her children taken away from her; Lucrezia tried, and she paid the highest price for it.

When I was offered to Rinaldi on a silver plate, I said yes.

But it was time to leave the stories of the past, now: the Uffizi was coming into view, and there Brando waited for me, and my work. The Bianca of yesterday made way for the Bianca of today.

CHAPTER 16

CASALTA, 1985

BIANCA

After three hours of sorting papers, my mind was lost in certificates of acquisitions, lists of expenditures, reports of restorations. Every once in a while some unexpected treasure passed by me – a green cigarette packet flattened in a folder, a postcard, a grocery list, little notes and personal letters... debris of lives long gone, snippets of moments past.

Brando came to crouch beside me, folding his long legs. His scent, wood and old books, filled my nostrils. For some reason, his attractiveness came as a surprise to me every time I saw him. *Every* time I was taken aback. Maybe because I'd never really noticed anyone but Lorenzo for years... all other men to me seemed invisible.

But Brando: I saw him.

'Is your friend okay?'

'Amarilli? She's as well as she can be... I'm worried, of course, but she's in good hands.'

'That's good. I hope she gets better soon. Come run away

with me? All the way to Caffè Medaglia around the corner, where nobody can *ever* find us?'

'Oh, yes,' I said gratefully. My stomach was gnawing at me, empty since this morning.

Brando treated me to a croissant and my usual cup of tea. 'Thank you. It's the first food I've eaten since last night; I'm famished! But we found a replacement for me at Legami, and she's lovely. So things will be easier, now...'

'Breathe, Bianca,' Brando said with a smile.

And I did. I sat back and closed my eyes for a second. When I reopened them, my gaze rested on the beauty of the church in front of us, and the windswept, dark blue sky of autumn.

I knew that while my eyes were closed, Brando had been looking at me. I felt the blood rush to my face – details of him jumped out at me as if through a camera lens finding its focus: long-fingered, delicate hands, a nose that wouldn't have looked out of place on a Roman statue, something in the curve of his shoulders that suggested a strong, solid embrace...

'You enjoying the work? Even if it's not among beautiful paintings, but dusty papers?'

'Very much,' I said wholeheartedly. 'And among dusty papers, there can be surprises. I found postcards, a grocery list, a little note with an appointment scribbled on it. It's fascinating.'

'Oh, yes. The archivist's little treasures. Theoretically speaking, we should keep the documents only, but in practice, nobody has the heart to get rid of those things or put them all together in a box – they'd lose their meaning. So they stay there, in between the folds of time. For the next person who finds it and thinks, oh, that morning of long ago he or she went to the shop, smoked a cigarette, got a postcard in the post from a friend, or a sweetheart... And your imagination starts running. Documents tell us of historical facts, but those little mementos preserve moments.'

I tilted my head as I listened. 'You're passionate about all this, aren't you?'

He shrugged. 'It's my life.'

'It's a *good* life,' I said with a smile. 'I suppose sometimes we forget how lucky we are to live where we do. You see all this day in and day out... the art, the architecture. I'm in love with my home, really... What?' He was staring at me.

'Sorry, it's just that... it's good to hear you talking.'

I laughed. 'Don't encourage me...'

'No, really! You were so quiet when we were at school.'

'You might come to miss those times,' I said. He was right – I was chattier than I'd usually be. Between being homeschooled, and therefore not used to people, and the secrets we carried as a family, I was always reserved. As children, we'd had to be so careful not to talk about our gifts, or about anything controversial happening in our family, and sometimes it had been easier not to talk at all.

'Bianca, I was wondering,' he began. At that moment, blood rushed to his face, and he was covered in red splotches. It was like seeing a lightbulb being switched on. The loquacious, cheerful man in front of me turned bashful all of a sudden.

'Yes?'

'Can I take you out tonight? I mean, I don't want you to feel... Because we're working together, and... Not if you don't want to...'

'Of course. I'd love to.'

Oh. Did I just say yes? It had come out before I could think, consider, turn things around in my head until I was exhausted with pondering. This was all new, for me.

'You would?'

This would be my first proper date, at age twenty-five.

Talk about momentous.

'Yes. I'd love that. Thank you,' I said decisively, before I could waver, find excuses and, most of all, before the insidious feeling of betraying Lorenzo could spark inside me.

'Oh, great! I'm looking forward to it!' Brando was his sunny, cheerful self again. His sudden shyness had been so charming. Not like Lorenzo, who believed the world belonged to him and everyone should do what he said.

No, *not* like Lorenzo.

And that sudden thought was unpleasant, and dry and dusty, and made me feel like the past would forever try to grab me back, even when I was walking away.

Tentatively, Brando touched my fingertips, all the while looking at me – his touch sent a shiver down my spine, and when he saw that I had no objection, he covered my hand with his, and entwined his fingers with mine. His face was so open, so... light. There was no history between us, no burden – his hand felt smooth and strong, and I couldn't help wondering how his lips would feel against mine...

'So, there's nobody else in your life, right now?' he asked.

I shook my head. 'No.'

'It seems impossible. I mean, you're... you're just so beautiful.'

I felt myself blushing. I imagined I'd be a shade of fuchsia, by now.

'What about you? I could say the same; why have you not been snapped up by some artsy girl?' I joked, to defuse the moment. Being called beautiful was lovely, but also a little embarrassing.

'Well, there *was* an artsy girl. But it didn't work out. You see... we came to a point where we either took it to the next level, or broke up. Neither of us could really see us spending our lives together. It fizzled out. We're still friends.'

I nodded. 'I can't imagine you deep in conflict or drama,' I said.

'Nah, that's not for me. But after Greta and I broke up, well,

I went through a real low. I asked myself if life was always going to be so... lukewarm. Going through the motions instead of living deeply. Authentically. You know what I mean?'

'Yes. I do.'

'When I saw you again... I couldn't believe it. I'm going to tell you something really, really embarrassing...'

'What?' I smiled.

'I wrote a poem for you. When I was... eleven? Twelve? You sat in the front row and I was in the back, and I used to look at your hair and I wrote a poem for you.'

'That's so sweet!' I laughed.

'It was a terrible poem. Really, really bad. Trust me.'

'Well, as much as I'd like to be sitting here being complimented, we need to go back to work,' I said.

A moment before I got up, he laid a gentle butterfly-kiss on the top of my head. A warm feeling rose from my toes to my face, my heart fluttering – that innocent, sweet show of affection had melted me, a long-frozen part of me coming to life again.

CHAPTER 17

CASALTA, 1985

BIANCA

Getting ready to go out with Brando was no small feat.

I was painfully aware of the fact that I'd never been on a real date before. The times I'd gone out with Enrico Rinaldi didn't count as dates. They counted as torture.

Lorenzo and I never met in public – it was always the two of us under the canopy of the trees, alone in our little world. Maybe having a secret relationship, keeping Lorenzo in my heart for so long after we broke up, had been damaging to me... Actually, scratch the maybe: it did damage me. But even so, I couldn't regret it. The whole thing was part of me; to erase it would have meant erasing part of my identity. As long as it stayed firmly in the past, where it belonged.

And as long as Tamara keeps her distance, I thought grimly.

The contents of my wardrobe were strewn on the bed and around my room, and I was mentally cursing myself for drowning in a glass of water. The choice was made harder by my recent change in look. Lulu had loaned me work clothes, and I had a pair of jeans, but nothing suitable for a date. What did you wear on a date, anyway?

I ran downstairs.

'Lulu! *Help!*'

Lucrezia looked up from her desk in what used to be my father's study, but had been since exorcised – I'm not using the word lightly – and was now hers.

'I have exactly the thing,' she said, and I breathed a sigh of relief.

Half an hour later I was wearing a black minidress with an aqua-coloured cropped cardigan, black tights and black pumps, with my hair down and pouffed by Lulu's hairspray. Having a fashionista sister had its advantages.

The girl I saw in the mirror wasn't really me – or the old me, anyway – but I liked her, I thought, twirling with my hands on my hips. This new Bianca wasn't bad-looking at all.

'You look beautiful!' Lulu was more generous than me. 'He'll be smitten!'

There was just time to slip in earrings and do my make-up – aqua eyeshadow and pink lipstick, apparently very *in* at the moment, Lulu assured me – before the bell rang.

I opened the door... and a part of me melted a little. Brando was painfully handsome, in jeans and a forest-green jumper, his dark blond hair tamed down – not for long, I predicted. It was good seeing him in the wild, so to speak, and not in an office, or archive, or library. *Very* good.

I realised I was standing there with my mouth half open, saying nothing, and felt my cheeks burn up. The curse of being pale was how quickly I blushed.

'Bianca... You look... well, you look amazing,' he said, and his awkwardness was a relief. At least I wasn't the only one.

He kissed me on the cheek, and handed me a bouquet of pink and light green peonies. A very artistic choice of colours. To be expected, I supposed. Just like the symphony of pinks and greens in my bouquet, everything else was textbook perfect, like in one of those films where there are fireworks in the sky at the couple's first kiss, or they dance to their favourite song in the street and everyone applauds.

With Lorenzo, everything had been askew.

Maybe I should stop thinking about Lorenzo, now.

'Thank you, please come in!'

I closed the door against the chilly air, and led Brando to the living room. There stood my three sisters. In a line. Like an interrogation committee. Or a firing squad.

Poor Brando stopped and smiled even more awkwardly than before.

'The three Fates,' he whispered, and I laughed.

In Greek mythology, the three Fates weave the thread of every woman's and man's destiny, and finally, they cut the thread when someone's life comes to an end. My sisters certainly looked solemn and a touch forbidding – Nora with her usual belligerent expression, Mia stern, Lulu a little lighter, with a half-smile dancing on her lips.

Poor Brando. I needed to get him out of there quickly.

'Well, have a good time,' Nora said, all the while looking at Brando. She had a way of making her lovely green eyes hard and grey like flint.

'We want to know everything when you come back!' Lulu said.

Mia said nothing, standing there looking a little otherworldly, in a long black dress and with those strange eyes, one brown, one blue.

I was pretty sure I heard Brando swallow.

'No pressure, then,' he said. This went down well: my sisters loved sarcasm. Lulu laughed and Nora chuckled, but Mia remained solemn.

'What time should I have her back?' Brando joked and I

commended him in my heart for standing up to the Falconeri sisters.

'Well, we're off!' I said quickly and grabbed my jacket.

'Sorry about that,' I said as soon as we were in the car. 'They're a little... *protective*.'

'No, that's good.'

'Really?'

'Oh, yes. Facing your sisters shapes the character. Separates the wheat from the chaff. Only the strongest and bravest remain.'

'Something like that! Where are we going?'

'Surprise. It's a bit out of the way... It'll be worth it, you'll see.'

His car was a muddy and battered jeep – I'm not much of an expert on cars, but this stood out to me because it was the kind of vehicle you'd see patrolling a national park.

'Sorry, not the most stylish car, but we're going off-road, so I borrowed my father's. He's a *guardia forestale*,' he explained while I climbed up, his hand on my back.

A forest ranger – maybe that was why Brando often smelled of wood, I thought. And then: *are we going off-road?* I thought of my dressy pumps...

'I can't wait for you to see the place I chose! It's off the beaten track,' he said. The car smelled of greenery and cut wood, like a moving piece of forest.

We chatted about everything and nothing as we drove on, the initial shyness dissolving into friendliness. After less than an hour it seemed like we were in another world, far from the gentle, domesticated Tuscany I belonged to. Hills and fields were replaced by dark expanses of trees, and there were fewer and fewer lights to obstruct the stars.

When he finally stopped the car, I climbed down and looked around, breathing the wind in. There were almost no lights nearby, except a few in the distance, gathered like a shiny bouquet. The night was dark and windswept and smelled of autumn, of trees and aromatic plants and night scents.

This wasn't the Tuscany of villas and bright sunshine, but a place wilder and darker, like it must have been hundreds of years ago, when between the towns and the castles there were stretches of ancient, wooded land inhabited by wolves, hogs and bears.

Brando took me by the hand and led me around the car – when I was facing the opposite direction, I saw a serpent of lights climbing up a small, round hill. 'We're going up there,' he told me, and his enthusiasm, his eagerness to impress me, touched me.

The natural gate to the hill was framed by two tall oak trees and two solar lights planted in the ground. The climbing road was dotted with solar lights too, a view that was ancient and futuristic at the same time.

'What's up there?'

'Pietrasanta,' he said with an air of mystery.

I played his game. 'And what's Pietrasanta?'

'Pietrasanta consists of three houses. That's the whole hamlet. And it's not on the grid.'

'No electricity? Hence the solar lights.'

'Yep. Torches would have been more striking, though.'

'Fire hazard.'

Brando laughed. 'You're a worrier!'

'It's a reflex. I pretty much brought my sisters up. I have the danger radars of a mother.'

'Well, it's time to relax, now, and let go a bit,' he said, and took my arm – thankfully, because my shoes weren't made for walking anywhere except on asphalt.

'No electricity, and no gas either?'

'Nope.'

'How do they cook?' I asked, imagining a great fireplace with a cauldron on it, and a fire with a hog turning on the spit.

'You'll see. I hope you're hungry.'

Distant voices reached us as we walked – laughter and chat and clinking of glasses. Louder and louder, until we arrived at a stone-paved clearing dotted with tables and chairs, all full but one. A blond-stone building, small and unadorned, stood as if being born out of the hill. On each table a cluster of candles shone – and the house was lit with flickering light.

'*Buonasera*, Brando!' A man with a grey beard and pure white hair, in a dark blue striped apron, came to greet us.

'Tommaso, *ciao*! This is Bianca. She'd like to know how you cook without electricity or gas.'

'Two ingredients: fire, and patience from our clients, because dishes take longer to cook. But they taste better. Come see,' he answered, and we followed him inside the house. The place looked like the kitchen of a castle: two huge pots, big enough to be witch's cauldrons, hung side by side in an open fireplace. On a table covered with a linen tablecloth was a bounty of bread, fat loaves neatly piled and protected by cloths, and cakes that made me drool; on another were bottles of red and white wine with handwritten labels, and uncut cured meats with enormous knives by their sides.

I was blown away. 'Ooooh!'

'What do you think?'

'This is wonderful, Brando. Thank you for taking me here. I'm starving!'

'Well, let's start with this,' Tommaso said and grabbed a bottle and two glasses. We sat at a table at the edge of the stone pavement, where the tiny restaurant ended, and the wood began. Tommaso opened the bottle and left us to pour the wine.

'There's no need to order; they only have what you saw, everything local.'

'Perfect. I see *why* you've brought me here!'

'Why?'

'To transport me to the past. To give me a taste of life long ago. Because you know that's right up my street!'

'Yes. I thought this would be very Bianca. Are you happy? Are you sure you wouldn't have preferred something a little more... civilised?'

'Absolutely not. What are those arches beyond the house? A castle?'

Brando looked dumbfounded. 'Arches?'

'Yes... like a cloister. A monastery, maybe?'

'There used to be a convent here, yes. But not any more... it was destroyed during the war.' He turned back, following my gaze. 'Do you really see something?'

I blinked. 'I...'

Yes, I was sure. There was a cloister beyond the restaurant, only partially illuminated by the flickering lights.

'No, it must have been a trick of the light,' I said, waving a hand in the air to brush the whole thing off.

I'd never before *seen* anything beyond the boundaries of Casalta.

'Then how did you know?'

'I must have read somewhere about Pietrasanta, and my mind filled in the gaps.' I smiled, cool as a cucumber although my heart was racing.

'Yes, of course. More wine?'

'Sure. Not Falconeri, I see, then,' I remarked.

'And not Orafi either. Your family and the Orafi are the main producers around here, but this is made with Tommaso's grapes.'

On hearing the name *Orafi,* my heart jumped. I really didn't want to have Lorenzo's name spoken, especially not there, not then.

Brando must have seen the cloud pass over my face. 'Bianca? I'm sorry, I didn't mean to criticise your family business, I...'

'No, no, not at all!' I wanted to change the subject fast. 'You know, my sister... my twin, Lucrezia...'

'Yes. Us boys were a little afraid of her.'

I laughed. 'Well, she's very sophisticated, and elegant, and she'd probably hate it here! So you took out the right sister.'

At that moment, Tommaso brought us a basket of bread, a butter dish and bowls of fragrant soup. '*Zuppa di castagne*,' he announced: chestnut soup.

'The flavour of autumn,' I said, tucking in.

We chatted companionably through a plate of cured meats and fragrant brown bread, and more wine for me as I wasn't driving. The burning torches against the dark of the night, the solar lights, the woods all around us – it truly felt like being back in time.

But what were those arches that I'd noticed? The convent that used to be here – had I really seen its ghostly remains? I hoped that Brando would forget all about it. I was sure that my excuse had been convincing enough for him to believe.

A sudden longing for my gift to return overwhelmed me, so intense that it almost made my eyes water. I resolved to talk about it with Mum when she arrived – maybe she could give me some advice.

In this setting, Brando looked like an ancient blond knight. By the time the cake arrived – honey and dried fruit – we couldn't look away from each other.

And this frightened me a little.

And I was even more frightened by the intensity of feeling and desire as we walked down the winding road, as close as we could be, without talking. I was acutely aware of his presence, of the warmth of his body, of the strength of his hold on me.

And then, something happened. I looked up and for a moment, a fleeting moment, I was startled – because I thought I'd seen a pair of serious brown eyes dotted with speckles of gold looking back at me. I thought I'd seen Lorenzo's eyes.

But then the moment passed: I was back in the here and now, and it was immediately forgotten.

They were Brando's eyes.

∽

The evening ended with a beautiful drive back through the Tuscan countryside – I was full and sleepy and relaxed and quite happy.

When we arrived in Casalta, Brando came to open my door. We stood there in the semi-darkness, close to each other, and embracing and kissing felt natural, without embarrassment or effort. His kiss was sweet and gentle. So now I knew what they felt like, his lips on mine... And pulling away was harder than I thought it'd be.

'Thank you for tonight,' he said, his voice a little huskier than before. 'I hope we'll do this again...'

'Of course, I'd love to.'

'Listen, I drive to Florence every day from Biancamura; if you want I can give you a lift in the morning?'

Oh. I didn't really want that. The train ride was my time to read Viola's diary and be alone with my thoughts. Also, we already worked together – I didn't want it to be too much, too soon.

'Don't worry. I enjoy taking the train. I have some quiet time to read and think.'

I was sure that Brando understood the words unspoken. 'No problem. Goodnight, then.' He seemed reluctant to let me go. And I was reluctant too.

It was supposed to be one last peck on the lips, but it turned into another kiss, tasting of my lipstick, of wine and of Brando, under a sea of stars. Neither of us pulled apart.

∽

Later that evening, Lulu was in the living room, reading a book by the fireplace as I went to sit beside her.

'Hello there, how did it go? You smell of... something burning?'

I laughed. 'Yes, Brando took me to this place with torches all around, pretty magical. The torches in the night... it was dreamy. I had a really good time! He makes me laugh. He's so funny. And intelligent, and kind.'

'Will you see him again?'

'Of course. He's one of the sweetest people I've ever met,' I said, a little piqued.

Lulu looked a little unimpressed, and I didn't know why. 'Well. Goodnight,' she said, then hugged me quickly and went upstairs.

''Night.'

I was left alone, staring at the slowly dying fire for a long time. I could still feel Brando's kiss on my lips as I thought about Lulu's reaction.

And as I stared into the embers, I could still see Lorenzo's eyes looking back at me.

∼

I woke up with a jolt, melted with longing. I couldn't believe that that moment I'd had with Lorenzo a long time ago had come back to me in a dream.

Our first kiss – light as a butterfly, almost reverent. And then warm and deep, as our bodies grew closer. Desire gripping me in a way I hadn't known was possible, like I'd turned into a creature of pure passion, pure instinct, pure heart.

A creature on fire.

Would I ever feel that way again?

CHAPTER 18

CASALTA, 1985

BIANCA

As morning broke, I stretched in bed, considering the day ahead.

Amarilli was being discharged today, Teresa was going to start working at Legami, and everything was falling into place. I couldn't wait to go to work, to read more of Viola's diary, and to be with Brando.

Yesterday's date came back to me. Unconsciously, I touched my fingertips to my lips...

Being with Brando had felt so good, and I couldn't wait to see him again. Thinking of Lorenzo while I was with Brando, seeing Lorenzo's eyes looking back at me, had just been a blip. A passing thought of no importance. I sang under my breath as I got ready. My reflection stared at me from the bathroom mirror as I brushed my hair, and I looked happy and relaxed.

I was still humming under my breath when I went downstairs. It was finally too cold to have breakfast outside. We huddled up in the kitchen, ignoring Nora's protests.

'The early morning cold will reinvigorate us!' she claimed.

'If it was left to you, we'd live outside! In a *tent*!' Lulu said, and Mia laughed.

'That'd be good,' Nora replied.

'If you have breakfast in the garden, you'll all get *pneumonia*,' Matilde said dramatically. Now she opened a fragrant paper bag and arranged the croissants she'd picked up at the bakery on a plate.

'I forgot to tell you, Mum called yesterday while you were at work,' Mia said, eyeing the croissants. 'She's moved her ticket; she's arriving tomorrow.'

'Finally, a proper plan! With dates and all,' Lulu said, and took a sip of her espresso.

Nora was silent. Her relationship with Mum was still a little strained.

But I was glad. I could ask Mum about my gift, if there was anything she knew that could help me. Mia didn't look enthusiastic. I thought I guessed why, but I wasn't sure.

'Well in time for Gherardo's party,' I said. The idea of seeing my mum still gave me butterflies – having believed her dead for so many years, it was still surreal that she could actually be there, with us. 'It's good, isn't it, Mia?' I said tentatively.

She shrugged. 'Oh, yes. It's great. I can't wait to see her. But...' She studied the croissant on her plate without touching it.

'But you're going to have to tell her something definite about going to London,' Lulu intervened.

Mia nodded.

'If you don't want to go, you don't want to go,' Nora said matter-of-factly.

'If you feel it's too much, for you...' I began.

'Don't let fear get the best of you, Mia. You've never left Casalta; how do you know that you don't enjoy travelling? Maybe you'll find out that you do,' Lulu argued.

'I don't even enjoy going down to the village. I like being here and on the hills—'

'But you've never known anything different,' Lucrezia interrupted.

I bit my lip. Part of me wanted to wrap Mia in cotton wool, protect her from a world that was bound to not understand her; part of me understood Lulu's reasons for encouraging her to fly. As for Nora, I knew she just didn't really want to see her sister far from Casalta and in Mum's world: it was selfish, but I understood her reasons, sunk deep into our family history.

'I'll think about it,' Mia said.

But she'd been *thinking about it* for weeks.

On my way out to go to work, I kissed her dark head.

'It'll all fall into place,' I whispered, and she gave me one of her slow, warm smiles that were so very Mia.

∽

At the station, I refused to look left and right to see if drama happened to be there, in the form of Tamara or Lorenzo's car – I kept my eyes down, determined not to see.

I didn't need to be pulled back into the past, I didn't need any confusion now that life was smooth – for once.

On the train, I opened Viola's diary again.

Dear Liala!!!

I have wonderful news! Federico pulled some strings and I officially am... in employment at the Uffizi!!!!

I smiled at the happiness that shone from the page. She'd written this last sentence in a fancy cursive and decorated it with stars and flowers. I was there, beaming at the little book, when the ticket inspector appeared in front of me. I felt myself blushing – again – and I pursed my lips together.

'Good book, yes?'

I nodded. I'd been so lost in Viola's narration, I'd forgotten I was in public – even though, granted, the train was always half empty. I composed myself and resumed my reading.

Federico came to get me in his beloved Ardea and we stopped at the Caffè Medaglia, where he treated me to coffee and a chocolate pastry, because there, where the best of Florence go, war scarcity is just an echo.

I smiled to myself again. I couldn't help wondering if I'd sat where she sat, at the Caffè Medaglia!

Today, over the noise of conversations mingling together, someone uttered the words: 'bombs falling from the sky'. The five words resounded over the tangle of voices. The place almost hushed after that, as if the air itself had been shattered in a million pieces. Even Federico went pale.

But I almost forgot that even happened, when we were greeted by Giovanni Poggi, the Sovrintendente alle Arti, and given a tour of the museum. I've been to the Uffizi before, of course, but I'd never seen it this way.

'Our Duce and Adolf Hitler himself have walked down the Corridoio Vasariano,' Federico declared. Being in public, he was his magniloquent self. 'No doubt the foreign leader was in awe of our homeland's grandeur!'

I wanted to roll my eyes, but of course I didn't.

I had the feeling that Poggi tolerated Federico's presence, but definitely didn't enjoy it. My feeling became a certainty when I was introduced to my colleagues.

I was so happy with the whole situation, I resolved to ignore the dirty looks I received from my would-be colleagues. I can only guess the looks are because of the way I found this employment, through Federico.

I was introduced to everyone quickly and I don't remember all their names. Three of them stood out to me, two for the way they looked down on me, and one because of her sweet welcome.

'This is Laio Cardellini, my assistant,' Poggi introduced colleague number one. He was a small, thin, bookish type with thick glasses and a serious expression. He looked at me like you'd look at a pet. And in fact, in their eyes, I'm Federico's pet.

And now to colleague number two. 'This is Pietro Sarti; he's been working here the longest. He's our guard dog,' Poggi said and touched Pietro's back. I was a little shocked to hear Poggi refer to someone like that, but Pietro, even if he looked as stern as Laio, maybe even more so, seemed amused.

Colleague number three is by far my favourite! Tiny Lisetta, who smiled and shook my hand and showed me around while Federico and Poggi were talking – or, to be more precise, Federico was lecturing Poggi on the role of the Fascist Party in the conservation of Italian art. Because he knows more than Poggi on this, obviously.

'So, is this the uniform?' I asked Lisetta. Matching blue skirt and jacket, with a black shirt underneath.

'It is! Isn't it pretty?' She turned around to show me. Lisetta is tiny and has the loveliest profile, like a film actress. 'It'll look so nice on you.'

Out of the corner of my eye, I caught Pietro giving us a supercilious look. When he met my gaze, he felt obliged to say something horrible.

'I suppose this is just a little pastime, a hobby to earn some pocket money until you marry wealth,' he said.

'You don't know the price I pay for this. So, shut up,' I hissed.

He. Has. No. Idea.

Lisetta's eyes went wide, and Pietro, too, seemed caught by surprise at my rebuttal. But he ignored my polite request of shutting up.

'If you think that sleeping with a Fascist is going to get you anywhere in life, think again.'

I had no answer for that. The part about 'sleeping with' got to me so deep and hard that my eyes filled with tears, and I hated myself for it.

But I won't let that vulgar, cruel individual ruin this, my one and only chance to work before I'm buried at Palazzo Valsecchi to be the wife of an old man.

When Federico and I left the museum, I felt like there was a tug of war going on in my heart and mind, and I was the rope itself, pulled between joy and elation, and shame and anger after what that horrible man said.

'So, are you happy, cara?' Federico asked.

'Very! Thank you.'

I couldn't let that man's awful words spoil my day. 'If you think that sleeping with a Fascist...' Argh! How dare he judge me without knowing me at all?

Federico tucked my arm under his and we walked across the river, until we reached a square building with an elaborate wooden gate and a coat of arms painted at the highest point.

'Palazzo Valsecchi. My humble abode.' Yes, he did say 'my humble abode'. Liala, you'd be proud of him.

'I'm not sure it's appropriate for us to be alone in your house...' My knees had gone weak.

I felt beads of sweat on my forehead. An unwelcome memory had flashed in my mind: Rinaldi and me out for dinner, and then him insisting we'd go back to his house. He offered me a tour, and lingered at the door of the bedroom.

'Do you like it, Bianca? Do you like how it's decorated?' His words were strange, surreal – he was saying something and meaning something else entirely, and I knew what it was. I'd been terrified, and when we returned to the living room, my knees were shaking.

If something happened there, nobody would help me.

The relief when Rinaldi took me home was immense, but not complete. I knew it was just a matter of time.

That night again, Mia had slipped into my bed to sleep with me. She had no idea what was going on, and neither did Nora; there was no way I could explain.

'We're not going inside,' Federico reassured me and we walked around the building to a back street. He unlocked another gate that opened onto a damp, dark room. When the sun illuminated the gloom, I saw what was inside: a black Fiat Topolino.

'There. Now, mia cara, you'll be so kind as to drive us home.'

'You're doing really well, my dear!' Federico shouted over the din of the car.

A man on a bike pedalled past us. He took his hat off and waved. I was clasping the steering wheel so hard that my knuckles were white.

'We can even go a little faster,' Federico said hopefully.

'Are you sure?'

'Perfectly sure. We might arrive before tonight.'

I leaned on the side of the Topolino, hurting all over after having tensed all my muscles. I almost had to prise myself from the wheel.

'I did it,' I said weakly.

Federico looked proud, if a little pale. 'You did it!'

'Thank you for this, Federico. I've been wanting to drive for ages! Really, I'm grateful.'

'Well, now your father doesn't need to drive you to Florence every day. You can drive yourself to work and back. With a bit of practice. And leaving three hours earlier.'

'Oh, no, that's not going to happen. Papà will never allow me to use his car,' I said, peeling the gloves off my stiff hands.

'You're back! Oh, what a hassle for you, Conte, I'm so very sorry she asked for all this...' Mamma rushed out of the house. 'Oh.'

She looked from me to Federico and back.

'She can't possibly have...'

'...driven us back. Yes, she did. And she'll get better and better.'

I was astounded. This man is my prison. The prison I'll be confined to forever. But when he came into my life, he brought with him the chance to work, and now the chance to drive a car. It's such a contradiction, I don't know how to handle it in my mind and heart.

Mamma tried to protest. 'But surely, a woman driving...'

'Signora cara, please forgive me, and I mean no offence, but you're old fashioned,' Federico replied and my astonishment reached a new level. 'Consider this a wedding present,' he added to me.

So now I have a job, and a car, and I'll drive myself to and from said job. Without a driving licence, but in the current chaos, who's checking?

I was lost in thought as I walked towards the museum.

What Federico was doing to Viola was awful – the selfishness of using his wealth and position to tie a young girl to him. And I knew what it felt like, your own father selling you down the river.

But in a weird way, Federico was also opening her world up, with the job at the Uffizi and teaching her to drive. He was freeing Viola from the limitations her parents had laid on her. It was all so arbitrary: Viola had to live by someone else's rule, constantly, whether it was her father's or her fiancé's.

Yes, Federico was being kind to her: still, it seemed to me that he was a kind *master*. And nobody should have a master. His generosity wouldn't have had reason to exist, had he not bought her.

A likeable man in a world governed by unjust rules, who took full advantage of those same rules.

And that colleague of hers, Pietro? What was wrong with him! How could he speak to her like that! Good on Viola for answering the way she did.

I was passing by Caffè Medaglia when I heard Brando calling me – I was so deep in my thoughts that I jumped out of my skin. Seeing him sent warmth into all my limbs again. The contrast between everything I was remembering and his kind, clean face was startling.

'Sit down for a minute before work?' he asked, and gestured to the empty chair across from him.

'I'd love that.'

We ordered tea and coffee, and a chocolate pastry for me: an homage to Viola's breakfast at that same place.

'I had a good time in Pietrasanta. With you. A really, really good time,' he said.

'Me too. It was lovely.'

And not just because the place he'd taken me was lovely and perfect and right up my street, but because Brando was so upbeat and light-hearted. He seemed to have an inner light... I'd forgotten to ask Lulu about his aura – I made a mental note to do so. I supposed none of us were exempt from problems or heartache, but Brando seemed untouched by shadows.

He seemed to be waiting for me to say something more, but it was my turn to blush the way he had when he asked me out for the first time. I stared at him. He stared at me. Both waited for the other person to make a move... And then we spoke at the same time.

'Maybe we could...'

'I was hoping to take you out again.'

I made an instant *and* firm decision not to berate myself for being awkward or insecure. You couldn't go from homeschooled sisters' keeper to social butterfly in the space of a date.

'I'd love to. Thank you,' I said.

'Oh, great! This is great. I'm happy.'

I smiled. 'Me too...'

'No, I'm really, *really* happy. My strategy worked.'

'Your strategy?'

'In middle school. Remember I told you I had a crush on you? Well, I ran away every time I saw you. That was my strategy, you see.'

I laughed. 'It did work! Actually, we're invited to a party next week, my sisters and my mum and me. We're celebrating a friend's sixtieth. Would you like to be my plus one?'

'I'd love to be your plus one, Signorina Falconeri.'

CHAPTER 19

CASALTA, 1985

BIANCA

As soon as I got home, I phoned Camilla for news of Amarilli – I couldn't call Villa Lieta in the evenings, because they were busy with dinner and then their night routines, when the guests would be given their medication and helped to get into bed.

'Teresa and I went to see her today. She's good, tired and a little shaken by it all, but good. She might need some treatment...'

'Treatment?'

'Maybe a small operation... She asked after you.'

An operation. Oh.

The old, familiar pang of guilt made itself felt again. I couldn't wait to see for myself that Amarilli really was good, that it wasn't just Camilla being the positive person she always was.

'I'll go see her tomorrow and then come mentor Teresa,' I said.

'Perfect. She's doing great, Teresa, just as we thought. She has a lovely manner; she's practical and efficient. People are a little wary at the change, but they'll get used to her. She's good at this, you'll see.'

I took a deep breath. Thank goodness. 'Thank you, Camilla. Have I told you lately how much I appreciate you?'

'No. But I know you do.'

∼

After dinner, Lulu asked me to join her on the stairs outside. She had a plaid blanket, and when I sat beside her she opened her arm to envelop me in the blanket's warm embrace.

We sat very close, and she laid her head on my shoulder – her scent was so familiar, even after twelve years apart, and seeing her flaming-red hair mixed with mine awakened memories of many nights slipping into each other's beds and sleeping together, as close as we had been in the womb. I didn't know how we could have been apart for so long: she was the other part of me, and I loved her with all my heart and soul.

'Did you summon me to have a proper chat about something, or for the pleasure of my company?' I said in a mock-solemn tone that hid a pinch of worry. She'd been acting a little strange that evening: pensive, distant.

'Both, oh my perceptive sister.'

'Go ahead. Is there something bothering you; can I help?'

'No, no, everything is good with me. I just wanted to talk to you about Brando.'

'Brando?' That caught me by surprise. 'What about him?'

'Well... do you like him?'

'Of course I do. I told you!' I shifted uncomfortably. 'What's not to like? He's fun, and considerate, and always in a good mood... and handsome. He's a handsome man.'

'Yes to all that, but... do you like him *like him*?'

'Like *like* him? What are we, thirteen?' I snorted. Lulu was venturing into a conversation that disquieted me; I didn't know why.

'It's just that...'

'What?'

'I don't know,' Lulu said maddeningly and shrugged her shoulders.

What kind of an answer is that?

'Lulu. Everything is working out for me. I'm embracing the new. And Brando is part of the new.'

'That's good. I just wanted to say, well, I'm so glad you're moving on in life, so have we all in the last few months, as you know, and... so many good things have come of it all. Like being by your side again,' she said and wrapped her arms around me, like she might have done when we were little girls. 'But...'

'But?'

'But you don't need to settle.'

'If it's Brando you're referring to, we've only gone out once. You're talking like I should go and choose a dress soon.'

'You will. A bridesmaid dress...'

'You... you and Vanni?' A wonderful warmth spread inside me. My twin was engaged!

'We'll be announcing it at Gherardo's party, but I wanted you to know before anyone else!' she said, her eyes shining with what looked suspiciously like tears. My Lulu had built an armour around her, and every time her feelings broke the surface, my heart melted. I felt tears filling my eyes too. 'I'll tell our sisters and Matilde tomorrow.'

'I'm so happy for you!' We hugged and kissed each other on both cheeks, and the joy on her face was the fulfilment of a wish I'd had for a long, long time: to be close to my twin again, and to see her happy, at last.

It was the best feeling in the world.

'You and Vanni are meant to be,' I whispered, and I touched her face lightly, gathering a tear on my finger.

'That's what I mean. Don't settle. True love is too precious to let it pass by.'

I couldn't help the gut-wrenching feeling in my stomach, because I already had. I had already let true love go.

∽

Alone in bed that night, I wrestled with memories for a while, trying to avoid the longing and bittersweet feeling of having loved and lost.

But it was a lost cause. I looked back at our whole arc: from the first time Lorenzo and I met and he told me to stay away from his family, to when we both returned to each other without quite knowing why, and then the years of friendship – two children holding onto each other in a crazy world – until we weren't children any more, and our bond turned into something else. It'd been seamless, smooth, like it was meant to be, from the very beginning. And the recollection of a specific night was too tender, too happy not to give in.

The easiest time for us to meet had been late at night, when we were least likely to be discovered. And that specific night, marked forever in my heart and soul, the sky was full of stars, thick like dust over our heads. We used to light candles – sometimes Lorenzo even lit a little fire at the foot of the tree – but not often, for fear of being found out. His presence, the fire and the stars made me feel like I was in another world, one where I was safe and happy and nobody would be sent away from their family, nobody would be scared into submission.

'Can you imagine, if it had been just you and me in the world? Thousands of years ago. When the world was still empty. We could have found a shelter and lived together, you and me, and the sun and the moon and the stars, and nothing else.'

'And bears and sabre-toothed tigers trying to eat us,' I said.

He always laughed at my jokes. It was hard to believe now, but with me, Lorenzo laughed often, in spite of his trademark seriousness.

That night – one moment we were sitting side by side, looking up at the stellar expanse, the next I leaned my head on his shoulder. He wrapped his arm around my waist, and kissed my cheek. Then my temple, my nose, my eyes, gentle kisses that made me smile and giggle, and it was in a smile that our lips met.

All of a sudden, I wasn't giggling and he wasn't smiling, and we were no longer two children, but a young woman and a young man who kissed hesitantly, and yet fervently.

We knew so much about life already, after what our families had been through – and yet we knew nothing. There was a whole world to be discovered ahead of us, everything to learn and everything to experience.

Life had seemed burdensome to me, a yoke of worries and endless vigilance, but now, with Lorenzo, it opened in front of me like a spring meadow.

'You're my whole world,' he said to me. 'I'll never leave you, unless you want me to.'

Little had I known that I would leave him, and break both our hearts.

CHAPTER 20

CASALTA, 1985

BIANCA

The phone on my bedside table rang too early, way too early. Still half asleep, I answered, curling up with the handset against my ear.

'Good morning, sleepyhead...' It was Brando, and his voice made me smile already. It was a lovely way to be awoken... and yet, the conversation I'd had with Lucrezia was still going round in my mind.

Don't settle.

But of course I wasn't settling! That was nonsense.

'Bianca?'

'I'm here. Good morning...'

'I won't be seeing you at work today...' It sounded like a mild protest.

'Not today, and not tomorrow. Part time, remember? I still have a lot to do at Legami.'

'When will I see you again, then? Please don't say Monday. It's too far away.'

'I'm at Villa Lieta, this morning. It's not far from your house, no? How about we have breakfast before you set off to Florence?'

'Great idea. See you in half an hour?'

'See you then.'

I got dressed quickly and bade goodbye to my sisters, already gathered in the kitchen.

'Having breakfast with Brando, bye, girls!' I called.

'Don't be late; Mum will be here in a few hours!' Mia said, half happily, half anxiously.

'I won't, promise!'

For the first time that year I wore a coat, cosy and warm. The wind was biting, and yellow, red and gold leaves rustled on the branches. The mornings were getting colder and colder and night was drawing in earlier and earlier, while fireplaces were beginning to be put to use all over the Tuscan countryside.

Brando was waiting for me in the little square in front of Villa Lieta, and greeted me with a kiss. We went to the coffee shop beside the home and sat at a tiny table for our breakfast.

'It seems that every time we meet, I'm eating!' I joked.

'It's because you're so busy!'

'Talking about busy... I have to go soon, but... Do you have five minutes to meet Amarilli? She'll be happy.'

'Of course, it would be a pleasure,' he said in that sweet way of his.

'You'll be undergoing an inspection,' I warned him.

'Old ladies like me. I'm nice. Also, I passed the trial by fire with your sisters... I can face anything,' he said, quite serious.

Amarilli was sitting in the common room by the window – it was a relief to see her dressed and up, and not in bed. She looked like she'd lost a little weight, and she was pale, with two ruddy spots on her cheeks. She didn't look too unwell, or frail – but there was something about her that squeezed my heart. At that moment I wished that Lulu had been with me, so that she could read Amarilli's aura and maybe tell me something more about her health.

'Good morning,' I called and smiled like I wasn't worried at all.

'Bianca, look at you – I didn't recognise you without one of your lovely dresses,' Amarilli said in a voice that was a little hoarser than before, a little feebler.

'My new look,' I said, and twirled in front of her in my jeans and jumper.

'And is *he* part of the new look?' she said naughtily.

'Signora, Bianca always mentioned you by your first name, so I didn't know it was you. Remember me? My mum used to come help you with the house.'

'*You* are Brando? The little boy that came up to my knee?'

'I am, yes. A bit taller, now.'

'It's good to see you again, and how's your mum?'

'She's great. I'll tell her you asked after her.'

'Please do. I remember her fondly. So, you two...'

It happened again. Brando lit up, turning completely red. I'd never met anyone who could be so relaxed and easy-going, and then turn shy and self-conscious in an instant.

'Well, we...' I began, but I wasn't sure what to say.

We're together? He's my boyfriend? We only went out once.

'We work together,' I settled on.

'Ah, yes,' Amarilli said with an *I wasn't born yesterday* look.

'And I'm going to be late for said work, if I don't leave now,' Brando said in his cheerful manner. 'It was good seeing you again, signora. I hope you'll feel better soon.'

'I feel perfectly fine, my dear,' Amarilli said proudly.

There was an unbelievably, unbearably awkward moment where Brando and I went to kiss each other, then somehow froze under Amarilli's and the other guests' gazes, and ended up almost knocking foreheads. Brando's face was the colour of beetroot.

'Well. Brando is a lovely child, from a lovely family,' Amarilli said when he'd gone. I smiled inwardly at her calling him 'child'. A six-foot-tall child. 'Also, *nail drives out nail.*'

'Pardon?'

'If you hammer a nail in, the nail that was there before will be dislodged.' She showed me with her hands.

'Oh.'

Amarilli attempted to look innocent, like she hadn't said anything controversial *at all*. 'I wish you and Brando the best, my love.'

'You don't mean it, Amarilli,' I said.

First Lulu, now Amarilli. What was wrong with them? Brando ticked all the boxes, and still both of them seemed vaguely disapproving. Well, not disapproving as such, but... not quite ecstatic.

'I do! I do wish you the best! Only...' She muttered something.

'I have no idea what you're saying.' I crossed my arms.

'Can you read me a story now?' she asked, changing the subject and handing me *The People's Companion* from beside her.

'No story until you tell me what you said under your breath.'

She sighed. 'It's just that he doesn't seem like the right one for you!'

'Why?'

She shrugged sadly. 'Because he's not the Orafi boy.'

∽

It was a long, busy day, showing Teresa the ropes and helping build connections and trust between her and the people we assisted. Amarilli's words, though, flashed in and out of my mind like a neon sign. Age had made her both blunt and insightful. And I didn't like what she saw.

But I couldn't wait to get home – Mum was going to be there! I was dying to see her, and I ran all the way from the car to the house...

And there she was, dressed in a boho-style flowing skirt and dangling earrings. Her eyes were very blue and sparkled with joy. She looked like she'd just stepped out of a Pre-Raphaelite painting, with her long hair, dark red like Lulu's, but now streaked with grey that she refused to dye away. She said she'd *earned* the grey hair and the lines on her face through life experience, and she wasn't going to try and erase either.

She still had her coat and scarf on, a symphony of jewel-green and peacock colours, purple and blue – she must have arrived just a moment before.

'Mum!' I threw myself into her arms, my cheek on her soft hair and breathing her scent in – vanilla and paint – until she pulled back a little, to look at my face.

It was still a shock to see our mother standing there, in the Casalta living room! Her gravestone still sat in the Casalta cemetery, protecting the secret that my father had built around her many years ago. I wondered how I was going to explain all that to Brando – my family history defied logic.

'You look different,' she said, and laid a hand on my cheek.

'It's my clothes! I changed style,' I said.

'No, not just that...'

'Well, I have a lot to tell you. I'm so glad you're here.'

'Are you sure it's not inconvenient for you girls? I don't want to take for granted that you'll put me up...'

Lulu and I protested, while Mia hugged both Mum and me, still linked together, in that childlike way of hers.

'Mia said it for us all,' I said, but out of the corner of my eye, I saw Nora looking down. The relationship between her and Mum was cordial, but not as warm as mine, Lulu's and Mia's.

It wasn't just that Nora hadn't forgiven Mum for leaving us, even if it had been very much against her will – it went deeper than that. Nora had been close to our father, though her depth of feeling wasn't reciprocated – I wasn't sure if Father ever loved any of us, because I didn't think he knew how to love at all. Maybe the first person who could truly reach him had been Gabriella, his second wife, to whom he was married for a short time before passing away.

It'd been surprising for us to hear from Gabriella that our father had considered Lulu his favourite – the daughter who was the most similar to Mum, and the one he'd sent into exile for years. As for me, I'd always been like a docile puppy to him; I was the one who tried to appease him the best I could, so he wouldn't harm my sisters.

But Nora was the one among us most akin to him, in looks and personality – though Nora's heart was warm and kind, which certainly couldn't have been said for Father's. Nora desperately wanted to be a Falconeri, without a hint of McCrimmon in her genetic make-up – to the point that she denied her gift, and nobody except her knew what exactly that was.

When Mum returned six months ago, Nora couldn't find it in herself to give her a chance, and only softened when Mum saved Casalta – and Nora's stables and horses with it – from being sold. My mother had rescued Nora's most precious thing, while our father almost lost it: this made Nora look at our family dynamics in a different light. But she'd told Mum that she needed time, and I couldn't blame her. Everything had happened so fast.

'Have you eaten? Please don't say, *I've eaten on the plane*, because that's not food!' Lulu said. 'I made you some pasta with pesto, and Matilde made you a blackberry *crostata*. She had to go a little earlier today; she says she'll see you tomorrow.'

'Great! A million times better than plane food, for sure!'

Mum laughed. Her voice, her Italian accented with a little Scottish lilt that she'd never lost, was music to me. 'I'll just go refresh and change, and then please, do feed me!'

~

After dinner when Mum went to sort her luggage, I climbed upstairs to speak to her in private.

She could have stayed in the master bedroom, but she said she couldn't bear sleeping there, that the room was too full of memories of my father and their unhappy marriage; she'd asked if we would let her sleep in her former studio.

We protested, but she had insisted – sleeping on the floor in a place where she'd been happy, and where Mia was happy now, would be a million times better than sleeping in a comfortable room full of bad memories. Mia had made her a nest of blankets on top of a soft duvet cover, and now she was sitting on it, cross-legged, sorting her minuscule amount of luggage into a pile.

My mum had had her paintings exhibited all over the world, she was featured in glossy art magazines and coffee-table books, and had set aside enough to buy Casalta from us – but she was still a flower child at heart, travelling with a tiny bag and sleeping in a nest on the floor. No wonder she hadn't fitted in with Father's strict family, with the conventions of life in a small Italian village.

'My love, come in!' she said when she saw me peeping.

'Can I talk to you for a moment?'

'Of course.' She patted the place beside her, and I sat at her side.

'Are you comfortable here?'

'Very. I'm surrounded by the fruits of Mia's talent. She's so much more talented than me!' She gazed around at Mia's canvases, scattered about the place – her materials, tidily organised on her table – and the frescoes decorating the walls. Our eyes fell on the small fresco she'd been working on when Father died – Judith beheading Holofernes – which carried more meaning than we cared to remember. We both averted our gazes at the same time. This was a secret between the Casalta women and Gabriella, my father's second wife – a secret that refused to be spoken aloud ever again. And not the only one. Mum didn't know what had happened between Lorenzo and me. And most definitely, she'd never, never know how Father tried to tie me to Enrico Rinaldi, how I'd had to endure... no, I didn't want to think about that.

'Mum...' I searched for the right words. She looked at me calmly, waiting for me to be able to articulate what had been in my heart for so long. 'Have you ever lost your gift?'

She thought for a moment. 'No. Well, maybe once, for a short while. When I was painting Lulu's room. I knew I'd have four daughters, I knew their names, and I could see snippets of their future.

'I painted your meadows and flowers and trees so easily – but when I moved on to Lulu's room, after painting the red roses, I saw black. No, not black: *blank*. I moved on to Nora's and Mia's rooms, thinking I'd get back to Lulu's when my Sight opened up again, and they flew out easily too.

'But when I went back to Lulu's, I still saw a blank. I even feared it was a bad omen, that she wouldn't be born. But thankfully, she was born healthy and happy...

'Now I know what it meant, that she'd leave Casalta and be away for a long time. But I'm going to finish it one of these days that I'm here – now I know what to paint.'

'That was just temporary, then. Losing your gift. You see... When Lulu was sent away, I lost mine. I haven't seen anything since then. You remember what my gift was, don't you?'

'Of course I do! I remember Viola... you know, when you used to tell me about being able to see times past, I was jealous!'

she laughed. 'So much better than catching glimpses of the future, like I do, too vague to rely on and sometimes frightening. Lulu is burdened with the way people can't really lie to her about how they feel—'

'And sometimes it's better not to know the truth.'

'Exactly. Mia is a galaxy unto herself, the most powerful of us. And Nora...'

'Nobody knows.'

'Nobody knows.' Mum took both my hands. 'Bianca, I do *not* believe you've lost your gift,' she finished unexpectedly. 'Not forever.'

'But I—' I began to protest.

'Your Sight is just obscured. Yes, it's been for a long time. But truly, I'm sure your gift is still there. And it will come back. It might do so in another form, though... you'll have to recognise it.'

'But when? When?'

'That, I can't tell. But I know. This is *my* gift, remember?'

I took a deep, deep breath of relief, and smiled.

'Yes.'

'Do you believe me, my little Bianca?'

'I do,' I said truthfully. 'There's something else...'

'You're seeing someone?'

'Your gift?'

'No, your sisters filled me in,' she laughed. 'Are you happy, my love?'

I answered quickly. Too quickly. 'Yes, of course. Of course.'

'But?' she coaxed.

I put my hands up.

'No, no. No buts. Not at all.'

Mum didn't know about Lorenzo. Or did she? Between their gifts and the family grapevine, I couldn't be sure. However, talking about Lorenzo was almost impossible for me – even with Lulu, even with Mum. It was a secret I'd kept for so long, and having to be quiet about it was so ingrained in me that discussing it out loud, bringing it into the light, felt almost sacrilegious.

Mum tilted her head – the same mannerism Lulu had, and I was sure she didn't believe me.

And then I noticed that Mum moved her gaze from my face to somewhere over my shoulder, beyond me. I turned around, and saw that she'd noticed Mia's little addendum to her fresco – the small, dark face with the black hair that surveyed the scene, a little removed.

'It's the celebration of yours and Lulu's return,' I said. Mum laid her fingers on the wall, gently. 'She painted herself looking over us all… but she forgot that her eyes are two different colours!'

Mum kept her hand on the picture for a moment longer, but said nothing.

'Well, goodnight, Mum,' I said and hugged her.

'Goodnight, my love,' she replied.

But she looked lost in thought, far away.

∽

And now the house was asleep, it was my time – mine and Viola's time.

It was too cold to sit on the stairs – the wind was whooshing around my window and whipping the branches of the trees, making them creak like the timbers of an old ship. I looked outside and took in the beauty of Tuscany at night, its hills teetering somewhere between sweetness and an ancient type of starkness.

The white roses painted above and around me danced and settled as I took refuge in my bed, holding Viola's diary.

But of course, that was just a trick of the light.

CHAPTER 21

CASALTA, 194-

VIOLA

Dear Liala,

I know it's a long time since I wrote, but days and night pass so fast now, I'm so busy and there's so much I need to learn, as quickly as I can – because I love, love, love my work, because I try my best to forget that I'm engaged, because I must prove myself in the eyes of those who believe I'm good for nothing, that I'm here because of who I know (true) and that I won't bring anything useful to my position, in fact, I'll barely be able to do it (not true).

This is my little world at the museum:

Giuseppe Poggi: the Supreme Authority. When I first started he was almost always in his office, but now he wanders the rooms and corridors a lot, with the weight of the world on his shoulders and without talking to anyone, except...

Laio, the Supreme Authority's assistant: his name sums it up. He assists Poggi and he does his best to pretend I don't exist. When he accidentally looks at me, his eyes move on smoothly as if he'd been gazing at an umbrella stand.

Pietro: annoying, insulting, condescending, pretentious, thoroughly unlikeable. But a good teacher. A really good teacher. He took me under his (uncomfortable) wing, surely at Poggi's request, and he's helping me memorise and understand all I need to know about the artwork kept in here. He couldn't be drafted because he had polio as a child and limps a little – I suspect he's self-conscious about it, but I don't think it takes away from his good looks. He's as handsome as he's unlikeable, I suppose. It happens.

Lisetta: sweet Lisetta! She never loses her good mood, she has delightful dimples and behind her pretty exterior she hides an encyclopaedic knowledge of the museum. She's the first daughter in a family of nine and supports all her younger brothers and sisters with her work.

I love my job. I'm trying to delay this marriage as long as I can, but I don't know how long I'll be able to hold on.

'Why wait?' my mother keeps saying, on and on...

'It's better to wait until it gets a little warmer. I don't want to wear a cape on my wedding dress.'

'You said this before. A little warmer, a little colder, cape, no cape! Who cares? You'll be beautiful. This horrible war... I shouldn't be saying that, it's a glorious war... but who knows what's going to happen? We must seize the day. What if Federico gets tired of the delays? What if you wait too long and he meets someone else?'

'Just a little longer, Mamma. Just a little longer.'

But I fear she's right. How long is too long? I can feel my father's breath on my neck.

But I neglected to say that I finally visited Palazzo Valsecchi! With my parents, of course. Yes, it's beautiful – a palazzo with narrow climbing stone stairs, frescoed rooms and ornate furniture, beamed ceilings and tapestries, every room drenched in history and art. Casalta is prettier, though. And Palazzo Valsecchi is full of ghosts, dark and heavy.

We stood side by side on the balcony, looking out to the city and to the river with its many bridges. It was an enchanting view, one that soon I'll see every morning when I awake. Federico said something, but I was lost in thought.

'I beg your pardon. I didn't quite hear.'

He seemed a little irked. 'What's in that head of yours, always daydreaming?' he said pleasantly enough, but I detected a little annoyance. He'd made allowances for the young, shy bride-to-be who knows nothing of the world – but soon, I'm sure, I'll have to start dancing to his tune.

'I said to please tell me if there are any improvements you want made to the place. I've lived there alone for a long time now; I do think you'll want to decorate a little.'

'Thank you. I'd love to do that.'

I looked up into Federico's face, searching for a hint of kindness, of affection – and I found them both. Buried underneath the pomposity, the self-importance, the boasting, there's a man who doesn't mean me harm. Who cares for me, in his own way.

They have me in a corner, I suppose – prisoner of my obligations: but Federico doesn't take advantage, treating me like I'm something fragile, to be cherished and protected.

These words comforted me a little. At least he didn't treat Viola like a doll of his own property, like Rinaldi had treated me.

Maybe it'd be easier if he were odious... like Pietro.

Because oh, Pietro surely is the most odious man who walked the earth!

Mmmm. The ending of this entry left me a little dubious.

For despite him being the most odious man to walk the earth, Viola was giving Pietro quite a lot of thought.

CHAPTER 22

CASALTA, 1985

BIANCA

Lucrezia and I were in my room, getting ready for Gherardo's birthday. I was looking forward to the party, but not to seeing Lorenzo and Tamara together, especially because Brando had bailed on me.

'I'm sorry Brando won't be there,' Lulu said, her voice uncertain, as she zipped up the aqua-coloured dress she'd loaned me, short and with a beaded belt around my waist.

Lulu was radiant in a short dress with an A-line skirt in a light blue colour that set off her eyes and contrasted beautifully with the brightness of her hair. Tonight she and Vanni were going to announce their engagement, and her joy and excitement were palpable.

'Yes, so am I. His dad has food poisoning and his mum is away, so he has to hold the fort... Well, me and Mia and Nora are going together. Unless... Is Nora taking someone?' I asked. 'She'd be perfectly capable of turning up with a boyfriend we never knew about.'

'That'd be very Nora. But as far as I know, she's not seeing anyone.'

As she often did, Mia materialised among us as silent as a cat.

'I'm not taking anyone either, but maybe I'll meet someone there,' she said in a serious, calm tone.

It was the first time ever that I'd heard her mention a possible relationship. I was half excited, half horrified – my *little sister*? Tonight she'd departed from her usual black and had gone for a long blue dress in her customary flowing style, with minuscule silver dots embroidered on the bodice, like tiny stars. She looked stunning. And not little any more...

'Wait, is this your gift talking?'

'Wouldn't you like to know,' Mia said. 'Anyway, if Tamara bothers you, I promise I'll give her the *malocchio*, the evil eye!'

Lulu grabbed the hairspray. 'Do you really believe in the evil eye? Seriously?'

'Well, no. But Tamara doesn't know that. And with my eyes, I look the part!' She blinked ostentatiously, like an owl, and we all laughed.

Nora walked in. 'I can give her a piece of my mind. That'll do the trick,' she said calmly. She was wearing a forest-green blouse with see-through sleeves, as well as trousers of the same colour, an outfit that highlighted her long legs and slender figure. With her short dark hair and moss-green eyes, big and slightly slanted, she reminded me of a wild doe.

'Well, I have my sister squad to keep me safe,' I laughed. 'But no need to worry. Tamara won't dare speak to me like that in front of the Orafi; she doesn't want them to know this side of her. Also, I don't care.'

'Ready?' Mum called from the hall. She wore a long black dress, her hair down as usual, delicately tangled as if on purpose, and dangling silver earrings. Both she and Mia had the ghosts of old paint stains on their hands, and this only added to their allure.

'You look amazing!' I cried.

'Why thank you!' Mum twirled. 'Vintage dress, of course, bought at a market in London, for a song. Oh, my beautiful girls! Everyone will admire you!' She opened her arms, and we joined her in a family hug.

I love these women so much, I thought, not for the first nor the last time.

∼

Gherardo had asked us to go a little earlier, so we could have a drink and a chat before everyone else arrived, and he'd sent his car to collect us.

The villa was all lit up with strings of fairy lights, striking against the dark sky. Now it looked so free and open, compared to the days when the feud between our families put the Orafi under siege.

Vanni opened the door in his wheelchair and we each bent down to kiss him. I thought that his dark looks, with eyes that seemed circled with kohl and long eyelashes, made a stunning contrast with my sister's Celtic complexion. His tousled hair went down to his shoulders and he wore a formal evening suit that would have looked stiff on anyone else, but which he turned into a second skin.

Vanni had been through so much, with the car accident that had paralysed him and his family falling apart – I had so much affection and respect for him.

'I can't wait for the announcement,' I said as I hugged him. 'I couldn't wish for a better brother-in-law.'

'Thank you, Bianca. I feel very much the same. Not you though, Mia,' he joked. He and Mia were always teasing each other, but the bond between them was strong.

'I *totally* dislike you too, Vanni,' Mia said and hugged him tight.

'Signora,' he greeted my mum.

'Please, please, drop the signora! Call me Emmeline,' she said.

'Emmeline, thank you for being here.' There was a moment of silence – we all held our breath for a second. Vanni wasn't just talking about flying over for the party, of course – he was reminding her that she was welcome in the Orafi house.

'Thank you for having me, Vanni,' my mum said in her proud, yet tender way.

Gherardo's feelings for my mother had driven Vanni's and Lorenzo's own mother away: Gherardo's estranged wife lived in the Italian Riviera and barely kept in touch with her sons. Even if Mum and Gherardo never got together, the two sons would have had good reason to resent her. But the tangle of acrimony and spite between the families had been uncoiled with my father's death – like a cascade, all resentments had been healed or at least lessened.

Almost all, I thought, bracing myself to see Lorenzo.

Vanni led us through the marble hall. 'You're all beautiful,' I heard him whispering to Lulu as we walked on, and a mixture of joy and longing filled me.

I wish I had what Vanni and my twin have.

We walked past the main reception room, bright with lights – through the open door, I caught a glimpse of tables set with covered plates, bottles, pyramids of glasses and bunches of flowers, with servers in black trousers and white shirts giving the last touches to the displays. The hired band was setting up their instruments on a low wooden platform; a woman dressed in gold was tapping her microphone lightly.

We came to the family reception room. Gherardo was sitting in his favourite leather armchair – since the accident he hadn't been in good health and struggled to walk – but not even this had affected his cheerfulness and good temper. I often thought of Gherardo as the antithesis of my father, his complete opposite.

He opened his arms to encompass us all, and Mum ran to him. They held each other tight. Gherardo had loved my mum forever, we all knew that, and she reciprocated his feelings. But life had kept them apart, until now...

'I'm so glad you made it,' Gherardo said, looking my mum in her eye in a way that moved me. His feelings couldn't be concealed.

We all greeted him the Italian way, with two kisses – all except Nora, who shook his hand and looked away. She had found it hard to move past the rivalry that our father had first lit, and then stoked over and over again – and I didn't blame her for it. She kept her composure and honoured Lulu's happiness – I couldn't have asked for more.

And then, the spell of joy was broken.

'*Bee-an-cah!*' Tamara enunciated, as if seeing me had made her evening.

I turned around and saw Tamara and her mother, the interior designer, walking towards me. Behind them was Lorenzo, his expression serious as usual. He was handsome as always, unreachable as always, and, I knew, still angry with me.

Tamara's chemical floral smell assaulted my nose, as I accepted her hug and stretched my lips in a smile – both her hug and my smile were rigid. I had to admit that she looked lovely in a pink chiffon dress and TV-ready make-up, while her mother seemed to have borrowed a tropical bird's outfit, all colours and chaotic patterns topped by a huge perm.

'Bianca,' Lorenzo said and offered his hand.

The hand I'd held so many times before...

No.

Tonight belonged to Lulu and Vanni, and to Gherardo, and I wouldn't let anything spoil it. I shook it and looked away – a server came in with a trolley laden with liqueur, wine and sparkling glasses, and I was thankful for the interruption. After a short while guests began to pour in and we all moved to the main reception room, where the band began to play.

A few words from Gherardo opened the dances. Nora was aloof and even a little irritated in the middle of a group of men who gravitated around her, as always happened; Mia danced by herself, attracting quite a few glances; and I stood beside Gherardo and Mum, sipping white wine – the wallflower.

The room was warm – I decided to slip out for a moment. I made my way towards the oval balcony ensconced in its wrought-iron balustrade, but there were a few guests there, probably looking for some fresh air too, so I stepped out onto the terrace. At the bottom of the terrace was Vanni's apartment, an outbuilding with only one floor, to facilitate his independence. I walked on the terracotta tiles along the dark hedge, until I reached a small opening – I threw my legs over and let them dangle over the parapet, not very ladylike. The chill of the wind was a relief after the stuffy room, and I closed my eyes.

'May I sit?'

A voice behind me.

His unmistakable voice.

I turned around to see Lorenzo, unsmiling, serious as he always was – the warmth emanating from his body negated his cool demeanour.

'Such a lovely evening,' I said neutrally. I was desperate to bolt and run back inside.

I felt in danger, and not from him, but from myself.

'Not for long,' Lorenzo said, and I did a double-take. Why was he saying that? But then I saw that his hand was stretched out flat towards the black sky, and I noticed that only a few stars here and there peeped out of the expanse of clouds. 'Rain is coming.'

'We should go inside.'

'Yes. I don't want to ruin my hair,' he said and made me laugh. I turned to look at him. Lorenzo's default setting was seriousness – severity, almost.

'You're in a good mood.'

He shrugged. 'It's that I'm happy for my brother. Sometimes, after his accident, you know... he's been so low for a long time. Almost giving up. But with Lulu's return, everything changed.'

'Do you remember...' we said at the same time.

'You first,' I offered.

'Do you remember the day of the storm?'

'When we did exactly what you're not supposed to do during a storm?'

He laughed. 'Yes. Be under a tree.'

'Thankfully we weren't hit by lightning! We're alive to tell the tale!' I said. And then, after the laughter, there was a moment of silence. He was serious again, while a few drops of drizzle began to fall.

'It was long ago.'

'Yes, of course. Long ago.' I shook my head. Yesterday. Today. Now, my heart was saying – in a way, I was still there, under the rain, beside Lorenzo. I never moved on.

The realisation hit me so hard, I almost gasped. What had been the point of finally taking his photograph down – it'd just been a meaningless act. This wasn't healthy! I couldn't possibly still be clinging to...

'This is the first time, you know?' Lorenzo said, interrupting my uncomfortable thoughts. 'The first time we've talked about what happened between us... calmly. Without arguing. I was so hurt, I could only see my own reasons.'

'I should have trusted you,' I said, and I couldn't quite believe I was speaking those words, acknowledging my regret. Allowing myself to see life the way it could have been, a life where Enrico Rinaldi had never crossed paths with me, where his hands had never touched me.

'Bianca...' he began, but we were silenced by the downpour. All of a sudden, the drizzle had turned into cold, fat drops. Lorenzo took my hand and helped me over the wall and onto the terrace – we ran under the rain back inside, wet and laughing.

'Oh, here you are!'

Brando?

All of a sudden he was there, all smiles, gathering me to him, sealing me with a slightly proprietorial kiss. He offered Lorenzo his hand. 'Hello, I'm Brando, Bianca's boyfriend.'

If expressions had a noise, Lorenzo's would have sounded like broken glass.

'Lorenzo Orafi.'

'I know who you are. Everyone around here does,' Brando replied – he seemed not to have picked up on anything weird, because his eyes were without shadows and his smile sincere.

'Well, it was nice catching up, Bianca,' Lorenzo said, nodding to Brando and turning around.

We were swept apart again, the currents of our lives flowing in two opposite directions.

Now Lorenzo was walking away towards Tamara and Brando was beside me, very, very close, and it felt wrong, like this wasn't the way it was supposed to be.

No. It was me who wasn't supposed to feel this way. It was all good, and I shouldn't have been outside with Lorenzo, stirring memories of times gone and closed forever.

'You made it,' I said to Brando.

'My sister came to look after Dad, so I thought I'd reach you. Sorry, I'm a little wet!' Brando explained.

'That's great, thank you,' I said truthfully. Now that the spell of me and Lorenzo talking alone and running under the rain like children was broken, I was relieved. Reliving old memories was a useless exercise, like dusting off a sand dune or trying to force a river away from the sea.

Brando swept my damp hair from my face – on the other side of the room, out of the corner of my eye, I saw Tamara sweeping raindrops from Lorenzo's shoulders, mouth smiling but eyes flinty.

At that moment, the music stopped, and the sound of cutlery tinkling on glasses called our attention. A semicircle formed along the walls, with Lorenzo, Gherardo, Vanni and Lulu at its apex, and the small orchestra behind them. The Orafi brothers announced a toast to Gherardo's health and the band played 'Happy Birthday', while Gherardo smiled and shook his head, as if to challenge the spotlight being on him.

Helped by Lorenzo, he stood and leaned behind his chair with one hand, holding a glass of wine with the other.

'Thank you all for coming here tonight to celebrate with us, but never mind the birthday of this old man' – protests from the crowd, waved away by Gherardo – 'I'm so glad to announce that our family has wonderful news.'

It was time! I slipped along the semicircle with Brando following me, until I reached my twin – I wanted to be beside her when they told everyone. Gherardo quietly thanked the waiter who refilled Vanni's and Lulu's glasses, then nodded to his son and all eyes moved to Vanni.

'I'll try not to be too sentimental or soppy,' Vanni began. 'But I can't give any guarantees!'

'Oh, no, here he goes!' a friend shouted and was met with laughter. Vanni raised his glass towards him. Mia's little hand slipped into mine – Lulu, with her shiny eyes and hair like tumbling flames, was more beautiful than I'd ever seen her before.

Oh no! I couldn't possibly start crying before the announcement!

'I've been looking for the right words, to write a proper

speech. But nothing sounded meaningful enough.' He shrugged. 'No words can describe my happiness right now, my gratitude that Lucrezia Falconeri has agreed to become my wife.'

Cheers and words of congratulations filled the room as Lulu bent over the chair to kiss Vanni, and then turned around to hug me, Mum and our sisters.

'Congratulations, Lulu,' I whispered in her ear.

Friends and family crowded around them – Lorenzo was towering over the others, with a rare smile on his face. He kept himself removed, until the little crowd dispersed, and he could embrace both Vanni and Lulu. The way he held Vanni, tight and deep, would have surprised anyone who didn't know him – who only knew his cool exterior and couldn't imagine that he was a man of profound emotions.

His eyes met mine.

Right at that moment, the ding-ding-ding that announced a toast sounded again.

This time it came from Tamara. What was she up to?

She stood there, waiting for all eyes to converge on her. Her face was split in two by her trademark wide smile, but her eyes were hard. It was like her face belonged to two different people.

She turned her gaze to Lorenzo, raising her chin in an adoring look. 'I know we wanted to keep the secret for another little while, but what better than sharing the moment with our brother and sister?'

Hey, Tamara. Vanni is not your brother. And as sure as hell, Lulu is not your sister.

Lorenzo's eyes widened. He was frozen. Probably nobody noticed, but I did. I realised I was gaping, and made a conscious effort to close my mouth.

'It's not exactly traditional for a woman to do this, but we're over old and useless limitations for us women!' Everyone was looking at her, confused. 'But enough chatting! You know me, *the moment* I'm in the limelight I start blabbering! That's TV people for you!' A self-satisfied laugh, and then her face turned solemn, changing expression easily and quickly, like she was made of Play-Doh. 'What I'm trying to say is that Lorenzo and I are joining the happy couple here! We, too, are engaged!'

Tamara looked up at Lorenzo, who stood rigid as a lamppost.

Had it not been tragic, I'd have found it funny.

She took his arm and clung to him like ivy strangling a tree. Noises of congratulations mixed with bewilderment filled the room.

I could only see Lorenzo's face, working, pulled between different emotions. Our eyes met across the crowd for the second time: and then he looked away, and composed his face in a smile. It was a formal smile – I couldn't see any joy behind it – but maybe that was just me, looking for a hole in his apparent happiness, clinging to nothing.

I wouldn't be the thirteenth fairy, the one who in folk tales begrudges and curses a happy gathering.

Brando's arm was around my waist, and he kissed my hair.

I lifted my glass and joined the toast.

∼

A few hours later, we were ready to go. Lulu was staying at the Orafi's for the night, so we hugged goodbye.

'Congratulations, *cara*. I love you,' I whispered in her ear.

'I love you too,' she said, but then she hissed: 'Speak later,' and threw a glance towards Lorenzo and Tamara.

On the other side of the room, Gherardo's face was set in a grimace – whatever he thought about Tamara's announcement, he wouldn't show it in public.

I felt cut in two between my joy for Lulu and a sense of loss after Lorenzo's engagement, so I simply pasted a smile on my face – I'd resolve my feelings later, alone.

'Thank you for coming to celebrate *Lulu and Vanni*, girls. I'm so glad we're part of the same family, now,' Gherardo said when we took turns to kiss him goodbye, stressing the *Lulu and Vanni* part. I foresaw a storm as soon as we left.

Brando gave me a lift home, and when we arrived, I sensed he was waiting to be invited inside. 'It's been a long day, Brando. Do you mind if I turn in?'

'No, of course not.' But his face said otherwise. 'Is there something wrong?'

'No, no, not at all! Thank you for coming.'

'Thank my sister; she saved the day. Or the night. *Buonanotte, amore,*' he said and opened his door to come and open mine, but I laid a hand on his knee.

'You'll get soaked. I'll just run in. *Buonanotte.*'

Once we were home, everyone began dissecting what happened – I would have liked to join Mum, Nora and Mia on the sofas, in their pyjamas, sipping tea. But for some reason I felt empty, drained. So much emotion, so much had happened. I slipped away upstairs.

In my room, I couldn't be bothered to undress.

I couldn't be bothered to remove my make-up.

I just lay there, curled up, listening to the sound of the rain against the window. I raked a hand through my hair where Brando had kissed me...

Nothing stays still, I realised.

Even if you embrace change, change will always come faster than you want.

CHAPTER 23

CASALTA, 1985

BIANCA

It was the morning after the night before.

I hurt everywhere – maybe I'd caught a cold... It took a few moments for yesterday's events to come into focus. And then I remembered.

Lorenzo was getting married.

It seemed impossible.

So what? I told the woman who looked back at me from the mirror. *You don't have time to brood. Life charges on. Remember, you've moved on? You're seeing Brando. Lorenzo is a ghost from the past, shadowing your present. Don't let it.*

But if Lorenzo getting engaged upsets you so much, should you be going out with Brando at all? Does Brando not deserve better than half a heart?

The thought was too painful, too guilt-inducing to consider now. I set it aside – I'd let it rip me apart later.

Breakfast with my family was a quiet affair – quiet on my part, because everyone else kept dissecting the party. Mum,

Nora and Mia didn't seem concerned by my silence and paleness, thankfully – it seemed that only Lulu was in on my secret. This was a relief – but also a bit of a surprise, in a way.

'Busy day ahead, love?' Mum asked.

'Not too bad. I'm going down to Legami a little later; I'm mentoring Teresa. Remember Maestra Teresa, the primary school teacher?'

'Oh, yes, of course! She'll be working with you? Tell her hello from me,' she replied, and her gaze lingered on me a moment too long.

Had my family really not guessed anything was wrong?

~

I needed a moment alone before facing the world.

I threw on my coat against the chilly air and went to sit among the autumn roses, trying to get the day going. I was gazing at the soft white mist embracing the hills when Lulu appeared, walking down the slope. She was resplendent with joy and with the morning sun at her back.

'*Buongiorno*,' she called. She stepped lightly in the grass covered with morning dew.

'*Buongiorno!* Did you walk all the way from the Orafi house?'

'*Sì*. I wanted some fresh air. And I wanted to see you alone for a bit. I'm glad I caught you before you went to work.'

Lulu sat beside me on the bench, in the same place where she'd seen our mother appear all those years ago, when everyone thought she was dead. She covered my hand with hers.

'Congratulations again, you look so happy!' I said. 'You were beautiful last night. You'll be a stunning bride. You look like me, after all!' I joked.

'Thank you, silly. How are you?'

A seemingly innocent question, but both Lulu and I knew that it was a laden one.

'I'm fine. Wasn't it nice of Brando to turn up last night?'

'It was. Are you *fine*, though?' She looked over my head and around me. My aura would give me away for sure.

'I will be. Which colour is my aura? No wait, don't tell me—'

'I can't tell you; you almost don't have one. Seriously, you're... switched off.'

'Mmm. Well, last night was a bit of a surprise. You know, Tamara's announcement.'

'I know! Lorenzo was furious. *His* aura made me wonder if he was going to explode. It was bright red and acid yellow, really awful. All wrong. I still can't believe what she did.'

What? 'Wait... he didn't know she was going to announce the engagement?'

'He didn't know he was engaged!'

'You mean... he didn't... It was all Tamara's idea?'

Lulu shook her head. 'Yes. Apparently, it was a surprise. Shame that Lorenzo looked like he wanted to punch the wall.'

I clasped a hand over my mouth. 'I did think it was strange, that she'd be the one to announce it and not Lorenzo... And his face! But I thought maybe it was just nerves...'

'Apparently, she'd announced the engagement *to* Lorenzo too, as well as us. And he's going along with it! I can't believe it! We're talking about Lorenzo, the guy who orders people about, not who's ordered about. I thought he'd incinerate her with one look. But no...'

It made some kind of perverted sense to me. Yes, Lorenzo was the one who gave the orders, and insisted things had to go his way. Except for one thing: his family. His love and respect for his family trumped everything else.

'Well, wait till I tell you what happened when everyone left.

Gherardo looked like he'd eaten a lemon. You know him, it takes a lot to make him angry, but this... He was furious.'

'And... and Lorenzo?'

'Well, Lorenzo is difficult to read. When it was all finished, his aura lost all colour. It's hard to explain. No happy colours, no angry colours. It was as if... How can I put this in words? It was as if he'd buried his emotions so deep, not even his aura showed them. He's so reserved, he's reserved *with himself* as well.'

'Sounds like him, yes,' I said sadly.

'Actually, he looked switched off too. Like you.'

I nodded and said nothing.

'With Tamara, the poor guy is going to be crucified. What does he even see in her!' my loyal sister commented.

'Well, she's beautiful, she's extroverted, she's head over heels in love with him, that's clear to see, she's going to drag him out of his isolation...'

'Yes, *drag* is the right word. She's going to drag him to the altar kicking and screaming.'

This made me laugh, but my laughter ended in a sigh.

'You regret ending it with him,' Lulu said.

'I've regretted it every day of my life. But at the time, I was simply too afraid.'

'Tell me, Bianca. Please, tell me. Don't keep it all in; it'll eat away at you.'

I took a breath. It was time.

'Well, as you know, we met in secret for a long time. Until he didn't want to any more. He wanted me to be with him out in the open, together properly, he said. He wanted to speak to Father. At first I accepted, then it turned out that Father knew about us, somehow, and threatened Mia and Nora, and you as well – you were away, but in my mind he was all-powerful, Lulu. I was sure he could reach you too and do something horrible. We were all convinced he'd killed Mum. And Lorenzo believed it was him who tampered with their car...'

'You don't need to explain how afraid you were; I know! I know what he was capable of.'

'You more than anyone,' I said sadly. 'Lorenzo said he'd protect us, that we'd be safe with him, with the Orafi. At that time, while you were in exile, there was a feud between our families. The night that Lorenzo was supposed to come speak to Father, I lost heart. Completely. I was sure he was going to do something evil to us, to our little sisters. I had to stop him.

'So I wrote a letter to Lorenzo and ran to their house in the middle of the night. I didn't see him again after that, Lulu, not until he and Vanni came to pay their respects after Father's death. I didn't trust Lorenzo to protect me, to protect us. He never forgave me for that.'

'But things changed! Father changed, you said – he married Gabriella, and then... well, he died. Surely if there was still something between you, you'd have spoken about it?'

'I wanted to. But I hurt him so badly, I couldn't...'

'Yes, I understand he was hurt, but surely he could see why you did what you did! Did you discuss it at all?'

'No. Not for years. Then Tamara came on the scene, and...'

Lulu's eyes widened. 'You didn't speak for *years*?'

I shook my head. 'Not until he came that day with Vanni, when you'd just returned. Father was still alive, and I was frightened for Lorenzo. For our sisters. I was... Father's property.'

I'd never tell her what happened with Rinaldi. I'd never tell my twin I was to be currency for the alliance between two men. Nora and Mia would never know either: it had to stay that way.

'You and Lorenzo Orafi. I'd like to knock your heads together,' Lulu concluded darkly.

In a way, I agreed with her.

Walking down the winding road towards the village, I thought back to the day Lorenzo had come to give his condolences for our father's death – the day Vanni and Lulu met again after all those years apart was also the first time Lorenzo and I met. Vanni and my sister went to sit in the rose garden – she had no idea of the conversation that happened in the meanwhile.

The man sitting in the Casalta living room was not my Lorenzo, not the man I'd loved so, so much – but a stranger in one of those immaculate, tailored suits he'd started to wear since he'd taken over the family business. He played the part of the hard, cold-blooded businessman so well that people bought it completely.

And yet I knew who he really was – I knew the kindness of his heart, which he shared with his brother and father.

And yet, that day, he stood there cold and removed, close to me and yet worlds away.

'How have you been, Bianca?'

The mundanity of those words, after all we'd been through, was jarring.

'Better now that we're free of Father,' I said, but there was a tide of other words that gathered in my throat and attempted to flow out – I pushed it all down. 'I can't believe we never spoke since...'

'Since you wrote me that letter,' he said.

'Since I wrote you that letter. Yes. Lorenzo...'

'Please, Bianca. No.'

'But I need to tell you, I have to tell you—'

'What, Bianca? What do you have to tell me? That you didn't really want to send that letter, that you were afraid for your sisters? That your mum disappeared, and Lulu was sent away and you were terrified? I know all that already.'

'Then you *can* forgive me!'

'There's nothing to forgive,' he said – but his eyes said otherwise.

I was silent. Unshed tears burned my eyes, as I kept it all inside. I stood in front of the wide windows – I could see Vanni in his chair, and my twin sitting on the bench beside him, among the roses.

'There is. And you clearly haven't forgiven me.'

'Rinaldi,' he said, and almost spat out the word.

My heart sank. No, no, I didn't want Lorenzo to know; I couldn't bear that Lorenzo would think of that disgusting man and me.

'How do you—'

'He was the mayor; he was a businessman from one of the big families here! Of course I knew!'

'It wasn't my choice; it was my father—'

'I'm sure it was. Because you didn't let me take you away. You never stood up to him—'

A spark of anger lit up inside me. 'I was afraid out of my mind. Can you not understand that? I needed you to stand by me, not to force my hand that way—'

'Force your hand to do what? To leave that maniac of a father of yours and come to me. With your sisters too, and...'

'*And* he tampered with your car! And exiled my twin, and God knows what he could have done to my little sisters! You have no idea what it was like. Harm came to your family from the outside – from my father – but for me and my sisters, harm came from our home, from our blood, from the person who should have protected us! You have no idea, Lorenzo. No idea.'

My breath was ragged and my heart throbbing – until that moment, I hadn't realised that I wasn't only angry at myself – but at Lorenzo too.

'I'll always be there for you and your family. But like I said, there's nothing left between us.'

'If there's nothing left, then don't speak to me again.'

'We haven't spoken in years. Not much will change,' he answered so calmly, so seraphically, you'd have thought he felt nothing.

When we called Vanni and Lulu back inside, we were calm, composed. They had no idea of what was said between us.

Next time I saw him, Tamara had come into his life.

And it had been too late.

CHAPTER 24

CASALTA, 1985

BIANCA

We waited and waited that morning, but there was no sign of Teresa.

We had a meeting with a social worker about a mother of three who was going through a rough patch, on how best to help her; I wanted to be there, to make sure that Teresa had a handle on things. Camilla had a few prescriptions to collect at the chemist in Biancamura, and deliver to elderly people in the local area.

But Teresa was still nowhere to be found.

I was stacking boxes of donations – it looked like boxes were my fate, these days – and looking at my watch repeatedly. 'You have to be in Biancamura in half an hour. Where is she?'

Camilla opened her arms and let them fall back on her hips. 'It's not like Teresa to be late; you know how organised she is. I'll call her. Maybe she's on the way, but I'll try.'

I watched Camilla dial Teresa's number, and we waited.

'Teresa?' Camilla said when someone answered. 'Oh, hello. It's Camilla, from her work. We were just wondering... Seriously? Oh, no! Is it bad? Of course, I'll leave the line free in case they call. Thank you. Please let us know. Bye.'

While I listened to the conversation, I felt the blood drain from my face.

'What happened?'

'That was her neighbour. Teresa fell down the stairs early this morning and, wait for it, broke her leg. They're putting her in a cast.'

No. No, no, no, no, no. I covered my face with my hands. This was awful, both for Teresa and us. I was too overwhelmed to speak.

'With a broken leg, she'll be out of action for a while. For sure,' Camilla said despondently.

'For sure,' I said, and my voice came out small.

'Well. We'll look for someone else to fill the gap. Like we found Teresa...'

'No.'

'What do you mean, no?'

'I can't put this on you. I did everything in the wrong order! I should have secured someone for Legami first, then looked for something else!'

'Bianca, this wasn't your fault. Teresa fell. It was an accident. We'd be set, if it wasn't for this hiccup.'

'I can't leave you in this situation. *Again.*'

'Bianca. Stop this now. I'll hold the fort until we find someone else. And you're working part time anyway. We'll manage!'

I went through the day in a haze. Guilt had become a way of life, at this point. I was now going to leave Camilla to do it all. Again. Or could I ask Brando for a few more weeks of grace to keep my part-time hours?

Why, why aren't there two of me?

One thing was sure. I wasn't going to cancel my meeting with Amarilli, no matter what else was there, tugging at my sleeve. She was putting a brave face on her daughter's move to Arizona, but I knew she wasn't herself – and my job wasn't only about sorting practical problems, but also making the people we assisted feel cared for.

I'd promised I'd take her to choose a new winter coat and then for a cup of tea, and some people-watching. I didn't want to let her down, even if we were swamped.

We walked slowly down the main street, towards Boutique Tomaselli, the small but reliable shop where the elderly ladies of the area went for its affordable prices *and* updated gossip. I couldn't help but notice that Amarilli hung onto my arm more heavily than ever before.

'So, how are things with your boy Brando?' she asked.

'I'll tell you after we choose your new fancy coat.' I smiled.

A few minutes later, Amarilli was turning left and right, admiring herself in a long burgundy coat, while the owner, Marisa, stood by with a matching scarf which no doubt she'd try to sell her as well. At that moment, a woman I didn't recognise stepped out of the changing rooms, wearing a fuchsia skirt and top. It looked like being punched in the eye would feel.

'What do you think, Marisa?' the woman asked, making poses in front of the mirror.

'Perfect! You'll steal everyone's attention, I'm sure of it!'

The woman laughed. 'You flatterer. I don't think so. It's for the oldest Orafi's wedding. The bride is stunning.'

Urgh. Just what I needed today.

'Oh, yes. The girl from the TV! Well, no wonder Lorenzo Orafi chose a beautiful wife. He's gorgeous himself.'

'Oh, I know. Both of them. The younger one, poor man, in a wheelchair! But that makes it all even more romantic, in a way. He's getting married too. To one of the Falconeri twins, the fancy one. Strange family.'

Marisa's eyes threatened to bulge out of her face. She threw a panicked glance at us.

Silence descended on the shop as the woman saw my unmistakable hair, and it occurred to her that a member of that *strange family* was right there.

'Some of us are strange; some of us are completely dull, uninteresting, plain and entirely forgettable,' Amarilli said in a loud voice. I wished for a hole to open under my feet and swallow me whole – but sadly, it didn't happen. I kept my eyes firmly on Amarilli as the woman escaped into the changing room, no doubt after having spotted my bright red hair as the unmistakable Falconeri trait.

'Your sister will be a beautiful bride! Feel free to come and have a look at bridesmaid dresses!' the shopkeeper said in the merriest tone she could muster – her eyes were darting from me to Amarilli to the curtained cubicle door.

I couldn't find it in myself to answer, and after having paid and with a hurried 'Thank you' and 'Goodbye,' I left the shop as quickly as I could, almost dragging an incensed Amarilli behind me.

∼

'Can I wear my new coat already?' Amarilli asked me as if she were a little girl.

'Of course. Show it off,' I said, and I folded her old coat in the shop bag.

She held herself proudly as we walked in the coffee shop, delighted with her new outfit, looking left and right for people we knew. Because her health didn't allow her to go out often, she was enjoying every moment. And I suspected the drama in the boutique had added to her enjoyment of the morning out, instead of detracting from it.

'*And* can I have a hot chocolate?' Amarilli asked as soon as we sat down.

'Well, your doctor wouldn't be happy, but we won't tell

him!' I went to order Amarilli's hot chocolate and my usual tea, then returned to sit across from my surrogate granny.

'Don't pay any mind to what that woman said about your family, *bambina*. She's jealous of you and your sisters.'

'No, of course not. Don't worry.'

But it did bother me. Sometimes I felt so tired of being the different one, the strange one. Lulu was so confident, Mia was oblivious and Nora didn't care – but I minded.

'I should have used this,' she said grimly and lifted her walking stick – it made a dangerous arc in the air, an inch from a punter's head.

'Er, no, please no weapons,' I said and discreetly moved the stick out of her grasp.

Truth was, every time someone mentioned or alluded to the strangeness of our family, it stung a little. Some parts of our 'strangeness', like our gifts, or our mother being foreign and not exactly a run-of-the-mill person, were a source of pride – our complicated history, our father's shadiness, our isolation, not so much. But obviously, the woman's reference to my family wasn't what had upset me the most.

Lorenzo's marriage was an imminent reality. And soon it'd be me buying a dress for it. There was no way I could avoid it, of course – not with him being my soon-to-be brother-in-law. I could never bring myself to wish that my twin had fallen for someone other than Vanni – they were so perfect for each other – but sometimes having history with Vanni's brother truly came at a price.

I still couldn't believe Tamara had stolen my sister's thunder that way, and that Lorenzo had gone along with it.

I looked up to see Amarilli studying my face. 'What's troubling you, *bambina*?'

'Teresa had an accident; she won't be able to work for ages. I'm due to go full time. Camilla will be on her own again. I'm going to ask if I can work part time for a little longer. Or maybe...' I looked down. 'Leave my new job and come back to Legami.'

She laid her hand on mine. 'Don't go backwards, Bianca. Listen to me: go forward. There'll always be something calling you to the last crossroads you passed, tempting you to take the other direction instead. But you stand by your choice. Us old people and sick people and all the rest of us will manage.'

'But—'

'You're young, you're healthy, this is your time! You chose to move on; stick by your decision. Listen to your decrepit friend!'

'You're not decrepit!'

'I *am*. But I don't mind.'

'Thank you, Amarilli.'

'You're welcome, *bambina*.'

~

That night, after a few hours leafing through wedding magazines with my sisters and Mum, I decided I'd forget everything about the world and just curl up on my bed with Viola's diary, the white roses Mum had painted on the walls surrounding me.

Apparently, as storm clouds had gathered in my life, the same had happened to Viola.

Dear Liala,

Something strange is happening at work. Something very, very strange, and I'm here stewing in doubt and worry.

I suspect that Laio and Pietro are stealing artwork, probably to resell it. I know it's a serious allegation, but I can't ignore what I saw...

I felt cold, and blood rose to my face... I'd stolen this diary too! *Never mind, let's just pretend it never happened.*

But let me tell you everything from the beginning.

Pietro has always walked to work, but one day he turned up in a car. I have no idea how he can afford it, as he is supporting his mum and his little siblings.

'This afternoon we have a school visit from Valdarno. I'd like you to take it,' he said, which surprised me. So far he hadn't seemed to have much confidence in me.

I'd been trying to convince him to let me do a guided tour, even if under his supervision, but he'd always dismissed me – not to mention the fact that now visitors are few and far between. I'm scared that the museum will have to close soon, and without warning. I'm scared that we'll soon hear the sirens and the noise of planes in the sky.

'Seriously?'

'Did I not just say so?'

'You did. Thank you!' I couldn't help the enthusiasm, even if the customary desire to slap him was still there. It never goes away.

'Well, then. Don't let me regret it.'

'I won't!'

So I started the visit. It went very well, although I was a little nervous; the teacher in charge kept the children in line with a ferocious look, but was smiley and sweet to me. I was deep into Medici history, with my back to a window and the children in a semicircle in front of me, when out of the corner of my eye I spotted Pietro driving away. It was strange for him to leave during work hours, and he didn't return until much later.

So this was why he'd finally asked me to take a group – there was something he had to do.

That was the first time he drove away during work hours –

and then it happened again and again. The car, the disappearances: something isn't right.

But it's not just this. The whole atmosphere has changed. With every day that passes, Poggi, Laio and Pietro, and Lisetta too, are getting more secretive. It's not that they're not involving me, it's that they're hiding something from me.

Outside, the city is holding her breath, keeping up a semblance of normality in the middle of a war – inside the museum, something is happening, something I'm not supposed to know about. I'm determined to discover what it is.

I approached Lisetta, trying to remain as vague as I could. 'Pietro has been busy, recently.'

'He always is.'

'I mean, he drives away in that new car, then comes back after a few hours.'

She nodded casually. She didn't seem interested.

'Do you know where he goes?'

'He runs errands, I suppose. Why so worried? Don't you think we have enough to worry about already?'

'True. Just, it seems a little unusual...'

'Tesoro, is there anything usual at all about these days? The world has gone crazy. I know the Duce has our destinies in hand, but well, you can't deny that these are strange times.'

I refrained from rolling my eyes. I get propaganda funnelled into me every time I see Federico, especially if my parents are there too; I have little tolerance for it left.

'Strange times indeed.'

'Anyway, I don't think Pietro will mind if you ask him. Or if you ask after him,' *she said.*

'What do you mean?'

'He has a crush on you! I can't believe you didn't notice!'

She's talking nonsense. Pietro can't stand me, and I can't stand him. And he doesn't miss a chance to show me how much he despises me.

'Nonsense. Also, I'm engaged.'

'Yes. Which is why Pietro is always so cranky, lately.'

No further comments were made by yours truly.

It's the middle of the night and I got up to write this. Next time he drives away, I'll follow him.

Yes, Pietro did have a crush on Viola. I'd guessed right, even from the few references in her diary. But what were her feelings for him, I wondered.

Dear Liala,

Today, again, Pietro slipped out. I was there doing nothing, because both the museum and the whole city are emptier by the day, so I found myself a strategic place from which I could see his car – the moment I spotted him, I made my way downstairs, praying that nobody would see me.

I jumped in my Topolino – you must have guessed that a part of me was enjoying the whole secrecy and adventure – and followed Pietro through the city streets. There are military trucks everywhere, both belonging to us and to the Germans, but they've become such a fixture now that I wasn't more alarmed than usual.

Pietro kept going and going, and I was so focused on not letting the black car out of my sight that I barely noticed we were out of Florence, the city's skyline in my rearview mirror as we drove on. Then, the city disappeared entirely and we were further and further inland, among hills and fields I didn't recognise. The roads were empty but for buggies and the occasional tractor, and it was strange to be somewhere not dotted all over with black and green uniforms: we've been at war for so long, it's all I've known for such a long time.

Suddenly, I couldn't see Pietro's car any more. The road was completely empty. How could that be? He hadn't turned left nor right, I was sure – he couldn't have disappeared into thin air. I was in the middle of nowhere; I didn't even know where – they'd certainly have noticed my absence at work by now – I couldn't just keep going, but I didn't want to turn back – would I even find my way back? I was cold, so cold – without a coat in the winter air, this was such a bad idea...

And then, someone jumped in front of my car – I slammed on the brakes and felt my heart and lungs trying to escape my body. When I mustered the courage to look up, two things happened: a flash of pain travelled down my neck, and I saw Pietro's furious face close to mine, so close that our noses nearly touched. He dragged me out of the car by the arm and pushed me to the side of the road, out of sight, behind a tree.

I thought I was about to die.

'Are you hurt?' was the first thing he said.

'What? Yes, I'm hurt! My head almost went through the windshield! And I almost ran you over! And you ask me if I'm hurt?'

He looked relieved. And then furious again. 'Viola, this is not a game. Why did you follow me?'

'Because I know that something's up. You keep disappearing. You're all whispering. Even Laio. Even Poggi. You...'

Pietro took me by the shoulders and pushed me against the tree. 'You're going to get us killed,' he hissed.

'You're selling artwork, aren't you? You're stealing it, and selling it!'

'What? Is that what you think?'

'What else is there to think?'

'Viola, listen to me. I'm going to tell you all. I'm going to show you.'

'And then you'll kill me?' I said in a feeble voice.

He rolled his eyes and, without a word, Pietro took my arm again and led me to his car. Only then I noticed a lilac hue in the sky: the short winter afternoon was turning into evening. I was freezing, and a shiver travelled through me: Pietro took his coat off and wrapped it around my shoulders.

We drove on in silence – by the side of the road, I saw a sign: Pietrasanta.

I remembered how isolated Pietrasanta was, how dark, even now, forty years later. 'Surely Pietro is not going to harm her,' I said under my breath.

Of course he wouldn't.

Would he?

I was terrified, with a touch of curiosity. Soon I'd know – and I'd find out if knowing had been worth the consequences.

'If I disappear, they'll come looking for me. My parents and my fiancé. They won't let you get away with—'

'Can you please stop with this thing about killing and disappearing and such?'

'But I'm about to discover your secret.'

'You really, really need to be quiet now, Viola.' He slammed a fist against the steering wheel.

That silenced me.

We came to the bottom of a hill and Pietro stopped the car. In silence, he got out and I followed. There was no point in asking 'Where are we going?' so I kept walking, climbing up the hill until the columns and arcs of what looked like a cloister appeared among the greenery.

The convent I'd caught a glimpse of that night with Brando – but I'd only seen shadows! It'd been destroyed during the war, Brando said. My blood ran cold. It wasn't a good omen at all.

We kept going until our feet stood on stone, and not on grass any more. A man with a patchy grey beard, dressed in a cap and a jacket that was too big for him, stood beside a small, dark door.

'Signor Ardito,' he greeted Pietro. He didn't give his name and touched his cap towards me. 'Will I go down and fetch...'

Ardito? That's not his second name either. Why is he known as Ardito?

'I have nothing, today. Just came to check. This is Tina. Forget her face; you won't see her again.'

Tina. And he should forget my face.

'Follow me,' Pietro said.

There was nowhere to run, so I did – I followed him inside.

The place was icy, echoey and now deserted. The man who probably acted as a custodian was outside. Pietro and I were alone: I'd lost all curiosity, all excitement. Now I wanted to cry. I'd be killed here and nobody would ever know what happened or they would pretend they didn't.

We climbed up a steep set of stairs, passed a landing – I caught a glimpse of wide, empty, freezing rooms – then up and up again, until we came to what looked like a storeroom. Leaning against a wall was a ladder – Pietro climbed on it and opened a hatch in the ceiling. For a moment I considered grabbing the ladder to make him fall, but as I was pondering this, Pietro extended his hand to take mine.

'It's old wood,' he said. 'Be careful.'

'Can you please make a decision?' I grumbled as I climbed up the rickety ladder.

'What?'

'You've dragged me here, you kidnapped me, and then you're nice and telling me to be careful, can you please... oh. I can't fit through here. What now?' I said, half squashed.

'Crawl all the way to the wall.'

I'd never been claustrophobic before. I can safely say that this has changed now. I was about to start screaming, when Pietro pushed upwards, and removed a whole portion of the ceiling – another hatch, this time so perfectly camouflaged as to be invisible.

I scrambled onto my knees and then stood, a little unsteady, still hyperventilating.

It took my eyes a few seconds to adjust to the gloom – when they finally did, I saw wooden crates, and white sheets covering painting-like shapes. I let myself fall on the floor again, my legs giving way to claustrophobia.

'Please, let me out of here,' I said, and my voice came out feebler than I'd thought it would.

Pietro helped me down – I coughed and coughed because of the dust and pulverised plaster. 'You need fresh air,' he said.

'You're doing it again.'

'What?'

'Being nice. You're supposed to be threatening.'

'Save your breath.'

Finally, we were outside in the cold air, at last. The sky was darkening, and all of a sudden all agitation left me, and I was a rag doll with dusty hair and shaking hands.

'So it's here. The artwork you stole.'

'We're not stealing it, Viola! We're trying to save it! Can you not see? The Germans will be here any day...'

'That's impossible...'

'You're still believing the propaganda? That we'll be glorious winners in this pathetic war? They'll invade us, and plunder us. And not just that. Bombs will fall on our cities. It's inevitable. It will happen.'

Could it really be?

I suppose it's easy to lie to those who're desperate to believe the lie. It's easy to delude those who'd rather embrace delusion.

But a tapestry of lies always, always frays.

'If you give us away we'll be thrown in prison, or worse. All of us. Poggi, Laio. Lisetta and the girls, everyone.'

'Poggi?'

'He started this. He told us that when Hitler came to see the Uffizi, when they walked down the Corridoio Vasariano... he knew. Poggi knew that the Führer's sights were set on us.'

It did make sense. Poggi lived for his work; it was plain to see: it was his sense of duty itself that had made him break every rule, break the law, put himself and his people in danger.

'You're all in on it?'

He nodded.

'All except me?'

He nodded again.

'Why did you not tell me? Why am I the only one left out?'

'Because we don't trust you. We never trusted you.'

'You don't trust me because of Federico.'

'Does it seem strange to you? Do you know how high your fiancé is in the party? Or is your head so empty...'

'My head is not empty. My head was never empty, Pietro.'

There was a moment of silence.

'No. I'm sorry.'

'You always assumed it was, though. A young, empty-headed girl looking for a pastime before getting married to a rich man. An older man she's marrying for money.'

'Are you marrying him for money, Viola?'

'Does it matter? Do my reasons matter at all?'

'Maybe it matters to me.'

It was then that he kissed me.

I've been kissed before.

But I was never kissed before.

Never, never, before Pietro kissed me.

I laid the diary on my chest, breathless. There was so much to take in! *Oh, Viola – 'I've been kissed before. But I was never kissed before...'*

You were all set in the cage your parents and your sense of duty had built for you – when life ambushed you.

And what was going to happen to the hidden paintings, when the convent was going to be razed to the ground?

But I had to get on with my work – I could only steal one last page.

I convinced my parents that my car had broken down; I'd wandered off looking for help, got lost, found someone who fixed the car, driven home shaken, but safe and sound.

They didn't question it: they were too relieved that I'd come to no harm. They had no idea what I'd been involved in. Things that good girls most definitely don't do. Such as stealing state property.

Such as kissing someone who's not their fiancé.

I can't sleep; I feel I'll never sleep again.

I keep thinking of the paintings in the false ceiling. I keep thinking of the danger Pietro and the others are in, and now, me too.

I keep thinking of Pietro's arms, Pietro's eyes. His lips against mine and his hands holding my waist.

I don't know who I am; I don't know who I've become. I've always been a good girl. This is the kind of thing fearless Marita would do, not me.

How seriously, how solemnly Pietro looked at me as we parted. But I can offer him nothing.

Then why am I counting the hours until I see Pietro again?

Being with someone while thinking of someone else. I could relate to that; I could relate to Viola's words in a way that was too uncomfortable to bear. The memories crossed my mind too quickly to be nipped in the bud. I closed the diary with a stronger thud than usual.

How could I have thought that Lorenzo didn't know about Rinaldi? A handful of men controlled every branch of power in these villages, dividing the spoils among themselves like hyenas. I'd been one of those spoils.

Keeping secret Father's plan to tie our family to the Rinaldi, and using me to do that, had been one of the hardest things I'd ever done. Until my father summoned me to his study – every conversation with him happened there, as if we were serfs receiving an audience with the landowner. I can only remember seeing him in my room once: the night that Mum had disappeared.

'So. How are things going with Enrico?' he'd asked.

What was I supposed to say? *He's as old as you, he has two sons my age, and he revolts me?*

'Fine.'

'Good to hear. That makes me happy. With Lucrezia away and your mother gone, we don't want your sisters to be put through any more upheaval.'

'No, of course not.'

'We also don't want your reputation to suffer, though. I spoke to him, and I made sure he won't leave you in limbo for much longer. He'll make things official. He has an ex-wife, but she's no trouble...' I wondered about her. She was 'no trouble'. Maybe she, too, had been sold and bought like me?

'I understand.'

'You're such a joy, Bianca. The most docile of my daughters. Not the smartest, but the most devoted.'

Maybe I wasn't the smartest, but I certainly wasn't devoted. I was terrified, that's what I was.

A question came into my mind, too powerful to contain. I swallowed and steeled myself.

'Why did you marry Mum?'

Usually I weighed every word I spoke to him, and I certainly didn't go looking for trouble. But I recalled my mother's words of love for him, before he turned on her. It seemed so strange to me, that he should have married her for love, and that she loved him like she did, as deeply as she did, and now look at our family. Look at what he'd done to us, what he was doing to me just then.

Father's face worked, and for a moment I thought he'd shout, or strike me. But he didn't.

'I was someone else, then,' he said, and looked down at his papers. The conversation was over.

I made my way upstairs, and Mia was on the landing. I composed my face into a smile.

'Bianca?'

'Yes, *cara*, it's all good, we were just sorting some things out,' I finally said, and my words sounded hollow, like my heart was. 'It's all good.'

I had been sure she didn't know what was happening. But I knew now how much I'd underestimated her gift.

CHAPTER 25

CASALTA, 1985

BIANCA

As soon as I stepped out of the house and felt the chilly wind on my skin, my thoughts went to Amarilli, and how I needed to remember to pack her warmest dressing gown for the hospital.

My pragmatic mind worked on details and practicalities. I'd had a childhood where I couldn't control the big things, like my father's temper or whether my twin and I could stay together, where I couldn't keep our mother home with us, but I could at least control the little things. I'd pack the perfect bag for Amarilli; she'd have all she needed.

I couldn't wait for it all to be finished.

Routine operation, a common procedure for heart problems and nothing to worry about, I said to myself for the thousandth time.

I looked at my watch – lunch and after-lunch activities at Villa Lieta were now finished. I'd been good at keeping Amarilli's operation out of my mind as much as I could, but now it was looming, and I couldn't fight the anxiety any longer. There was no way I'd pass on my anxiety to her, though – so I painted a smile on my face. I hoped with all my heart that her daughter had driven through from Rome, but something told me she hadn't.

I found Amarilli sitting on her bed, all packed and ready.

'Hello, *cara*. How kind of you to come and see me today,' she said while slipping something into her little bag – I couldn't see what.

'You're all done! I was going to help you. Did you remember the dressing gown? Your warmer one, not the summer one. And your slippers?'

'I remembered both dressing gown and slippers. I packed up already because I was hoping you'd read for me. You know, so we can spend the afternoon in a pleasant way and forget about tomorrow. Not that I'm nervous!' she hastened to add.

'No, of course not! Neither am I. It's a routine operation; being nervous would be a waste of energy. Now. Shall we make a start on *The Heiress and the Rebel*? It looks great.' The cover displayed a corseted woman with flowing blonde hair and a man with his shirt ripped open – he was probably the rebel. I was always a little embarrassed to buy those books at the newsagent, and always made sure to say they were for Amarilli and not me. Rina, the owner of the newsagent, would just smile and nod as if to say, *Yes, sure*.

I'd never admit I enjoyed them.

'Good idea,' Amarilli said – but instead of getting up and sitting on the armchair as she always did, she pushed herself back and leaned on the pillow – I helped lift her legs gently onto the bed.

'Chapter one,' I began.

Just a routine operation, I told myself. She was going to be fine.

∼

Dear Liala,

It seems to me that the person I was when I began writing this diary is not the person I am now. That my childhood lasted forever, and then, all of a sudden, I was pushed out of it – and that little step out of the world I knew turned into a breathless run, and everything began to change at a pace I can barely keep up with.

Radio bulletins today were terrifying, and the most frightening thing is that we can't make out what's going on. We've lost the war – the Allies are coming – invading us? Saving us? The Germans are coming – they're on our side, they're our enemies – our Duce is not abandoning us – our Duce ran away – we're resisting, we've surrendered. Nobody knows what's really happening. Papà has gone to fight, in spite of not being in good health. He'd had enough of being treated like a weakling, he said. Mamma is out of her mind with worry.

Everything is falling apart. We're not going to reap victory for Italy's sons and daughters; we're not going to reap anything but chaos and destruction.

I'm not wiser than my parents, I'm not less credulous than anyone else, but I felt it coming: maybe because I allowed myself to see it, and my parents didn't. They were too afraid to accept that we'd put our trust in a handful of empty slogans.

Mamma tried to stop me from going to Florence.

'I'm sorry. I'm going,' I said simply, even if I knew I was giving her more worry.

I couldn't tell her that I had to help protect the paintings, that my place was with Poggi and his people. That I needed to be with Pietro, because in the space of one night, my unspoken promise to him had become stronger than my forced promise to Federico. When things calmed down a little, I'd tell her that I refused to be married. And together we'd see where life took us next.

So Viola *was* refusing the marriage!

She'd been stronger than I ever was, because I'd never had the courage to say no. The reason why Rinaldi and I weren't married now, and why he'd moved away from here and never come back, had nothing to do with me. All I knew was that not long after the dreaded conversation about my reputation, Father told me that *the deal* was off.

After a while of living in terror, dreading that he'd change his mind, I finally accepted that I'd never feel Rinaldi's disgusting hands on my body again, that toad's mouth on my skin, and I'd never be tied to him in marriage. The Falconeri and the Rinaldi wouldn't seal an alliance, after all, for reasons unknown to me.

I still hadn't told anyone about this, and I was devastated that Lorenzo knew.

It was my secret, my shameful secret. I hadn't stood up for myself, I couldn't, but someone must have been watching over me from above.

Pietro was waiting for me, dark shadows under his eyes, but his back straight and his chest open, as if to say, World, I won't go down without a fight. *He gathered me in his arms and held me so tight it almost hurt. It wasn't a greeting – it was a goodbye.*

'Viola.' I held my breath. 'You belong to someone else.'

'No, no, I don't, not any more!'

'What...'

I wanted to explain, but there just wasn't time. Poggi called us – Pietro took my hand and led me to the basement where many times they'd met without me. This time, I was allowed to be there.

Poggi's eyes were hard, like I'd never seen them before. He hadn't given in to the chaos around us: his hair was perfect and his shoes shone, as always. Not even war on our streets could make him dishevelled. At that moment, incongruous as it was,

I was glad I'd worn my Uffizi uniform: I, too, was ready for battle.

'And so, Signorina Innocenti, you know,' he said.

Laio, by contrast, seemed to have slept in his clothes. His eyes were febrile. 'She can't be trusted.'

'Excuse me, I'm right here. And I can be trusted. In fact, I'll help.'

'The best way to help is to stay out of it,' *Laio insisted, and Pietro took a step closer to me.*

'Why are we wasting time discussing my loyalty?'

The three men exchanged looks, a silent conversation that seemed to decide my fate: whether they liked it or not, I was in.

'Welcome to our club of madmen,' *Poggi said, a hint of humour in his eyes.*

'And madwomen,' *I said.* 'Where's Lisetta?'

'I'm here,' *Lisetta said, slowly, calmly opening the basement door and stepping inside. I had to do a double-take, because she almost didn't look herself, with a dress worn to the bone and too big for her.*

'Well, let's get to work,' *Poggi said.*

Pietro still hadn't uttered a word, his face dark and focused. There was much to do, and we had to do it fast: I didn't have time to think of anything else, to even ask myself what was going to happen tomorrow. There were heavy wooden doors to close, windows to bar, crates as big as coffins to be taken to the road and onto a waiting truck, vaguely military-looking but unmarked.

I knew where we were going, though the destination hadn't been spoken aloud. Lisetta climbed into the back, but Laio went to take the place beside Pietro.

'Laio, get into the back and check on the crates,' *Pietro instructed – grudgingly, Laio did as he was told, and Pietro and I were left alone in the front.*

Outside the windows a strange world unfolded – the worst

> *of it being people with their belongings rolled up in sheets on their shoulders, women carrying babies with toddlers hanging onto their mothers' hands, old people leaning on walking sticks, everyone escaping from the city – and going where?*
>
> *I had to tell him, and I had to tell him now, even if Laio and Lisetta would hear us, even if the engine was so loud, I had to shout. 'You said I belong to someone else. But not for much longer, Pietro!'*
>
> *I looked at his profile, his face as tense as a fist and yet vulnerable. 'Viola, you're getting married. I can't... you can't...'*
>
> *'No. I won't get married,' I whispered – I thought that with all the noise he wouldn't hear me. But he did, because he squeezed his eyes shut for an instant, and then he took my hand and brought it to his heart.*

A voice interrupted my reading suddenly, too suddenly. The whiplash almost made me dizzy. *Not now, not now, I need to know what happens next!*

'Oh, hello, Bianca. I spotted your hair from the next carriage!'

I looked up and saw Ester, a nurse who used to work at Villa Lieta. Closing the diary was almost physically painful.

'Hello,' I said, trying to infuse my words with some enthusiasm. Ester began to chat about something or other and I managed to intersperse her monologue with appropriate words, all the while thinking about Viola.

She might not make it. Viola might have been killed, and Pietro too. I knew that Florence was bombed during the war, more than once.

When the train began to slow down and came into the station I wanted to stomp my feet like a disgruntled child – Ester had stolen my time with the diary, and now I had to go to work. Argh. And I couldn't take the diary out again either, given that I stole it, which was a fact I was trying to forget. I bade a falsely cordial goodbye to Ester and began my usual walk to the museum, to the heart of Florence. Everywhere I looked I could see imprints of Viola, what she'd seen, what she'd said, what she'd done. Now more than ever I wished my gift was back, so I could know more, see more, see the story unfolding.

It seems to me that the person I was when I began writing this diary is not the person I am now, Viola had said, and equally it seemed to me that since I'd begun reading her diary I'd changed more deeply than I'd ever thought possible. It was as if her story had brought old wounds to the surface, to help them heal.

What's going to happen next? Will war swallow her; will she survive?

I tried to come back to the present. Florence was too gorgeous not to get lost in her beauty, on this luminous autumn day. The sky was so blue, the light low and golden, reflecting equally golden specks in the Arno waters. But thoughts of Viola kept coming back, and I felt liminal, in between two worlds, in between past and present.

As I walked up the stairs to the archive, I kept trying to see Pietro with my mind's eye: I painted an image of him, then scrapped it and started again. Dark hair, dark skin, blue eyes, thin: but how long was his hair; was his skin darker or lighter than Mia's? Were his eyes cornflower blue like mine, or aqua, like Lulu's? Was he thin and wiry; had poverty taken a chunk out of him? How did his voice sound? I imagined it deep and soft...

I stood in front of the door for a moment, absentmindedly, until the door opened.

'Excuse me?'

I had to blink once, twice, because for a moment I thought Pietro was in front of me – but it was Brando, looking confused.

'*Ciao*, Brando, sorry, I was lost in thought...'

'Bianca, it's you!'

Now I was confused. 'Of course it's me.'

'Sorry, for a moment there I didn't recognise you! You looked different.'

'Really? Different, how?' I asked.

'Like... someone else. Black hair, short. I mean, short hair and short person. I don't know. I only saw her for a moment. Must have been the glare,' he said and turned towards the window from which the morning sunshine seeped. But there was no glare.

It sounded like he'd seen Viola. I thought I knew what just happened – past and present had blended together like they sometimes did around me. But I could hardly explain that to him without revealing too much about my gift.

'Must have been.'

'That was so strange,' he said. 'Anyway, it's lovely to see you. As always.' He looked left and right before kissing the top of my head – we'd agreed that we both preferred not to be too affectionate at work.

I sat with my boxes overflowing with documents, and settled in. I knew there wouldn't be any news of Amarilli for a little while, between getting her ready for surgery, the operation itself and then coming out of the anaesthesia. I couldn't wait to see her, but I knew that for now, all I could do was wait.

But a sudden bout of cold filled me. I couldn't stop shivering – my hands were icy. The feeling of dread in the pit of my stomach made me stop what I was doing, and turn towards the door.

At that moment, Brando appeared on the doorstep. 'Your sister is on the phone,' he called to me.

I raced to the receiver.

'Bianca, it's me.'

'Mia? Are you well?'

'I'm good, we're all good. But... I'm sorry, Dottor Artibani called from Villa Lieta. Oh, Bianca... Amarilli has passed away during her operation.'

CHAPTER 26

CASALTA, 1985

BIANCA

Over the next few days, the hard, tight knot inside my stomach wouldn't go away.

I kept seeing Amarilli out of the corner of my eye, a shadow just out of reach – every elderly lady was her – I heard her voice calling me. But it was all just an illusion, the deeply human desire to fill whatever void we meet.

Phantom pain I suppose, like when you lose a limb, but still feel it.

I was tasked with packing away Amarilli's things at Villa Lieta while her daughter, Anita, began to empty her house. It was all so fast, but Anita's move to Arizona was looming. I asked myself if Anita knew how much her absence, her silence, had troubled her mother – Amarilli had always made a point not to complain or pile any guilt on her daughter.

'I want her to be free. I want her to live her life,' she'd said many times, almost every time that Anita was mentioned. Privately, I thought that there had to be a happy medium between yoking sons and daughters to the family, and having them disappear from your life.

I sadly looked at the pile of magazines on her bedside table: *The People's Companion, La Signora*, the book with the corseted lady in the arms of a Mr Darcy lookalike on the cover. Even in sorrow, I smiled. It was all so Amarilli.

A plastic zipped pocket labelled 'Documents' had been gathered while she was in the hospital and given to me for safe-keeping – I was going to give it to Anita without opening it, but through the clear plastic I saw an envelope with my name on it, written in shaky capital letters.

I took out the envelope. There was one of Ortensia's stickers – a little duck – in the bottom corner, and again, it made me smile.

The writing inside was all lopsided – with Amarilli's eyesight being so bad, I was surprised she'd managed to write at all.

My dearest Bianca,

You've been like a daughter to me. Thank you for keeping me company; thank you for sharing stories with me. Your youth and sweetness have been a joy to be around. I'm writing this because I feel the end coming, and I think I won't come out of the hospital alive. I don't know why, it's a feeling I have, even if it's you who has a sixth sense and not me. Please, don't be sad. I've had a good, long life and I'm ready to go, even if I'll miss my grandchildren so much, and you, of course! There's something I need to tell you, and you need to listen to me very carefully. Promise?

'I promise,' I murmured between the tears.

Here goes.

Be true to your heart.

You gave me, and many other people, so much of yourself. You had the courage to start something new: don't look back. If you do, you'll find yourself twenty, thirty years from now wondering why you didn't take your chance when you could.

In every way, bambina mia, *be true to your heart.*

I hope your life will be full of fun and full of love and that all your dreams come true.

With all my love,

Amarilli

Tears were streaming down my face – but they weren't entirely tears of sorrow. Amarilli had left a little crumb trail for me, to help me out of the confusion.

Be true to your heart.

Yes, I would.

I put the letter back in the envelope and folded it in two, carefully, and slipped it in my jeans pocket. Then, I zipped Amarilli's little bag closed, and stood to leave. But when I turned around, right by the door was Lorenzo.

Be true to your heart, bambina.

Before I knew what I was doing, before I could think – before either of us could think – we were in each other's arms. He took my face in his hands and our eyes locked us into each other – neither of us could look away. I forgot where I was, I forgot about Brando, about Tamara, about the whole world.

He was here again, the Lorenzo I knew – before the disappointment, the betrayal, the long silences, the walls we'd built around our hearts.

We embraced slowly, and every moment, every inch that took my body closer to his was heavenly – it seemed impossible we could ever, ever let go. We settled into each other – all that

I'd held inside came out in a long, long exhale, and the same happened to him, because I felt him lean on me – the strong, enduring, Orafi eldest son, the heir and linchpin of the family, his father's and brother's defender and caretaker... leaned on me.

I love you, Lorenzo. I've always loved you since the day I met you. I love you, I love you, I love you.

Opening my heart to the truth felt good, and right, and real. I knew I'd lost him, but at least I didn't have to pretend I'd moved on.

Once I decided to be true to my heart, there was no need to pretend about anything.

'Signor Orafi,' a voice – Dottor Artibani's voice – broke the spell, and I pulled away. For a moment Lorenzo kept me close – and then he pulled away too, and we were once again apart.

Dottor Artibani looked vaguely embarrassed – I knew he'd seen us. He and Lorenzo exchanged a few words, then Lorenzo, with a nod to me, left.

Did it really happen? Did we really find each other; did we really melt into each other? It'd been so fast, so quickly over.

When I walked out of Villa Lieta, I was reeling with it all. After our embrace, Lorenzo had almost run away from me, and I had no idea what he thought, what he intended to do. He was engaged. I had no control over that. But I had control over my own choices: I could be truthful; I could do what I knew was right. Amarilli's letter, with its simple wisdom, had shone a light on my next step.

In my car, I leaned back on my seat and closed my eyes for a moment.

Oh, Lorenzo.

Did it really happen?

CHAPTER 27

CASALTA, 1985

BIANCA

The dresses I'd discarded after my identity crisis were in two rattan bags, carefully folded with sachets of dried rose and lavender. I picked my favourite dress, blue with tiny aqua flowers, took off the jeans and off-the-shoulder T-shirt I was wearing, and slipped it on instead. I swept my hair in a half-up, half-down style, with one of my hairclips.

The jeans and the suits ended up in the bags, while my beloved dresses claimed back their rightful place, hanging in the wardrobe all in a tidy colourful line.

How could I have ever allowed a stranger's venomous words, and my own insecurity, to dictate who I saw when I looked in the mirror? The way I chose to dress had nothing to do with anyone else, friend or lover, or enemy. Certainly not with Lorenzo's girlfriend.

I looked at myself in the mirror.

Yes. This was *me*.

The rose garden at Casalta had seen so much, I pondered as I sat there with Brando. So much of our story and of those who came before us. I wondered how many women and men before me must have sat here, in this very place, ready to make or break someone's heart.

Brando and I were wrapped up in coats and scarves, black branches over us and a carpet of dead leaves under our feet. The golden autumn had morphed into the colder, darker second half, the bleak month of November and its short days. And still, pink-yellow roses bloomed, their beauty even more touching, because they bloomed in the cold.

'Can I make you coffee?' I asked. Focusing on the practical helped my nerves a little.

'No, thank you, I'm good. You sounded awfully solemn, on the phone,' Brando said. I sensed his anxiety.

'Yes. I... I called you here because...'

I'd barely started talking and already my eyes were full of guilty tears. I was about to hurt this kind, generous man, and all because I'd thought I could lie to myself, and if I lied well enough, I'd end up believing it. And Brando had been caught in my clumsy attempt to move on from the past when I still wasn't ready. Because this particular piece of the past was actually present – I just hadn't wanted to admit it.

My heart belonged to Lorenzo, still. I knew that there was no future for us, but it didn't change the fact that I couldn't give my love to anyone else, until I'd moved on from him. And I couldn't let Brando be dragged into this mess, not until I'd sorted out my emotions. If I ever would.

'Are you crying? Don't cry! Whatever it is! I mean, I know it's probably not the best news for me, but *don't cry*.'

'I can't continue seeing you. I'm so sorry.'

He sat back on the bench as if I'd punched him in the gut.

'Oh. I see.'

I couldn't come out with anything better than 'I'm sorry.'

'I could feel it, you know? That your heart wasn't in it.'

'That's not true, Brando. It's not true that my heart wasn't in it. It's that I didn't quite know myself. I didn't mean to...'

'To use me to get over another man?' I was speechless. All the air had been pushed out of my lungs, and for a moment I couldn't breathe. 'Did you think I didn't know? I've seen the two of you together. Lorenzo Orafi. Who else?'

I looked down. 'We're not together. He's engaged; you know that – you were there.'

'But...'

Oh, no. Brando was dragging the words out of me, words that would hurt him, words I didn't want to say. 'But I can't be with anyone else because my heart is taken. By him.'

There. Saying it aloud was strange, uncomfortable. Wonderful, like a cold shower that hurt but washed away all that was stagnant, all that was old. 'I'm so sorry, Brando.'

Brando leaned his elbows on his knees. 'I might argue that being in love with a man who's engaged to another woman is not conducive to happiness.'

'I know. But I can't help it. And I can't involve you in this.'

'A bit late.'

'I thought I could forget him! I thought I was ready to move on. When I realised I wasn't... I had to stop seeing you. I'm sorry,' I repeated weakly.

'I know you are. But it doesn't make me feel that much better, to be honest,' he said with a small smile.

Silence enveloped us, as the chilly breeze made me pull my cardigan tighter and cross my arms to keep warm. Without a word, Brando took his scarf off and wrapped it around my shoulders. The gesture reminded me of when Pietro enfolded Viola in his coat, in the freezing night.

'Please don't be nice to me,' I whispered.

I searched his face for signs of anger. Maybe him being angry with me would have assuaged a bit of my guilt: I wanted him to be mad at me, to pronounce cutting, cruel words. There was no anger, though – maybe that's what I would have got from Lorenzo, but not from Brando. His eyebrows were knitted together and I was horrified to see that his eyes were shiny with tears. In my father's world, men didn't cry – but Brando had been brought up to be authentic with both joy and sorrow. The tears I'd been trying to hold back began to flow.

'I can't help being nice. If you want a brooding *I-own-the-world* kind of guy you know where to go. Please, don't cry...' Brando said once again.

I dried my cheeks. 'You keep saying that. But I hurt you.'

'Do you want me to comfort *you*, now?' He smiled.

'No, but...'

'Bianca. It's the cliché to end all clichés, but hearts get broken and hearts mend,' he said. 'It just takes time.'

I nodded.

'Something else,' he continued, and looked for my eyes. 'Don't let what happened between us influence your work choices. The project is coming to an end, and I don't know what you'll choose to do next. But please know that this will not change our working relationship; I'm in your corner, always.'

'I know. Thank you.'

'Good,' he said, and stood. I unravelled his scarf from my neck and took a step to accompany him to the car. 'It's okay. I'll just go. Take care.'

He went to lay a kiss on the top of my head, like he used to do – but he changed his mind, and walked away.

～

Being authentic has a price. I knew that already, in theory, but practice was a lot harder.

I spent the day doing my old job, now that Teresa was out of action – going through the motions helped calm the hurricane inside me. It'd been the longest, longest day, but Viola's diary was calling me.

I grabbed a torch and climbed out on the stone stairs, leaning against the cold wall. It seemed a lifetime ago that I'd left Viola on that truck with Pietro, driving on dangerous roads, but it'd been two days only. She'd just told him that no, she wouldn't get married to Federico Valsecchi.

...he took my hand and brought it to his heart.

A sudden bump made us both cry out – we were thrown forward and heard an ominous thumping sound coming from the back of the truck. I was about to cry out for Lisetta, hoping she wasn't hurt, when I saw a figure, two, more, surround the truck.

Pietro lowered the window.

'No way forward. The road is blocked,' the soldier said in a clipped tone.

'We're just going to—'

'The road is blocked,' he repeated, and his hand travelled to the weapon he was carrying. I was sick with fear. What if he decided to check the back of the truck...

'Please, let's go,' I whispered.

Pietro called out a cheerful, grateful-sounding 'Thank you,' and we turned around. 'Laio, all good back there?' he said, changing tone instantly.

'All good! What's going on?'

'They stopped us. No going ahead.'

Laio shouted an array of blasphemies. 'Everywhere else is too far; they'll stop us again.'

'Everywhere else?' I asked. 'Are there other hiding places apart from Pietrasanta?'

'Oh, yes. We couldn't have risked hiding everything in one place.' How had they managed that? I was in awe of these

people's courage and skill. 'But Laio is right, they're too far. We're turning back to Florence.'

'We can't!' Laio shouted.

Pietro thumped the steering wheel with his palm and made a sudden stop, throwing everyone forward once again. 'What choice do we have?'

'I have another idea,' I said. 'Casalta, my house. Nobody will think of looking for anything there.'

'Who lives with you?'

'My mother. She won't give us away. She won't give me away. And once the crates are hidden, everyone else will be none the wiser.'

'I'm going to go and tell Signor Poggi about the change of plan.' Lisetta's voice came from the back, and before anyone could stop her she'd jumped down.

'Lisetta!' I called her, but she didn't turn around.

The closer we came to Casalta, the more terrified I felt. It'd seemed a good idea when I first proposed it, now not so much. What if someone I knew saw me on that truck? How would I justify that?

We came to the bottom of the Casalta hill – terror rose to the point where I was about to burst into tears. But then a strange calm filled me. I couldn't cry; none of us could run away as there was nowhere to run, and we were responsible for irreplaceable artwork. And for our lives. Hysterics were not an option.

In the tiny mirror above me I caught a glimpse of a white face, the glimpse of a ghost. That ghost was me.

'I'd better go in the back,' I told Pietro and he stopped to let me climb down and up again. I kneeled on the dusty floor among the crates, with Laio staring at me from across the space.

'If you're taking us into a trap, I'll strangle you with my bare hands.'

'And good luck to you too, Laio,' I replied and crawled towards the front, so I could guide Pietro in case he needed it.

Mamma ran out of the house in a panic – when she saw that I was in the strange truck that had just approached her home, she looked even more confused.

'Viola, what's happening? Who are these people...'

I took both her hands. I was desperate to reassure her, but I knew I couldn't. 'Mamma, please. Don't ask me any questions. Not yet.'

When she saw Pietro and Laio, she inched closer to me and slipped her arm under mine, as if to protect me.

'I'm so sorry to impose on you, signora,' Pietro said, as if this was a social occasion. But his words and his tone were perfectly judged to calm her a little. Manners and politeness are my mother's very sustenance.

'Let's go make them coffee,' I said, and gently led my mother towards the kitchen – it was only then that I saw Zia Agnese was on the doorstep.

'What on earth, Viola?' she began. I shot her a hard glance from behind Mamma, and she got the message.

'They're starving, the men. They'd be so grateful for something to eat,' I said.

'Of course,' my mother replied, and I felt something squeeze my heart as I saw her so frightened, so desperate to cling to normality. I'd brought danger to her door.

Zia Agnese grabbed me by the arm and drew me inside. 'What do you think you're doing?' she hissed. From the window, I could see Pietro and Laio unloading the crates.

'There was no choice but to come here. Everything is going to be fine. I'll explain, I promise,' I tried to soothe her and ran outside to show Pietro and Laio the way to the attic. They followed me upstairs, carrying the crates of treasure.

'Too narrow,' Pietro said curtly, and proceeded to unlock the crates and take out the paintings, one by one, careful not to let the sheets covering them come undone. Sweat poured from his and Laio's faces as they worked – I climbed up with them and helped lean the paintings against the furthest wall, carefully.

I heard the vehicles approaching, before I saw them.

A German truck was here, and a black car I knew, I recognised.

Federico stepped out of it, fury painted all over his face. Another man followed him – I let out a small cry when I realised it was my father. But he looked like someone else, someone almost monstrous. He was pale, wrathful, merciless.

'I knew it. I knew it!' Laio shouted, appearing beside me with a pistol drawn – a pistol I didn't know he had. 'You betrayed us,' he said and I saw that his extended arms holding the gun were shaking.

'It wasn't me!' I whispered, with the overwhelming, all-consuming feeling that what Laio believed now didn't really matter, not any more. And I was right, because in the midst of our screams Papà shot him, just like that, pouring bullets into him like you'd water a plant. Even Federico looked horrified, as I worked hard not to fall on my knees, not to crumble in terror and despair.

It was then that I saw a blonde head appearing from inside the German truck – a slight, fair figure rose from the tangle of black – Lisetta.

'I'm sorry,' she shouted towards us. Useless, worthless words. She looked at Laio on the ground and covered her face with her hands. Laio drew his last, ragged breath and lay still, his eyes open to the empty sky.

Everything happened at once.

Mamma ran out towards Papà, calling his name, but she stopped, frozen, when she saw Laio in a pool of blood.

Her eyes darted from Papà to Federico to Laio's body to me,

confusion painted on her face as a lifetime of belief and trust shifted and liquified in her mind.

The people who'd arrived at Casalta to restore order — her own husband, who to her eyes embodied everything that was good and reliable and trustworthy — were responsible for the broken man on the ground.

'Giuseppina! Our daughter is a whore!' Papà shouted and then turned to me. 'You thought we didn't know that you were seeing that pathetic little man? That criminal dressed in rags?' He strode towards me — but before either I or Pietro could move, my mother stepped in front of me, her feet planted on the ground in a stance I'd never seen her taking before.

'Don't touch my daughter,' she said in a low tone, and if I wasn't crying before, I was now.

And so was I. Viola too had an angel that looked after her. Her mother had found the strength and courage to stand up for her.

Papà froze. His wife had never, never challenged him before. I could see the shock painted all over his face. Pietro was beside me at once — I felt like folding in two with terror, because weapons were pointing at us from all around, and I was sure I was about to lose my mother and the man I love.

Federico spoke. 'How could you do this to me, Viola? You made a promise. How could you?'

I don't know if he spoke any more; I don't know who did what afterwards — I was frozen in terror; I couldn't see nor think — I stood on the edge of a precipice, about to lose everything I loved, about to lose my life, about to nullify all effort to save the paintings.

All of a sudden no words mattered, nothing we could do mattered, because the sky wasn't empty any more, but full of roaring planes bearing a deadly payload. The bombs we'd feared for so long had finally materialised and began falling on us.

Pietro grabbed me and my mother and dragged us towards the house as the air around us exploded, and a terrible pain bloomed from the inside of my ears outwards. I heard nothing for a handful of seconds, and then the noise and screams came back, the pain of Pietro's hands digging into my arms as he dragged me away and inside the house, up into the attic to curl up beside the paintings.

'I love you, Viola,' he whispered and, somehow, I heard him over the din. And then he ran out again, why, why? I screamed after him but he didn't turn back. My mother, my aunt and I curled up together among the paintings, holding onto each other.

It was like being in a dream, kneeling among the paintings with my arms clasped over my head, deafened by thunder. But it wasn't a dream, and the noise wasn't thunder. Debris fell off the roof every time a detonation shook the ground and turned the sheets grey – one of them came loose: the perfect face of a Renaissance girl, bronze hair and dark eyes, a pearl hanging from a gold circlet on her high forehead, stared at me. I recognised Bianca de' Medici, a little dame immortalised in paint and gold.

The portrait that gave me my name, the painting by Bronzino that my mother saw in the Uffizi long before having us, and yet she'd known that one day she was going to have a daughter, and call me after little Bianca.

It's me, Viola... It's me, somehow, reaching out to you through rivers of time.

Viola, can you hear me?

I shook more and more at every roar that threatened to shatter my body and everyone, everything around me, and a prayer learned in childhood came to my lips. Thunder crashed around me; trees on fire glimmered beyond the broken windows – any moment now the wooden ceiling above me would go up in flames and the paintings with it, and we'd all be obliterated. I prayed and prayed and said goodbye to my family, to my life, to my love, who was lost somewhere, maybe wounded, maybe dead.

A moment of silence. The world seemed to hold its breath and hush, unmoving: the hills, the trees, the flames, the paintings scattered on the attic floor.

The serene eyes of the young Renaissance dame peeping through the sheet met mine once more – I saw Bianca's eyes blink slowly, her dark irises disappearing beneath her lids with the long, long eyelashes, and then reappearing. In my terror, I didn't question that a girl in a painting had blinked – and I didn't question hearing the little dame's voice in my head.

Viola. All will be well. I promise.

The thunder began again, but I didn't hear it any more – I took my trembling arms from my head, raised my chin, and sat still, waiting for the storm to end.

My cheeks were wet with tears as I read on. One, two fell on the paper and smudged the ink.

This was the last page.

Viola, my Viola, will I ever know what happened to you?

CHAPTER 28

CASALTA, 1986

BIANCA

Sometimes life resembles these hills around my home, full of ups and downs and change and choices. Sometimes it's like a pond, still and unmovable, and the only visible movement is the breeze on the water. The weeks and months following Amarilli's passing and breaking up with Brando were like that, a still pond where every day was like the day before.

I hadn't spoken to Lorenzo since that day at Villa Lieta. After we'd fallen into each other's arms, after we'd felt how deep and unbreakable the bond between us was, there was nothing more to say or do. No – *we* didn't feel an unbreakable bond; I did, not him. Clearly this bond was in my heart, but not his.

Had he wanted me, he would have come looking for me.

Even if I hated to admit it even to myself, I waited; I waited and hoped he'd come for me, but he didn't.

Lorenzo had no desire to shatter what he had and rebuild it back with me. He was engaged to another woman, he was moving on with his life, and I had to do the same.

The day would come when I'd have to stand at his wedding, and nobody was to see that my heart was broken. I'd smile a perfect smile and none, including Lorenzo, would know what was below the surface.

My love for Lorenzo would be my secret, and mine only.

Legami was out of my hands, with Teresa healed and having taken over my role in her thoughtful, considerate way. I helped only occasionally when an extra hand was needed. The project at the Uffizi had now ended, and I missed my work immensely: the funding had been renewed and Brando had asked me to continue, but I couldn't take the job and then leave them when I was about to start my course at the Scuola di Restauro.

Mum was almost commuting between Casalta and England, and Mia was still considering joining her in London – she said that it wasn't time, yet. My Mia, she was so fragile: I still felt I had to protect her at all costs. Nora was as busy as always, and Lulu was often travelling for work – her wedding was set for the spring.

Since I'd finished reading Viola's diary, since the night I'd experienced the abrupt end of her story, I'd had no hints, no signs of my gift.

It was gone, I was sure.

Yes, life was still: I was holding my breath for the next phase.

And then the response from the Scuola di Restauro came.

I sat on the stone stairs that had listened to all my confidences, all my troubles and happy moments, since I was a child and had sat there with Lulu and Mum. I opened the letter.

We regret to inform you that we cannot grant you a place in next year's course.

That was the only sentence that mattered to me, among words of explanation and best wishes on my future endeavours.

I was more disappointed than I could say. As strange, as unwise as that was, I simply hadn't considered the possibility of not making the course once I'd applied. Even if Brando had warned me that the school didn't offer many places. I'd been so busy asking myself whether I was clever enough, good enough to apply, I simply took for granted that if I overcame my own insecurity then I'd be given the chance to try.

I smiled to myself. And it wasn't a bitter smile. I felt in awe of life itself and its unpredictability. I'd done everything in my power to try and fit life into my plans, to give a shape to water: I'd earned enough money to pay for the course, overcome my insecurities to apply, tied loose ends so I could have a clean break, without leaving anything undone, or responsibilities unfulfilled.

I was ready for the next step, in every way.

And then, just as had happened to Viola when they were on their way to Pietrasanta, the road was blocked.

What now?

~

The cold kept us inside, in the cosy Casalta kitchen. Mum was back for a few days and she, Mia and I were sitting together at the table, an apple cake and a steaming teapot between us.

'Mia has something to tell you,' Mum said.

'I think she knows. You know, don't you?' Mia said to me, apprehensively.

'That you decided to go to London? Well, I don't have your gift, but yes. I guessed it,' I said with a smile. 'I'm so proud of you, Mia.' I really was. I knew how much courage she'd had to summon to make this choice. It was as if my own daughter was fleeing the nest.

'It's time to branch out,' she said seriously, making me smile.

'Are you okay with it, my love?' Mum said. 'I know you'll be busy with your studies...'

That was my cue. 'I didn't get into the course.'

Mum's eyes widened, and she leaned back on her chair. Mia was still and silent.

'When did you find out?' Mum asked.

'A few days ago. I wanted to sit on it for a little while before telling everyone.'

Mum covered my hand with hers. 'But...' she began. I tilted my head, waiting to hear what she had to say. '...don't let this setback discourage you. If art restoration is what you want to do, apply again.'

'I intend to. Brando *did* tell me it was hard to get in. I promise, I won't let this deflate me. It's just a delay, not a full stop.'

'That's my girl,' Mum said.

'I was wondering if it'd be too much trouble... if I could come and stay with you for a while, too. I know it'd be a tight squeeze, but...'

'Yes!' Mia hugged me. 'Yes, yes, yes!'

'Wait, it's up to Mum...' I laughed.

'I couldn't be happier!' Mum said.

We hugged and Mia hugged us both. I wanted to feel excited. I *was* excited.

But something inside me had no peace; something kept fluttering around like a bird in a cage, slamming against the walls of my heart.

Later that night, Mia knocked at my door. She'd spent the evening in her studio, and still smelled of paint and turpentine, her hands stained as always. She had dried blue paint on one side of her face.

'Do you actually use a canvas? Or do you paint yourself?'

She laughed too. 'Bit of both.'

'So, we're going to London.'

'Yes.' She came to sit beside me on the bed, and I wrapped my arm around her thin shoulders.

'Don't worry. I'll be there too. I'll always be there to protect you.'

'Thank you. So will I. I'll always be there to protect you,' she said solemnly. I smiled and tried not to laugh. My little Mia. 'Like I did when Father wanted you to marry that disgusting old man.'

That silenced me.

'What?'

'Rinaldi. You were supposed to marry him, weren't you?'

My mouth fell open.

'I protected you then.'

It took me a moment to recover myself, my mind empty and too full at the same time. 'What are you talking about? You were a child!'

'I spoke to Father.'

'You... How... What did you say to him?'

'It doesn't matter any more.' She gave me a peck on the cheek, playful, sweet. But when I looked in her eyes, those strange, cat-like eyes, one dark blue, one hazel brown, I almost shivered. 'So, it's time you stopped worrying about me.'

She was the angel who watched over me. My little sister, whom I'd always tried to protect, had protected me.

The question remained: *what had she said to Father?*

∽

I went to say goodbye to Florence – a temporary goodbye, I was sure, but I still felt the need to do so, and to do it alone.

While I was in the city, I decided to run some errands for my impending journey: my first stop had to be Feltrinelli, the biggest bookshop in Florence. I wanted a notebook to act as a travel diary, maybe a book about London's history and art, and a plain tourist guide.

My mind went to all the passages in *A Room with a View*, the novel by Edward Morgan Forster, where Lucy, the protagonist, consults her Baedeker – the guide of choice for British tourists, at the time... I'd be Lucy, but instead of leaving London for Florence, I'd be doing the opposite. I was also curious to check out *Signorsì*, the book by Liala that Viola was reading.

I was scouring notebooks, examining one with little butterflies all over – they reminded me of the butterflies Mia had painted on the stairs that climbed up to her studio – when a heavy, chemical fragrance filled my nose. I felt someone's gaze on me, and my skin almost prickled with unease.

I turned around.

Of course. I was bound to meet Tamara sooner or later; it was inevitable. If it didn't happen by chance, it'd happen through Lulu and Vanni. I was glad to think that at least in London, I wouldn't have to see Lorenzo, I wouldn't have to see his fiancée, I wouldn't have to speak to either of them or think of either of them.

'Can I speak to you for a moment?' she asked.

Er, no?

'I'm not sure what's left to say to each other, Tamara.'

'Please?'

She sounded... *pleading*. This was weird. Me being me, if I saw the smallest sign of distress in someone I couldn't help but try to alleviate it, somehow. I was wired that way.

I nodded, planning to disentangle from her as soon as I could, and followed her towards the tables inside the bookshop.

'Coffee?' Tamara asked.

'Tea. Thank you.'

Hopefully she wouldn't slip arsenic in it when I wasn't looking.

As she placed the order in front of me and sat down, I

noticed that she looked like she'd lost some weight, and that under her signature heavy make-up, she was a little pale. I fought the instinct to ask her if she was okay.

'Well, Bianca. Congratulations. You got what you wanted. I'm happy for you,' she said.

'I don't know what you're talking about, and in any case I doubt you'd be happy for me. But thank you.' I cringed at my own words. I might have learned to be catty, I might have developed a thicker skin, but I didn't like that side of me.

'I don't understand, Bianca. What's the point in pretending you don't know what I'm talking about?'

I was horrified to see Tamara's eyes fill with tears. The witch herself, crying? All of a sudden she seemed vulnerable.

'Tamara. I *truly* have no idea.'

She crossed her arms. 'You want me to believe that your twin didn't tell you?'

'Lucrezia has been away on and off for business; she's travelling a lot...'

'Lorenzo didn't tell you?' she snapped.

That was enough. 'No! Look, I'm sorry if you're having trouble, but I have to go...'

'He broke up with me.'

It took me a moment to digest what she'd just said and recover my composure. 'I'm sorry. But it has nothing to do with me.'

'You can't fool me, Bianca. There was always something going on between you two.'

'Believe me, there was nothing between us for many years. You said it yourself, he never spoke about me.'

'I lied. He did speak about you. He said that what happened was a fairy tale, an illusion... that it belonged to the past. But everything told me the opposite. I always knew he loved you.'

'Loved. Past tense. What happened between Lorenzo and me belongs to the past. I don't know the point of this conversation. Like I said, your breakup has nothing to do with me. You despise me...'

'I never despised you. I *admired* you.' She spat out the word as if it were an insult.

'Ha! Should I remind you of the things you said to me?'

'No need. I remember. I was jealous. I've always been jealous of you, the shadow in between my fiancé and me.'

The bookshop was busy; people whirled around us with mugs and trays and the air was full of the low buzz of conversation. Tamara's words could have been lost in the din, but instead I heard them all, loud and clear. Me, the shadow between them. I could see the sense in what she was saying, but it still sounded unreal, absurd. What had happened between Lorenzo and me had always been a secret, had never bled out to influence other people's lives.

'I suppose there's no more need to be jealous of you now. He called the engagement off. I should have known... I tried to tie him down with that, but... well, nobody forces Lorenzo's hand. I should have known,' she said again.

'Tamara, I told you: I haven't spoken to Lorenzo in a long time; I had no part in breaking your engagement.'

'You *exist*. That was enough.'

The sip of tea I'd just taken got stuck in my throat, and I had to make an effort to swallow.

'I never meant to cause you pain. I'm sorry.'

'What's the point in saying sorry? You came floating in with your stupid dresses and flowing hair, always so... unique. So poised...'

I had to laugh. 'You said I looked like your grandmother! And I'm hardly poised! You don't know me.' I repeated the same words I told her when we first met. 'You just thought you did.'

'I know I was horrible to you. But I was right, wasn't I? You took Lorenzo away from me, in the end.'

'Lorenzo *took himself* away from you,' I specified. 'Like I said, your breakup has nothing to do with me. There's no way back for Lorenzo and me. Too much has happened.'

Tamara lowered her eyes. She looked broken.

She loves him. She truly loves him. Maybe somewhere inside me there'd been the suspicion that Tamara was a social climber, that she was after the Orafi's wealth and prestige. But the heartbreak, true heartbreak, was painted all over her face, in her posture, in the sound of her voice. Every molecule of her spoke of love lost.

'I'm sorry that you're suffering,' I said, and I was sincere. She nodded. 'Whatever happens next, you don't need to worry about me any more. I'm going away for a while. Abroad.'

Tamara shrugged. 'Wherever you go, it's not going to change anything for him.'

'I know. He moved on, and so did I. Well, best of luck,' I said and stood. I was desperate to get away from that convoluted story, in which none of the players had come out with any peace or joy. I wanted to get on with my life.

'That's not what I meant,' she said, and the resentment in her eyes almost frightened me. '*It's not going to change anything for him.* Wherever you go, his heart will be yours.'

CHAPTER 29

CASALTA, 1986

BIANCA

'You all ready?' Lulu asked. She was trying to summon enthusiasm, but failing. I knew she wasn't happy about me going, even if, with all her travelling, she wasn't going to be home often.

'Extremely ready!' Mia exclaimed.

'Lulu, please cheer up! It's not forever, Nora will be here, and you're always gone anyway!' I begged her.

'I'm cramming in all I can before getting married... You're right though, I'm being selfish! I'm sorry. You'll have a great time...'

'Thank you!'

'But I can't wait to have you back!' she concluded and threw her arms around me again. Wedding preparations were making her sentimental. Very un-Lulu, I thought. I was determined not to let pre-emptive homesickness get the better of me.

But oh, how lovely Casalta looked as I turned around, and saw my home pulling away from me, further and further.

The trip to the airport was one long, silent panic attack,

crowned by the mishap of all mishaps. When we came to the check-in, my plane ticket was nowhere to be found.

'I can't find it! It's not here! It's not here!' Beads of sweat formed on my forehead, and I started feeling warm, then hot, then positively roasting with nerves. Bag, jacket, wallet, sunglasses, everything was jumbled up and taking turns to fall onto the shiny white airport floor. I was like a tree losing leaves. 'I'm sure I took it; it was on the coffee table in the living room, and I picked it up... It *must* be here...'

Lulu and Mum were trying to catch falling accessories and help me go through whatever bag or pocket came to hand, but Mia stood there as cool as a cucumber. 'Don't worry. You're not going to need it.'

'Mia, please, this is not the time for your cryptic statements.'

'It's not—'

'Mia, not now!'

At that moment, someone called my name. I heard it, but it didn't register at first because I was so flustered, the place was so noisy with people and announcements over the speaker, and my own thoughts were screaming in alarm in my head.

But when he called my name a second time, I knew who it was.

I turned around, and he was there.

Lorenzo.

For once, he wasn't impeccably groomed, nor calm and in control. He looked flustered and frightened, in jeans, T-shirt and an oversized black coat, and his forehead was beaded with sweat.

As for me, I too was sweaty and flustered and looking like a Christmas tree with bags hanging off me instead of baubles.

'Bianca!'

'Lorenzo?' I whispered.

This time, I didn't think; I didn't hesitate. Nothing, nothing, nothing was going to come between us ever again.

I ran into his arms, and as we held onto each other tight, tight, finally home – I heard Mia's little voice pipe up.

'I told you that you didn't need that ticket.'

∼

The night was so quiet, except for the faint sound of the wind brushing through the trees, that we could hear our own heartbeats. The moonlight spilled through the window, illuminating Lorenzo's bed in soft silver light.

I closed my eyes, breathing in the weight of the moment, and when I opened them his face seemed different. I'd seen him hundreds of times, but tonight for the first time he was truly mine, and I was truly his.

He took a step toward me, and I felt the air shift, as though the world around us had faded, leaving only this moment. Only him. Only me. And everything else was far away and didn't matter.

He closed the distance between us, his hand reaching for mine. I looked down at our joined hands, unable to meet his eyes.

'What's wrong?' he asked, searching my face.

I took a breath. 'When something feels this good, it's hard not to think it might slip away.'

Lorenzo lifted my hand to his lips, pressing a soft kiss to my knuckles, tenderly. 'It won't,' he said, his voice filled with quiet conviction. 'I won't let it.'

I looked up at him then, and the raw honesty in his eyes made my heart rejoice and ache at the same time.

'I believe you,' I said and a smile found its way onto my lips. But my heart was so full that tears welled in my eyes as well, and I fought to hold them back, but it was useless. They spilled over, and I felt a wave of vulnerability crash over me. He reached out, brushing a tear from my cheek with the pad of his thumb, his touch so gentle it almost broke me.

Before I could respond, his hands came up to cradle my face, and he leaned down, his lips brushing against mine in the softest, most reverent kiss I had ever known. It wasn't hurried or desperate; it was steady, deliberate, filled with all the words he didn't say aloud. His love was in every touch, every movement, and I felt it sink into me, filling the spaces life had emptied, giving me back all that I'd lost.

I reached up, my fingers tangling in his hair as I kissed him back. When we finally broke apart, his forehead rested against mine, and our breaths mingled in the stillness. His hands slid down to hold mine, and I could feel the strength in his grip, the unspoken promise he was making.

'You don't have to be afraid any more,' he said, his voice soft but certain. 'Not with me.'

I nodded, my throat too tight to speak, and he smiled, the kind of smile that felt like it was just for me. 'I love you,' he said simply. 'I love you more than I thought I could love anyone.'

He pulled me into his arms then, holding me so tightly it felt like he was trying to shield me from the world.

For a while, we just stood there, wrapped up in each other. His fingers traced slow circles along my back. I leaned into him, my ear pressed to his chest, listening to the steady rhythm of his heart. It was the sound of home.

'Do you ever think,' I murmured after a while, 'that we were meant to find each other? That this – us – was inevitable?'

He tilted his head slightly, as though considering my question. 'I don't know if I believe in fate,' he said. 'But I believe in you. In us. Maybe that's the same thing.'

I smiled, tilting my head back to look at him. 'I think it is.'

He brushed a strand of hair from my face, his thumb lingering along my cheekbone. I reached up, resting my hand against his cheek, and his eyes closed briefly at the touch.

When he kissed me again, it was slow and steady, the kind of kiss that could mend broken pieces and forge unbreakable bonds. And as his arms tightened around me, I let go of every fear, every doubt, and let myself fall completely.

In his arms, I was home.

∼

That night was the first time I was able to spend the whole night in Lorenzo's arms, the first time we could be together in peace, without fear of being discovered, without doubts about our true feelings for each other. Without misunderstandings or resentment from the past.

'I never stopped thinking about you,' he whispered in my hair.

'I never stopped regretting you. Why—'

'Why did we not tell each other? After you told me to stay away, well, I did. When your father died I didn't know what to do... I tried to read you, but you were so distant!'

I touched his face, following his profile with my finger. 'So were you! You even tried to buy Casalta...'

'I know. I hated that place, Bianca, I'm sorry, but I did. It was your father's domain. I wanted it to disappear; I wanted you to be free. I should have been honest with you, I should have told you how I felt, but I was...'

'Afraid. Me too. And then I met you at Villa Lieta with Tamara.'

He pulled me down to his chest, holding me tight again. 'I'm not proud of how I treated Tamara. I wanted to move on from you, from us. I forced myself to do that. But the night of my father's birthday, when we started talking, I was sure I couldn't keep living a lie. I just couldn't. And then Brando arrived; I had no idea you were seeing someone too. The way he looked at you. I thought I'd lost you.'

'And then Tamara announced your engagement—'

Lorenzo winced. 'Don't remind me. Nobody knew she was going to do that, except her mother. I was furious. But there you were, beside Brando, and you looked so suited to each other... All fight went out of me.'

'All fight went out of *you*? It's hard to believe!'

He smiled a lopsided smile. 'You two seemed so happy.'

'Maybe I should say that you and Tamara looked happy too, but well... you really didn't. You seemed miserable.'

'I was. But I shouldn't have gone along with it all. It wasn't fair on her.'

'It wasn't fair on Brando. That's why I left him. He deserved better.'

'But I was convinced the two of you were ideal for each other. That's why after we met at Villa Lieta, I tried not to contact you. God, it was so hard. But I wanted to let you live your life.'

'I wanted to let you live yours.'

He smiled. 'Thankfully Lucrezia had other ideas. She didn't know I'd called off the engagement, not for a while. She was always away, but when you decided to go to London, she came looking for me and told me. I had to come to you. I was so scared you'd just tell me to go away.'

'But I didn't. I held you tight. And I won't let you go, ever again.'

'Do you believe in me now, *amore mio*?'

'With my life.'

Amarilli was right. Only by being true to my heart had I arrived where I desired to be, and, as if in a cascade of goodness, I'd done the right thing for everyone around me as well. Lorenzo and I were together, Brando and Tamara were free to find true love, and my little Mia was flying solo, without her big sister following her every step.

Thank you, Amarilli, I said in my mind.

I fell asleep against Lorenzo's chest, his arms around me, skin to skin. Like it was always meant to be.

∽

I dreamed of Viola. She was standing somewhere among shelves and boxes, sunlight seeping through a window, dust dancing in the single ray of light. She was there and then she wasn't, disappearing behind a shelf, twirling among the boxes and papers, almost dissolving into dust and then becoming solid again, glowing with inner light.

I recognised the place: it was one of the archive rooms at the Uffizi – I'd crouched on that floor for hours, sorting out myriads of papers.

In the dream, Viola smiled. 'Come find me,' she said, in a voice that came from far away, and yet was so close to my ear that I felt her warm breath and smelled the scent of violets.

I woke up with the echo of her words still in the air. Instead of the sun, it was moonlight that filtered through the blinds. It made Lorenzo's jet-black hair shine with a silver glow, and when he opened his eyes, the moon reflected in his irises. I had to blink – for a moment I couldn't believe that my Lorenzo was there beside me. That face I loved so much, those features I'd imprinted on with my first love.

My first love, and the last.

CHAPTER 30

CASALTA, 1986

BIANCA

I made my way up the stone stairs where I'd first attended my interview, where Brando had stopped me from falling. Adriana, my former boss, was just on her way out, and we bumped into each other.

'Bianca! What are you doing here? Brando said you were moving to London!'

'Change of plan,' I said with a smile.

Lorenzo coming to find me at the airport had been surreal. I'd gone with him without hesitation, this time – and when I hugged Mia and Mum, who were leaving without me, I'd murmured a contrite 'I'm sorry.'

'Sorry? Look at you, you're the picture of happiness! Which means I'm happy too,' Mum had said. Mia kept her composure, even if her eyes were a little shiny. When they disappeared through the automatic doors, Mia's little black figure was still visible through the semi-transparent doors as she walked away.

And now, I was back at the Uffizi to tie up a loose end.

'You came to tell us you're coming back? Tell me that's why you're here!'

'Sorry, Adriana,' I answered, delighted with her welcome. I was so happy I'd left a good impression.

'Well. You look good. I never saw you in civvies,' she commented on my beloved dress, one of my favourites, blue with tiny embroidery around the neck and hem. I wore blue ballerinas and the usual hairclip in my hair, without any make-up. The old me. The real me. Oh, it was good to be back – back to myself, back here, where so much had happened.

My smile shifted into something a little fixed, a little rigid, when I remembered I had stolen goods from the archive in my handbag. Viola's diary was there, wrapped and protected in a linen sachet.

'Thank you. I hope everything is good with you, Adriana.'

'All peachy. Still wrestling with computers!' she laughed. 'Are you looking for Brando?'

'Yes, I was hoping to consult the archive one last time.'

'I'm sure it won't be a problem. Goodbye, Bianca,' she said and walked down the stairs with a wave.

I knocked at the door. All of a sudden, I was anxious – I hoped Brando didn't bear me any resentment. He'd told me he didn't, but I was still a little worried. When I heard his 'Come in,' I stepped into the office.

'Back to the scene of the crime?' he joked. His face was open and cheerful like I remembered it. Thank goodness – I shouldn't have worried, but even if leaving him had been the right thing to do for everyone, guilt still pricked me whenever I thought of him.

'I am! Do you have a moment? Not if you can't...'

'Of course, of course.' He pulled up a chair at his desk for me, and I sat. 'So, how are things? Everything... good? *Lorenzo?*' he asked, tilting his head a little.

Did I dream it, or was there a hint of hope in his tone?

That maybe I'd say something like *It didn't work out; I made the wrong decision?*

'Lorenzo is good, thank you, all good.'

He nodded and looked down. Guilt ambushed me again, but I continued.

'How have you been?'

'Good too. Not seeing anyone yet. Which is surprising, considering the appeal that archivists have. We're the Don Juans of our field.'

I laughed. 'Well, while we're on that subject, I'd like to consult the archive. With you, of course, if you can, if you have a moment. I know I don't have access any more.'

'Oh. Yes, of course. It's no problem. Come,' he said. We walked down the corridor I knew so well, up to the anonymous-looking door that hid marvels behind it. Brando took the keys out of his pocket, and when he opened the door the familiar smell of old papers and damp hit me again.

'So, what do you want to know?'

I couldn't tell him about the stolen diary, of course – I could hardly argue that Viola wanted it to belong to me, and not be lost inside a box. Somehow, I didn't think Brando – or the law – would be convinced if I told them that a voice had instructed me to take something from the Uffizi archive and bring it home.

I hoped I wasn't blushing too much.

'Long story short, I'm trying to find out what happened to the previous owners of Casalta, the Innocenti family. Their daughter, Viola, in particular. My grandfather bought the house from them after the war.' This wasn't exactly true: he'd bought it from someone who was looking after their estate. No members of the Innocenti family had been in Casalta at that time.

'Would your local registry office not be a better place to start?'

'I tried; there's no trace of them. They lost a good part of their archives during the war, and it seems that anything pertaining to the Innocenti family went up in flames at that time. But Viola was involved with the hiding of the Uffizi paintings during the war. I think this could be a link to her, a way to know more.' Also, Viola herself had told me to look for her here, but that was a secret.

'Oh, yes. That's an incredible story. Poggi is my idol, you know? Had it not been for him, so much would have gone the same way of those documents you were talking about.'

'Yes. Him, and his people.'

'You know, the hidden paintings were returned in 1945,' Brando said, opening a drawer and taking out two pairs of transparent gloves. He passed a pair to me and slipped the other pair on. 'Some had been stolen by the Germans, and they were relinquished to the Allies. Thankfully only a small number were destroyed, or we wouldn't be here.'

'The ones hidden in Pietrasanta? The convent was destroyed.'

'I never heard of anything hidden in Pietrasanta. Where did you read about that?'

Oops. 'I can't remember.' They must have moved them before the place was destroyed.

'Can you believe it?' Brando continued. '*Primavera* by Botticelli was almost turned to ash. I can't even think about it. Let me see...' he said while he gestured for me to follow him to the back, where the cabinets and shelves I remembered well were kept. Brando scoured around, opened a few drawers, and finally said, 'A-*ha*!'

He took out two folders and brought them to one of the tables for me to see. He spread the material out and pulled up another chair.

'Like a child in a sweet shop,' I told him with a smile. '*Grazie.*'

'*Prego*. I'll go back to my work, if you don't mind, or Adriana will kill me,' Brando said and I nodded.

I took a breath and began sifting – I knew it'd take me a while, but I also knew that what I was looking for was here, because Viola herself had called me. I lost all sense of time and kept going – I was about to take a break for coffee, when I came across a newspaper article:

> *The paintings stolen from the Uffizi were returned to the people of Florence by the Allied forces, in the person of Frederick Hartt from the Monuments Men, during a public ceremony in Piazza della Signoria. On instruction by Giovanni Poggi, Sovrintendente alle Arti, a banner was hung on the first truck entering the city: 'The Florentine artwork returns where it belongs'.*

Those words were touching, but it wasn't the article that arrested me: it was the photograph below it. I traced it gently with my gloved hands.

There she was – *Viola*.

She looked tiny and clearly the war had taken its toll. But her eyes were shining – she'd lost nothing of her zest for life. If anything, she looked more alive, more glowing. And the man beside her must be Pietro!

Finally I could see his face. Tall and almost gaunt, with trousers too big for him held in place by a thick belt – a strong, determined face and his arm around Viola's waist.

I blinked hard, happy and teary, and took the cutting to Brando, hoping to make a photocopy.

'You found her?' He seemed astonished.

'Yes. This is Viola.'

'You were lucky... or you have an instinct for archival work.'

'Well, neither of these... Viola told me where to find her,' I said calmly. Brando stared at me for a moment – I guessed he thought I wasn't making sense. Finally, he decided I'd made a joke, and gave a little laugh.

'Thank you for your help, Brando.'

'No problem. Out of curiosity, are you writing a book?'

I laughed. 'Maybe, who knows? Do you mind if I make a copy of...'

I couldn't finish the sentence.

I was sure I'd heard my name being called from the back of the room, beyond the shelves. But I was also sure that there was nobody in there with us. Could it be...

'Did you hear that?' I asked.

'What?'

I shook my head and turned around slowly.

Bianca...

'Bianca?' Brando echoed.

'Yes. Yes, sorry. It's just that... I'm sure there's something else I need to see.'

He looked at me quizzically. 'I'm not sure how to help you.'

I didn't know what to do either – this was uncharted land for me too. I turned around and around, hoping for a sign – my whole body was buzzing with strange electricity. I wished Mia had been there with me – she'd have known what to do. I was so self-conscious, I was burning up. How could I explain all this? And then, I saw that there was a small cardboard box in a corner.

'What's that?' I asked. In for a penny, in for a for a pound. Brando had already noticed I was a little weird, anyway.

'You look like a dowser, you know, those people who find water underground using a divining rod?'

'I know. I think there's water there.'

Brando crouched beside the box and I followed. 'Remember we spoke about the little treasures we find among documents and folders? The postcards, the shopping lists, food wrappers, dried flowers, even feathers. Well, we had some more boxes in from out of Florence; Adriana processed them and this is what we found. Debris. Memories' debris.'

He lifted the lid, and my eyes fell on a letter still in its envelope. It seemed to glow gold.

You found me.

'May I?' I asked. Brando nodded.

I lifted the letter up – it was addressed to Agnese Innocenti, Viola's aunt. 'I think this is what I was looking for.'

Brando shrugged. 'I don't think the Falconeri sisters will ever stop surprising me.'

Cara Zia Agnese,

How I wait for your letters from home! I'm always overjoyed to hear you're well, and I so wish you'd join us in America.

So that was why Viola had disappeared! She'd emigrated across the ocean, like many Italians had done after the war.

Mamma prays every day that you will, especially since Pietro's mother and siblings have come too, and they too have settled well. Mamma is well, thank God, though since Papà's death in the bombing she's become frail. Food is healthy and abundant here, so I trust she'll recover in time. Both Pietro and I have found work in a shoe factory owned by another Italian immigrant. We've been very fortunate up to now. Please know that there's plenty of work for everyone here. If we succeed in selling Casalta there'll be enough money for your fare, but I'm saving as much of my wages as I can anyway, and I hope that if Casalta doesn't sell then I can send you the fare. I think of Casalta often, and pray my roses are well...

They are! They still are, Viola!

Please, go lay flowers on Papà's grave on behalf of Mamma and me. And lay a flower on Laio's grave, and Federico's too. I still can't quite believe we survived that day! And that Casalta didn't burn down!

So her father had died that day, and Viola was compassionate enough to ask her aunt to lay a flower on his grave. And Federico Valsecchi had died there too. Casalta still being there was a miracle.

Dear Zia, I'm returning the note that Lisetta sent us through you. As you can see, it's unopened, but please, tell her that we forgive her.

I dream of Casalta all the time, you know? In my dreams I walk through the garden and I sit on the stairs outside. How I miss those roses; how I miss the hills of home. I'm so glad that I brought my little doll with me, Bianca! Nothing else reminds me of home, of my childhood, like she does!

But home is here now; home is wherever Pietro is.

Please try and join us as soon as you can.

All my love,

Viola

It was then that it hit me: I'd been waiting for my gift to come back, praying for it, longing for it. But I'd taken for granted that if it returned, it'd look just the same, it'd take the same form. Not for a moment had I considered that maybe my gift had changed, just like I had.

I was sure, now. I'd heard Viola's calls and followed her steps all the way here. My Sight was back; it'd just taken another form. I was whole again, and I couldn't wait to see what my gift would reveal to me next.

'Bianca! Are you crying? *Again?*' Brando looked panicked. 'What's wrong? Is it something I did? Is there anything I can do?'

'Don't worry. They are happy tears.'

'Ah. We like those. However, please don't cry over historical documents,' he said, and made me laugh between my tears.

CHAPTER 31

CASALTA, SPRING 1986

BIANCA

I won't cry. I won't cry. I won't cry.

But when I saw my twin walking down the aisle on Gherardo's arm, *obviously* I did.

Lulu looked perfect in her wedding dress, with puffy sleeves and a wide gown, inspired by Princess Diana's attire, of course – I wouldn't have expected anything different from my fashionista sister. Knowing Nora's and Mia's styles, though, Lulu had chosen simple outfits for us – sleek shift dresses just above the knee in a light blue colour that suited all three of us.

The men were in blue, and Vanni was so handsome in a navy suit with a red rose. Lorenzo, instead, wore a white rose as a buttonhole. Yes, white roses are my favourite: *not* a coincidence.

'Best man and bridesmaid, bit of a stereotype,' I said.

'Best stereotype ever,' he whispered.

'Everything is just perfect,' I sighed, overlooking the pews filled with guests.

Mum wore a silver and blue dress that made her look like

she'd just risen from the sea; Matilde looked splendid in a dark cherry dress that highlighted her tanned complexion; and Gabriella, our father's widow, was there to share our joy in her usual sweet, quiet way, wearing a dove-grey suit that suited her silver hair perfectly. The only dissonant note came from a tall, thin woman who looked just like Lorenzo: Signora Orafi, Gherardo's wife, who, knowing her ex-husband's feelings towards Mum, hated being in the same space as any Falconeri woman. I couldn't resent her; I simply couldn't – I saw her point of view and I was touched that she'd chosen to come to the wedding anyway.

As soon as I could, I moved a few steps to the pew where she sat, removed from us.

'Thank you for being here,' I told her in a low voice and leaned down to hug her.

I was surprised when she returned my hug: she didn't speak a word to me that night, but that hug was enough for me, and I did hope for a reconciliation when it was mine and Lorenzo's turn to get married.

And then, among smiles and tears, the solemnity of the ceremony gave way to a flurry of congratulations, rice and confetti thrown over the church steps as they walked out in the sunshine.

Lulu had decided she wouldn't throw her bouquet, but give a red rose to each of her girlfriends instead. I kept myself a little removed, so when she came to me, she had no more roses to give – her face fell, and she looked around in a mild panic.

Lorenzo unpinned his white rose from his jacket and handed it to me: a collective '*Aww*' was the soundtrack to our kiss.

'My brother will be next,' Vanni said, and I looked at Lorenzo with a little apprehension – someone else announcing his engagement. But Lorenzo was smiling, and the happiness he exuded dissolved all my doubts.

'We'll be next. Won't we?' he asked, his glass raised towards me.

'Yes,' I said simply and raised my glass too, meeting his in a silvery clink.

See, Amarilli? I followed your advice. I've been true to my heart, I thought as everyone cheered and my sisters hugged me in a cloud of chiffon and spilled wine.

∽

'Do you think they can spare us for a little bit?' Lorenzo asked as we danced, his arms around my waist and his lips against my hair. Casalta looked like a dream, luminous with fairy lights, wine and music flowing all around and filling the garden and the hills, down to the vineyards and olive groves.

'I'm sure,' I said, and even without speaking our destination aloud, we both knew where we wanted to go.

We walked hand in hand on the soft grass, fireflies dotted here and there. It seemed that the night itself had been made to order for Lulu's wedding – a warm summer breeze swept the fields and the hills, and whispered among the branches of the hazelnut tree. The same tree had seen the blooming of Lulu and Vanni's love, and mine and Lorenzo's. Maybe there was something magical among those branches.

We lay together, still hearing faint music from far away, a sea of stars above our heads – just like the night of our first kiss.

'A star for each of us,' I whispered, my fingers woven with Lorenzo's. 'One for Mum, one for each of my sisters, for Vanni and Gherardo and for your mother. A star for Amarilli, a little further away but still part of our constellation…'

And that star just above the hill, beaming intermittently, its light like a heartbeat: *That one is for Viola*, I thought. Maybe it was my imagination, but the air was filled by a faint scent of violets.

EPILOGUE

BIANCA

I was in Mia's studio, kneeling in front of the little scene she'd painted: the four of us and Mum surrounded by rose branches and their thorns. And, a little removed, there was the face of a girl who looked like Mia. The girl I'd thought was Mia as a child, when I'd first seen it.

But the more I stared at the little image, the more I felt that something wasn't right. The girl had brown eyes, not one blue and one hazel-brown like my little sister – I thought it'd been a slip-up, but now it seemed unlikely. Mia might have been scatty and distracted in her daily life, but she wasn't so in her art. When it came to painting, she was maniacally precise and particular, and the magical realism of her work hid rigour and care. She wouldn't have made a mistake about the colour of her own eyes.

I studied the painted face with its halo of wavy black hair, floating bodiless and mysterious, like a dream or a memory.

Who was this girl?

At that moment, Mia came to sit beside me, silent as a cat as she often was. It seemed to me that I was looking at something private, something secret, and I almost apologised, even if Mia never minded us visiting her studio to see her works in progress.

'Do you know who she is, Bianca?' she asked.

I shook my head. All of a sudden, there was an eerie feeling in the pit of my stomach.

'That's Francesca,' Mia said calmly, cheerfully, as if we were just chatting, as if what she was about to tell me wouldn't change our entire lives. 'She's our father's fifth daughter. She's our other sister.'

A LETTER FROM DANIELA

Dear readers,

Thank you for picking up *The Tuscan Sister's Secret*! If you'd like to stay up to date with my new releases, you can sign up at the following link. Your email address will never be shared, and you can unsubscribe any time.

www.bookouture.com/daniela-sacerdoti

I feel privileged that with so many demands on our time, you chose to read a story of mine. I love all four of the Falconeri sisters, but I have a soft spot for Bianca, for her strength and self-sacrifice in protecting her family. It was an emotional journey, to follow her as she takes her life in her hands and finds her voice and her power. Bianca's story unfolds alongside Viola's, a girl who lived in Casalta during the Second World War: Viola's diary helps Bianca understand and unravel her own life. I hope you'll forgive the liberties I've taken with history for the sake of a cohesive narrative.

Some of you have followed me since I started, with the Glen Avich quartet; some will have picked up *The Tuscan Sister's Secret* as the first book of mine: to all of you goes my immense gratitude.

Thank you for reading, and thank you for adding your experiences and your imagination to my plot and characters, and creating a story that is only your own. I hope Bianca will steal your heart like she stole mine, and I can't wait to know what you think!

Happy reading,

Daniela

HISTORICAL NOTE

Although the parts of this book set during the Second World War are based on true historical events, I've taken liberties with dates in order to compress events into a shorter period of time, including the aerial bombings Florence was submitted to.

In this book I pay homage to Giovanni Poggi, Sovrintendente alle Arti (Superintendent to the Arts) in Tuscany during the Second World War. Adolf Hitler's sights had been set on looting the Uffizi since May 1938, when Benito Mussolini accompanied the German leader to visit the museum, both the exhibit rooms and the beautiful Corridoio Vasariano. Moreover, air strikes endangered the artwork further.

In 1940 Giovanni Poggi began hiding paintings in villas and castles away from Florence, subsequently adding more and dividing them up between several more locations. Two of these locations were plundered by Nazi forces, but later liberated by the Allies, while in 1944 many precious paintings, including *Primavera* by Botticelli, almost burned during a bombing around the castle of Montegufoni, in the Tuscan countryside.

The stolen paintings were retrieved and returned to Florence; an official ceremony took place in Piazza della Signoria, attended by the whole city, cheering on the return of what rightfully belonged to them.

In *The Tuscan Sister's Secret*, I've tucked up the events in a shorter period of time. The preparation of the boxes of paintings to be hidden and the bombing of Florence by the Allied forces happen within a few months of each other. The fictitious locations of Pietrasanta and Casalta take the place of the real hiding places, such as Montegufoni Castle.

I hope my readers will forgive this poetic licence, taken while always keeping historical truth in mind.

Daniela

ACKNOWLEDGEMENTS

Thank you to everyone at Bookouture, the best team! Heartfelt, special thanks to my editor, Jess, to Saidah and Richard for giving wings to my stories so they can be read abroad as well, and to Jack Renninson for refreshing fantasy and science fiction book talk.

Thank you to my parents, Franco Sacerdoti and Ivana Fornera, for feeding me bread and books as I was growing up – sometimes I forget that all started from you and the stories you told me and read to me.

Thank you as ever to Francesca, Simona and Irene: every woman needs a women's tribe.

And, of course, to Ross, Sorley and Luca, the earth, the sky and the sun. Always.

Daniela

PUBLISHING TEAM

Turning a manuscript into a book requires the efforts of many people. The publishing team at Bookouture would like to acknowledge everyone who contributed to this publication.

Commercial
Lauren Morrissette
Hannah Richmond
Imogen Allport

Cover design
Sarah Whittaker

Data and analysis
Mark Alder
Mohamed Bussuri

Editorial
Jess Whitlum-Cooper
Imogen Allport

Copyeditor
Rhian McKay

Proofreader
Becca Allen

Marketing
Alex Crow
Melanie Price
Occy Carr
Cíara Rosney
Martyna Młynarska

Operations and distribution
Marina Valles
Stephanie Straub
Joe Morris

Production
Hannah Snetsinger
Mandy Kullar
Jen Shannon

Publicity
Kim Nash
Noelle Holten
Jess Readett
Sarah Hardy

Rights and contracts
Peta Nightingale
Richard King
Saidah Graham

Printed in Dunstable, United Kingdom